108課綱、全民英檢初／中級適用

英文作文示範

·劉雲湘 著·

Join the Writing Club!

◆ 文法技巧 ——
所有句型皆附例句與中譯
豐富寫作內容

◆ 字詞技巧 ——
遴選優質範文，逐句解析
一網打盡單字、片語用法

◆ 組織大綱 ——
從聯想問答得到寫作提示
釐清大綱與組織方向

三民書局

國家圖書館出版品預行編目資料

英文作文示範 Join the Writing Club!／劉雲湘著.——
初版十刷.——臺北市：三民，2021
面；　公分.——(英語Make Me High系列)

ISBN 978-957-14-5134-3　(平裝)
1. 英語 2. 作文 3. 寫作法

805.17   97023291

英語 Make Me High 系列

英文作文示範——Join the Writing Club!

作　者	劉雲湘
發 行 人	劉振強
出 版 者	三民書局股份有限公司
地　址	臺北市復興北路 386 號 (復北門市) 臺北市重慶南路一段 61 號 (重南門市)
電　話	(02)25006600
網　址	三民網路書店 https://www.sanmin.com.tw
出版日期	初版一刷 2009 年 1 月 初版十刷 2021 年 12 月
書籍編號	S806840
I S B N	978-957-14-5134-3

三民書局

PREFACE

The purpose of this book, consisting of forty units, is to help you write better in English. Each unit, beginning with a title along with either a writing genre or a combination of genres, is divided into five steps: Step 1 (Association), Step 2 (Organization), Step 3 (Model Composition), Step 4 (Analyzing Sentences), and Step 5 (Words → Sentences & Grammar Points → Sentences). All steps, except Step 2 in Chinese and Step 3 in English, are bilingual (in English & Chinese), which is designed to give you extensive practice in translation from English to Chinese and vice versa. This book also features the application of a triangle of skills, namely three-dimensional (3-D) writing skills (see diagram below): outlining skills, lexical skills, and grammatical skills, which can reinforce your ability to write in English.

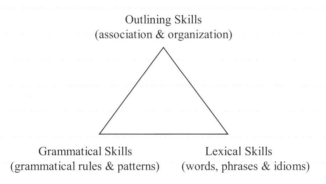

Outlining Skills
(association & organization)

Grammatical Skills   Lexical Skills
(grammatical rules & patterns)   (words, phrases & idioms)

Three-Dimensional Writing Skills

Step 1 (Association)

The skill of association inspires you to think creatively by generating ideas and/or capturing images in your mind.

Step 2 (Organization)

The skill of organization enables you to arrange your ideas in a coherent and logical sequence.

Step 3 (Model Composition)

Each model composition clearly presents the structure and content of the whole text for you to simulate spontaneously and recite repeatedly.

Step 4 (Analyzing Sentences)

Each of the sentences in the model is translated into Chinese and analyzed with the aid of words, idioms, and/or sentence patterns.

Step 5 (Words → Sentences & Grammar Points → Sentences)

Example sentences help you know not only the meanings and usages of the words and grammar points within the text but also how to use them to make sentences.

Overall, this book serves to help sharpen your writing skills step by step via model compositions involving a wide range of texts, a number of writing genres (expository, informative, narrative, persuasive, and procedural writing) and a set of 3-D writing skills (outlining skills, lexical skills, and grammatical skills).

Liu Yun-hsiang
HSNU, Taipei
November 25, 2008

一、本書編寫的目的是為了提升英文寫作表達能力。本書的目標著重在透過系統的步驟和技巧的傳授來奠定英文寫作表達能力的基礎。一旦具備優質的英文作文寫作技巧與能力，不僅可以增強考試實力，也可以應付實際生活及未來職場所需。

二、本書分成四十個單元，每個單元各自獨立，均附有文體、標題以及五個訓練步驟。其中步驟 2 以中文呈現，步驟 3 以英文呈現，其餘皆以雙語呈現，藉以達到訓練中、英文雙語互譯的功效。

三、本書的另一特色就是應用一組三角形的技巧，亦即三度空間寫作技巧（參考下列圖示），包含組織大綱技巧、字詞技巧以及文法技巧。這些技巧可用以增強英文寫作表達能力。

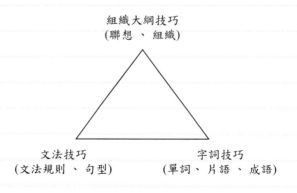

三度空間寫作技巧

四、本書各單元的五個步驟：

步驟 1（聯想提示）

聯想技巧可以讓寫作者的思考力發揮創意，藉以激發想像、捕捉靈感。

步驟 2（組織大綱提示）

組織大綱技巧可以讓寫作者在鋪陳靈感時，組織架構合乎連貫性和邏輯性。

步驟 3（範文）

範文清楚呈現全文結構和內容，期能激勵自發性模仿以及反覆背誦。

步驟 4（寫句實戰分析）

範文裡的每一個句子皆譯成中文，並附有單詞、成語以及句型分析。

步驟 5（用字遣詞、文法句型）

提供例句並幫助瞭解字詞及文法要點的用法及意義，進而應用於造句的表達。

五、本書透過範文撰寫，包括多元內容的取材、多種文體的呈現以及三度空間寫作技巧的嘗試，其目的就是要採取按部就班的方式來協助磨練英文寫作表達技巧。

六、本書中如有任何疏漏及錯誤，敬祈各界先進，不吝指正。

劉雲湘謹識

於師大附中

Contents

Join the Writing Club!
英文作文示範

UNIT
1

UNIT
2

UNIT
3

UNIT
4

UNIT
5

UNIT
6

UNIT
7

UNIT
8

UNIT
9

UNIT
10

UNIT
11

UNIT
12

UNIT
13

UNIT
14

UNIT
15

UNIT
16

UNIT
17

UNIT
18

UNIT
19

UNIT
20

UNIT 1

Narrative/Persuasive Writing　敍事文／說理文

A Big Decision　重大的決定

　　寫一篇文長約 120 字的英文作文。請以 "A Big Decision" 為題，敍述你曾經做過的一次重大決定，以及它對你所造成的影響。

　　Write an English essay in about 120 words under the title "A Big Decision." Write about one big decision you have made and how it affects you.

Step 1　聯想提示 Association　依人、事、時、地、物、原因和方法聯想與題目相關的事項

- 那個決定是什麼？　What was the decision?
- 我什麼時候做了那個決定？　When did I make the decision?
- 我對誰宣布了這個決定？　Who did I announce the decision to?
- 他們對我的決定反應如何？　How did they react to my decision?
- 他們為何如此反應？　Why did they react to it that way?
- 我從這個決定得到什麼好處？　What benefits did I get from the decision?

Step 2　組織大綱提示 Organization　依照想到的事項，定出寫作優先順序及細節

第一段

1. 主題句：兩年前的今天，我對同學宣布我要戒菸。

2. 支持句：

　a. 同學的反應及原因。

　b. 自己的態度。

3. 結論句：到目前為止，我仍信守戒菸的諾言。

第二段

1. 主題句：戒菸的好處說不完。

2. 支持句：舉例

　a. 外表的影響。

　b. 日常生活的影響。

　c. 金錢上的影響。

3. 結論：戒菸讓我受益匪淺。

1

英文作文示範

A Big Decision

This day two years ago, I was announcing to my classmates that I was ready to quit smoking permanently. I was booed and hissed off the platform after that, for I had tried and failed to quit many times. Even though they thought I might be fooling them again, I swore to myself that I would stop smoking for good this time. So far, I have been keeping my promise to quit smoking.

I think that the benefits of quitting smoking are unlimited. Here are some of them. First, quitting smoking helps me stop the bad effects of tobacco on my appearance, including stained teeth and yellow fingernails. Second, quitting smoking improves my day-to-day life substantially. For example, ordinary activities, such as climbing stairs, swimming, and running, no longer leave me out of breath. Besides, quitting smoking enables me to put aside the money I would have spent on cigarettes. Indeed, I have benefited greatly from my decision to quit smoking.

Step 4 寫句實戰分析 Analyzing Sentences

第一段

1. This day two years ago, I was announcing to my classmates that I was ready to quit smoking permanently.

兩年前的今天,我對同學宣布我要永遠戒菸了。

字詞提示
- announce *v.* 宣布
- permanently *adv.* 永久地

文法句型
- be ready to V 準備好要⋯
- quit V-ing 放棄,戒除
- 注意:句中的過去進行式表特定過去時間的動作持續進行。

UNIT
1

UNIT
2

UNIT
3

UNIT
4

UNIT
5

UNIT
6

UNIT
7

UNIT
8

UNIT
9

UNIT
10

UNIT
11

UNIT
12

UNIT
13

UNIT
14

UNIT
15

UNIT
16

UNIT
17

UNIT
18

UNIT
19

UNIT
20

2. I was booed and hissed off the platform after that, for I had tried and failed to quit many times.

講完後我被噓下台，因為我之前已經試過很多次，但都沒有戒成功。

> **！字詞提示**
> - boo *v.* 發出噓聲，喝倒采
> - hiss *v.* 以噓聲表達不滿

> **！文法句型**
> - fail to V　做某事失敗
> - 注意：過去完成式 had + V-en 比過去式發生的時間更早。

3. Even though they thought I might be fooling them again, I swore to myself that I would stop smoking for good this time.

儘管他們認為我可能又在騙他們，但我對自己發誓這一次要把菸永遠戒掉。

> **！字詞提示**
> - fool *v.* 欺騙，愚弄
> - swear *v.* 發誓
> - for good　永久地

> **！文法句型**
> - Even though + S + V, S + V....　儘管，縱使
>   Even though 搭配過去式子句，主要子句也通常搭配過去式。
> - stop V-ing　停止做某事

4. So far, I have been keeping my promise to quit smoking.

到目前為止，我仍信守戒菸的諾言。

> **！字詞提示**
> - promise *n.* 諾言，承諾

> **！文法句型**
> - so far　到目前為止
>   so far 常搭配現在完成 (進行) 式。

第二段

5. I think that the benefits of quitting smoking are unlimited.

我認為戒菸的好處說不完。

> **！字詞提示**
> - benefit *n.* 益處

> **！文法句型**
> - 第二段裡的動詞時態要轉成現在式，因為作者轉而說明他所認為的事實，而不再敘述過去的事件。

6. Here are some of them.

列舉其中幾項。

> !文法句型
> - Here + be + sth.　表示以下要介紹某些東西給某人

7. First, quitting smoking helps me stop the bad effects of tobacco on my appearance, including stained teeth and yellow fingernails.

第一，戒菸有助於防止我的外表不再受到香菸的不良影響，包括有汙垢的牙齒和黃色的指甲。

> !字詞提示
> - stained *adj.* 有髒汙的，弄髒的

> !文法句型
> - help sb. (to) V　幫助某人做某事

8. Second, quitting smoking improves my day-to-day life substantially. For example, ordinary activities, such as climbing stairs, swimming, and running, no longer leave me out of breath.

第二、戒菸大幅改善我的日常生活，諸如爬樓梯、游泳和跑步等一般的活動不會再讓我喘不過氣來。

> !字詞提示
> - day-to-day *adj.* 日常的
> - substantially *adv.* 相當多地；實質上地

> !文法句型
> - leave + O + OC　將…置於某狀態
> - out of breath　上氣不接下氣，喘不過氣來

9. Besides, quitting smoking enables me to put aside the money I would have spent on cigarettes.

此外，戒菸讓我能把原本會花在香菸上的錢存起來。

> !文法句型
> - enable + O + to V　使…能夠…
> - put aside　保留，撥出
> - would have + V-en　表示過去本來要做但未做的行為

10. Indeed, I have benefited greatly from my decision to quit smoking.

的確，戒菸的決定讓我受益匪淺。

> !字詞提示
> - benefit *v.* 獲益

UNIT
1

UNIT
2

UNIT
3

UNIT
4

UNIT
5

UNIT
6

UNIT
7

UNIT
8

UNIT
9

UNIT
10

UNIT
11

UNIT
12

UNIT
13

UNIT
14

UNIT
15

UNIT
16

UNIT
17

UNIT
18

UNIT
19

UNIT
20

Step 5

用字遣詞 Words → Sentences

1. announce [ə`naʊns] *v.* 宣布

   The famous actress announced her engagement to the media yesterday.

   這位著名演員昨天對媒體宣布她訂婚了。

2. permanently [`pɝmənəntlɪ] *adv.* 永久地

   Mr. Chen decided to settle permanently in the United States.

   陳先生決定永久定居美國。

3. boo [bu] *v.* 發出噓聲，喝倒采

   The singer sang so badly that he was booed off the stage.

   這個歌手的歌聲很糟，所以被噓聲趕下台。

4. hiss [hɪs] *v.* 以噓聲表達不滿

   The audience hissed at the speaker to show disapproval.

   觀眾對演講者發出噓聲，表示他們的不贊成。

5. fool [ful] *v.* 欺騙，愚弄

   You lie to me all the time. I am not going to be fooled again.

   你總是對我說謊。我不會再被騙了。

6. swear [swɛr] *v.* 發誓

   I swear to myself that I am starting all over again.

   我對自己發誓要重新開始。

7. for good [fɚ `gʊd] 永久地

   Jane is going to move to Europe for good.

   Jane 要搬到歐洲去，永遠住在那裡。

8. promise [`prɑmɪs] *n.* 諾言，承諾

   John kept his promise to visit his aunt regularly.

   John 信守諾言，定期去探望他的姨媽。

9. benefit [`bɛnəfɪt] *n.*; *v.* 益處；獲益

   The discovery of oil brought many benefits to the town.

   石油的發現帶給這個城鎮許多好處。

   I benefited a lot from the regular exercising habit.

   我因為規律運動的習慣獲益良多。

10. stained [`stend] *adj.* 有髒汙的，弄髒的

Mom soaked the stained clothes in cold water.

媽媽把弄髒的衣服泡在冷水裡。

11. day-to-day [`de tə `de] *adj.* 日常的

It is harder for the physically-challenged people to solve their day-to-day problems. 對殘障人士來說，解決日常問題更加辛苦。

12. substantially [səb`stænʃəlɪ] *adv.* 相當多地；實質上地

The daily costs have increased substantially. 每天的花費已經大增。

文法句型 Grammar Points → Sentences

1. be ready to V 準備好要…

Students are ready to learn to read. 學生們正準備好要學習閱讀。

2. quit V-ing 放棄，戒除

I've quit drinking. 我已經戒酒了。

3. fail to V 做某事失敗

Mavis failed to win the championship. Mavis 沒有贏得冠軍。

4. Even though + S + V, S + V.... 儘管，縱使

Even though it was raining, Oscar walked to work.

儘管下雨，Oscar 還是走路上班。

5. stop V-ing 停止做某事

Jeff couldn't stop laughing. Jeff 笑個不停。

6. so far 到目前為止

So far 常搭配現在完成式，為副詞片語。

So far, there's been no word from the two lost boys.

到目前為止，一直沒有那兩個迷路的小男孩的消息。

7. Here + be + sth. 表示以下要介紹某些東西給某人

Here are some advice. 以下是一些建議。

8. help sb. (to) V 幫助某人做某事

I helped my brother find the book. 我幫我弟弟找到這本書。

9. leave + O + OC 將…置於某狀態

Please leave the window open. It is hot here. 請讓窗戶開著。這裡很熱。

10. out of breath 上氣不接下氣，喘不過氣來

David is always out of breath when he climbs the stairs.

David 爬樓梯時總是上氣不接下氣。

11. enable + O + to V 使⋯能夠⋯

The software enables us to access the Internet in seconds.

這套軟體讓我們在幾秒鐘內就可以連上網路。

12. put aside 保留，撥出

Mary tries to put some time aside every evening to read to the kids.

Mary 試著在每天傍晚撥出一些時間讀書給孩子聽。

13. would have + V-en 表示過去本來要做但未做的行為

I would have become a doctor if I had studied hard enough when I was a student. 如果我還是學生的時候讀書夠認真，我應該會成為醫生。

UNIT 1
UNIT 2
UNIT 3
UNIT 4
UNIT 5
UNIT 6
UNIT 7
UNIT 8
UNIT 9
UNIT 10
UNIT 11
UNIT 12
UNIT 13
UNIT 14
UNIT 15
UNIT 16
UNIT 17
UNIT 18
UNIT 19
UNIT 20

UNIT 2

Narrative Writing 敘事文

A Big Surprise 大吃一驚

95 學測英文作文試題

　　根據下列連環圖畫的內容，將圖中女子、小狗與大猩猩之間所發生的事件作一合理的敘述。文長 100 個英文字左右。

　　Reasonably describe a whole series of events that happened to the lady, the dog and the gorilla in the following three-frame comic strip. Write your essay in 100 words or so.

Step 1　看圖聯想 Association 依人、事、時、地、物、原因和方法聯想與題目相關的事項

Step 2　組織大綱提示 Organization 依照想到的事項，定出寫作優先順序及細節

第一段 (圖 1)

　1. 一位婦人正在廚房裡忙著做飯。

　2. 一隻小狗靜靜地坐在一旁等待。

第二段 (圖 2)

　1. 突然間，一隻大猩猩出現在廚房裡，令這位婦人大吃一驚。

　2. 她嚇得把手上捧著的菜餚都打翻了。

　3. 盤子摔破了，小狗撲上前去吃散落一地的食物。

第三段 (圖 3)

　1. 然後，一位男士脫下了面具，露出真實身分。

　2. 男士獻給那位婦人一束鮮花，婦人臉上充滿欣喜。

UNIT 1
UNIT 2
UNIT 3
UNIT 4
UNIT 5
UNIT 6
UNIT 7
UNIT 8
UNIT 9
UNIT 10
UNIT 11
UNIT 12
UNIT 13
UNIT 14
UNIT 15
UNIT 16
UNIT 17
UNIT 18
UNIT 19
UNIT 20

3. 小狗也把地上的剩菜剩飯清光了，十分開心滿足。

Step 3 範文 Model Composition

A Big Surprise

One evening, Mrs. Liu was busy cooking in the kitchen and looking forward to her husband coming home for dinner. Meanwhile, their pet dog was sitting still behind her, smelling the delicious dish on the stove.

All of a sudden, a gorilla appeared in the kitchen, which scared Mrs. Liu. Such was her shock that she dropped the dish she was holding. The plate hit the ground with a loud crash and broke into pieces. The dog promptly made a dive for the food spilled on the kitchen floor.

Suddenly, Mr. Liu took off his mask to show his wife that it was only a gorilla costume. And then, to her delight, he handed her a bunch of flowers. The dog also helped clear the scraps on the floor and felt so happy.

Step 4 寫句實戰分析 Analyzing Sentences

第一段

1. One evening, Mrs. Liu was busy cooking in the kitchen and looking forward to her husband coming home for dinner.

某一個傍晚，劉太太正忙著在廚房裡煮飯，並期待丈夫回家吃晚餐。

① 文法句型
- be busy + V-ing　忙著做⋯
- look forward to + V-ing/N　期待⋯

2. Meanwhile, their pet dog was sitting still behind her, smelling the delicious dish on the stove.

這時，他們的寵物狗也靜靜地坐在她後面，聞著爐子上美味菜餚的味道。

① 字詞提示
- meanwhile *adv.* 同時，其間
- still *adv.* 靜止地

!文法
句型

- S + V₁..., and V₂.... = S + V₁..., V₂-ing....　分詞結構 V₂-ing 與主要動詞 V₁ 兩個動作伴隨發生，用分詞構句表示。

第二段

3. <u>All of a sudden, a gorilla appeared in the kitchen, which scared Mrs. Liu.</u>

突然間，一隻大猩猩出現在廚房裡，把劉太太給嚇著了。

!字詞
提示

- appear *v.* 出現
- scare *v.* 嚇著

!文法
句型

- all of a sudden　突然地
- ..., which scared.... 為關係代名詞的非限定用法，關係子句僅作補述之用，而不用以修飾或限定先行詞，關係代名詞前面一定要有逗號。

4. <u>Such was her shock that she dropped the dish she was holding.</u>

她嚇得把手上捧著的菜餚都打翻了。

!字詞
提示

- drop *v.* 摔落

!文法
句型

- Such be + N + that + S + V....　如此…以致於…

5. <u>The plate hit the ground with a loud crash and broke into pieces.</u>

盤子摔在地上，發出很大的聲響，並裂成了碎片。

!字詞
提示

- crash *n.* 撞擊聲

6. <u>The dog promptly made a dive for the food spilled on the kitchen floor.</u>

這隻小狗立刻撲上前去吃散落廚房地板上的食物。

!字詞
提示

- promptly *adv.* 立刻地，敏捷地
- spill *v.* 打翻

!文法
句型

- make a dive for　撲向，衝向

第三段

7. <u>Suddenly, Mr. Liu took off his mask to show his wife that it was only a gorilla costume.</u>

劉先生突然脫掉了他的面具，讓他太太知道那其實只是件猩猩裝。

字詞
提示
- mask *n.* 面具
- costume *n.* 服裝，裝束

文法
句型
- take off　脫掉

8. And then, to her delight, he handed her a bunch of flowers.

接著，令她感到欣喜的是，他獻了一束花給她。

字詞
提示
- hand *v.* 遞給，拿給
- bunch *n.* 束

文法
句型
- to one's + 情緒性 N　令某人覺得…

9. The dog also helped clear the scraps on the floor and felt so happy.

這隻狗也幫忙把地上的剩菜清光了，而且覺得很開心。

字詞
提示
- clear *v.* 清除，清理
- scraps *n.* 剩菜剩飯

Step 5

用字遣詞 Words → Sentences

1. meanwhile [`min͵hwaɪl] *adv.* 同時，其間

   Mother went shopping. Meanwhile, I cleaned the house.

   媽媽去購物。同時，我打掃了屋子。

2. still [stɪl] *adv.* 靜止地

   The child found it hard to stand still for a long time.

   這孩子覺得長時間站著不動很難。

3. appear [ə`pɪr] *v.* 出現

   Mary suddenly appeared in the doorway.　Mary 突然出現在門口。

4. scare [skɛr] *v.* 嚇著

   The thunder scared the dog.　雷聲把狗嚇著了。

5. drop [drɑp] *v.* 摔落

   Be careful not to drop that vase.　小心別把花瓶打破。

UNIT 1
UNIT 2
UNIT 3
UNIT 4
UNIT 5
UNIT 6
UNIT 7
UNIT 8
UNIT 9
UNIT 10
UNIT 11
UNIT 12
UNIT 13
UNIT 14
UNIT 15
UNIT 16
UNIT 17
UNIT 18
UNIT 19
UNIT 20

6. crash [kræʃ] *n.* 撞擊聲

Lillian heard a loud crash in the kitchen.

Lillian 聽到廚房裡很大的撞擊聲。

7. promptly [`prɑmptlɪ] *adv.* 立刻地，敏捷地

Dave promptly forgot what happened yesterday.

Dave 立刻把昨天發生的事情忘了。

8. spill [spɪl] *v.* 打翻

It's no use crying over spilled milk.

為打翻的牛奶哭泣是沒有用的。(覆水難收。)

9. mask [mæsk] *n.* 面具

The kids were all wearing animal masks.　這些孩子們都戴著動物的面具。

10. costume [`kɑstjum] *n.* 服裝，裝束

Julie wore her costume for the party.　Julie 穿了參加派對的衣服。

11. hand [hænd] *v.* 遞給，拿給

My boyfriend handed me a bowl of noodles.　我的男朋友拿了一碗麵給我。

12. bunch [bʌntʃ] *n.* 束

Miss Wang received a bunch of flowers from her secret lover.

王小姐收到一束仰慕者送的花。

13. clear [klɪr] *v.* 清除，清理

I helped clear the leftovers from the table.　我幫忙清理了桌上的剩菜剩飯。

14. scraps [skræps] *n.* 剩菜剩飯

We gave all our scraps to our dogs.

我們把所有的剩菜剩飯都給我們的狗吃。

文法句型 Grammar Points → Sentences

1. be busy + V-ing　忙著做…

John is busy preparing for the exam.　John 正忙著準備考試。

2. look forward to + V-ing/N　期待做…

We are looking forward to seeing you next month.

我們期待下個月見到你。

3. S + V$_1$..., and V$_2$.... = S + V$_1$..., V$_2$-ing....

He said goodbye, and waved his hand.

→ He said goodbye, waving his hand.　他說再見並揮揮他的手。

本句的分詞結構「waving his hand」與主要動詞「said goodbye」兩個動作同時發生，用分詞構句表示。

UNIT
1

UNIT
2

UNIT
3

UNIT
4

UNIT
5

UNIT
6

UNIT
7

UNIT
8

UNIT
9

UNIT
10

UNIT
11

UNIT
12

UNIT
13

UNIT
14

UNIT
15

UNIT
16

UNIT
17

UNIT
18

UNIT
19

UNIT
20

4. all of a sudden　突然地

　　All of a sudden, the lights went out.　突然間，燈熄滅了。

5. 關係代名詞的非限定用法

　　關係代名詞引導的關係子句僅作補述之用，而不用以修飾或限定先行詞時，關係代名詞前面一定要有逗號。

　　My brother didn't apologize, which made me angry.

　　→ My brother didn't apologize, and this made me angry.

　　我弟弟沒有道歉，這讓我很生氣。

　　I want this man, who can speak English.

　　→ I want this man, for he can speak English.　我要這個人，他會講英文。

6. Such be ＋ N ＋ that ＋ S ＋ V....　如此⋯以致於⋯

　　Such was Mandy's fright that she closed her eyes.

　　Mandy 很害怕，所以把眼睛閉了起來。

7. make a dive for　撲向，衝向

　　The goalkeeper made a dive for the ball.　這位守門員朝球撲了過去。

8. take off　脫掉

　　In Chinese culture, it is considered polite to take off your shoes before you enter a house.　在中國文化裡，進屋前先脫鞋被認為是有禮貌的。

9. to one's ＋ 情緒性 N　令某人覺得⋯

　　To our surprise, the manager quit yesterday.

　　令我們驚訝的是，經理昨天辭職了。

UNIT 3

Narrative Writing 敘事文

A Comfort Word 一番安慰話

北區公立高中 94 年第二次指考模擬考

請以「一番安慰話」為題寫一篇至少 120 個字的英文作文。第一段敘述你自己為了什麼事而哭過，或曾經見過什麼人為了什麼事而哭。第二段描述你是如何度過這次經驗，或是你如何安慰、陪伴或協助你所見到的哭泣者，以及這次的經驗令你有何體會、收穫或成長。

Write an essay entitled "A Comfort Word" in no less than 120 words. Narrate one thing for which you yourself or someone else cried in paragraph one; describe how you rode it out or how you comforted, accompanied, or helped someone you saw crying and what you realized, gained or learned from this experience in paragraph two.

Step 1 聯想提示 Association 依人、事、時、地、物、原因和方法聯想與題目相關的事項

- 誰是我安慰的對象？ Who did I comfort?
- 我如何安慰這個人？ How did I comfort this person?
- 我從這次經驗中學到了什麼？ What did I learn from the experience?
- 這個人發生了什麼事？ What happened to this person?
- 有那些具體的例子？ Specific examples?
- 這個人聽完我安慰的話之後覺得如何？

  How did this person feel after listening to my comforting words?

Step 2 組織大綱提示 Organization 依照想到的事項，定出寫作優先順序及細節

第一段

1. 主題句：我發現坐在我旁邊的同學在哭泣。

2. 支持句：我問她為何哭泣。

    原因： a. 她數學期中考不及格。

    b. 考試時因為太累而無法集中精神。

    c. 考前熬夜準備考試。

UNIT
1

UNIT
2

UNIT
3

UNIT
4

UNIT
5

UNIT
6

UNIT
7

UNIT
8

UNIT
9

UNIT
10

UNIT
11

UNIT
12

UNIT
13

UNIT
14

UNIT
15

UNIT
16

UNIT
17

UNIT
18

UNIT
19

UNIT
20

3. 結果：她嘆息並淚水盈眶。

第二段

1. 主題句：我盡力安慰她。

2. 支持句：

　　a. 如何安慰她：利用海倫凱勒的例子。

　　b. 她的反應：破涕為笑。

3. 結論：我也學到了一課：「成功是經驗一次又一次的失敗，卻不失去熱忱。」

Step 3　範文 Model Composition

A Comfort Word

　　Once I discovered that the classmate sitting next to me was crying. I turned aside and asked her why she was feeling so bad. She told me she was frustrated by her failure to pass her mid-term math exam. It was not because she hadn't studied hard before the exam, but because she had been too fatigued to concentrate during the exam. She explained further that she had stayed up all night preparing for the exam the night before. Then, she sighed deeply with her eyes brimming with tears.

　　I did all I could to comfort her. I told her that quite a few great women, like Helen Keller, could ultimately achieve success despite a succession of failures. My words really touched her, and she finally stopped crying and smiled again. I also learned a lesson from this experience. As Winston Churchill once said, "Success is going from failure to failure without losing enthusiasm."

Step 4　寫句實戰分析 Analyzing Sentences

第一段

1. Once I discovered that the classmate sitting next to me was crying.
　　有一次我發現坐在我旁邊的同學正在哭泣。

· the classmate sitting next to me = the classmate who was sitting next to me　分詞或分詞片語當形容詞，相當於簡化的關係子句。

2. I turned aside and asked her why she was feeling so bad.

我轉過去問她為何心情這麼差。

① 文法句型 · turn aside　(把頭或身體) 轉開

3. She told me she was frustrated by her failure to pass her mid-term math exam.

她告訴我她因為數學期中考不及格而感到挫折。

① 字詞提示 · frustrated *adj.* 挫折的

4. It was not because she hadn't studied hard before the exam, but because she had been too fatigued to concentrate during the exam.

並不是因為她考前不用功，而是因為考試時太累而無法集中精神。

① 字詞提示
· fatigued *adj.* 疲憊的
· concentrate *v.* 全神貫注

① 文法句型
· not...but....　不是…，而是…
· too...to...　太…而不能…

5. She explained further that she had stayed up all night preparing for the exam the night before.

她進一步解釋說，考前一整晚都在熬夜準備考試。

① 文法句型 · stay up　熬夜

6. Then, she sighed deeply with her eyes brimming with tears.

她深深地嘆息著，淚水盈眶。

① 字詞提示
· sigh *v.* 嘆息
· brim *v.* 充滿

① 文法句型 · with + O + V-ing　表附帶狀態的分詞片語

第二段

1. <u>I did all I could to comfort her.</u>
   我竭盡所能來安慰她。

   ⓘ 文法
   句型
   · do all one can to + V　竭盡全力

2. <u>I told her that quite a few great women, like Helen Keller, could ultimately achieve success despite a succession of failures.</u>
   我告訴她有許多偉大的女性，像海倫凱勒，儘管經過一連串失敗而終能成功。

   ⓘ 字詞
   提示
   · ultimately *adv.* 最終地，終極地
   · achieve *v.* 達成
   · despite *prep.* 儘管
   · succession *n.* 一連串，接續

3. <u>My words really touched her, and she finally stopped crying and smiled again.</u>
   我這番話讓她相當感動，而她最後破涕為笑。

   ⓘ 文法
   句型
   · 注意：stop V-ing　停止做某事
   　　　　stop to V　停下來做另一事

4. <u>I also learned a lesson from this experience.</u>
   我也從這次經驗得到一個啟示。

   ⓘ 文法
   句型
   · 注意：learn A from B　從 B 學到 A

5. <u>As Winston Churchill once said, "Success is going from failure to failure without losing enthusiasm."</u>
   正如邱吉爾所說：「成功是經歷一次又一次的失敗，卻不失去熱忱」。

   ⓘ 字詞
   提示
   · enthusiasm *n.* 熱忱

Step 5

用字遣詞 Words → Sentences

1. frustrated [`frʌs͵tretɪd] *adj.* 挫折的
   Jimmy felt extremely frustrated when he was turned down by Rosa.
   當 Jimmy 被 Rosa 拒絕時，他感到極度沮喪。

2. fatigued [fə`tigd] *adj.* 疲憊的

The manager was so fatigued that he couldn't pay attention during the meeting.

經理太疲憊了，以致於在會議中無法專心。

3. concentrate [`kɑnsən͵tret] *v.* 全神貫注

Max couldn't concentrate on a book for a long time.

Max 沒辦法長時間全神貫注地閱讀一本書。

4. sigh [saɪ] *v.* 嘆息

When the exam was finally over, Joe sighed with relief.

考試終於結束了，Joe 因為放鬆而嘆息。

5. brim [brɪm] *v.* 充滿

Nathan's eyes brimmed with tears when he was leaving his family.

當 Nathan 要離開家人時，他淚水盈眶。

6. ultimately [`ʌltəmetlɪ] *adv.* 最終地，終極地

Ultimately, the boss has to make the final decision.

最終，老闆必須下最後的決定。

7. achieve [ə`tʃiv] *v.* 達成

They could not achieve their aims.   他們無法達成目標。

8. despite [dɪs`paɪt] *prep.* 儘管

Bill was good at physics despite the fact that he found it boring.

Bill 很擅長物理，儘管他覺得物理很無聊。

9. succession [sʌk`sɛʃən] *n.* 一連串，接續

Nina had a succession of colds.   Nina 一直感冒。

10. enthusiasm [ɪn`θjuzɪ͵æzəm] *n.* 熱忱

Mr. Johnson never lost his enthusiasm for teaching.

Johnson 先生從來沒有失去教學的熱忱。

文法句型 Grammar Points → Sentences

1. turn aside   (把頭或身體) 轉開

I waved at Dave enthusiastically but he just turned aside.

我熱情的對 Dave 揮手，他卻只是把頭轉開。

2. not...but....   不是…，而是…

I like the actress not because she is beautiful, but because she is extremely talented.

我喜歡這個女演員不是因為她漂亮，而是因為她極有才華。

3. too...to...　太…而不能…

Jamie's far too young to go to school on her own.

Jamie 年紀太小了，不能自己去上學。

4. stay up　熬夜

Lani stayed up reading until midnight.　Lani 熬夜看書到半夜。

5. with + O + V-ing　表附帶狀態的分詞片語

The athlete landed on the ground with his body leaning forwards.

這位運動員著地時身體向前傾。

6. do all one can to + V　竭盡全力

The girl did all she could to cry for help.　女孩竭盡所能地大聲呼救。

UNIT
1

UNIT
2

UNIT
3

UNIT
4

UNIT
5

UNIT
6

UNIT
7

UNIT
8

UNIT
9

UNIT
10

UNIT
11

UNIT
12

UNIT
13

UNIT
14

UNIT
15

UNIT
16

UNIT
17

UNIT
18

UNIT
19

UNIT
20

UNIT 4

Narrative Writing　敘事文

A Dozing Dream in Class　上課打瞌睡做夢

94 年學測英文作文試題

請根據以下三張連環圖畫的內容，以 "In the English class last week, ..." 開頭，將圖中主角所經歷的事件作一合理的敘述。

Reasonably narrate a whole series of events that the leading character experienced through the following three-frame comic strip. Begin your writing with "In the English class last week, ..."

Step 1　看圖聯想 Association　依人、事、時、地、物、原因和方法聯想與題目相關的事項

Step 2　組織大綱提示 Organization　依照想到的事項，定出寫作優先順序及細節

第一段 (圖 1)

1. 主題句：上禮拜英文課時，王老師正在上第三十課。

2. 支持句：

　　a. 那是關於「四海一家」這首歌的一課。

　　b. 每個學生都很專注地聽這首歌，除了我以外。

第二段 (圖 2)

1. 主題句：我當時正在打瞌睡，並且在做夢。

2. 支持句：

　　a. 在我的夢境裡，我是個英文老師。

　　b. 我正在教我的學生英文文法。

UNIT 1
UNIT 2
UNIT 3
UNIT 4
UNIT 5
UNIT 6
UNIT 7
UNIT 8
UNIT 9
UNIT 10
UNIT 11
UNIT 12
UNIT 13
UNIT 14
UNIT 15
UNIT 16
UNIT 17
UNIT 18
UNIT 19
UNIT 20

　　c. 全班都很安靜，只有老師一個人喋喋不休地講授細節。

　　d. 所有的學生都在打瞌睡。

第三段 (圖 3)

　1. 我很生氣的敲打前面的桌子。

　2. 我大吼：「醒醒吧！」

　3. 突然間，我聽見王老師說：「醒醒吧！」

　4. 我這才知道每個人都在看我打瞌睡。

Step 3　範文 Model Composition

A Dozing Dream in Class

　　In the English class last week, Mr. Wang was teaching Lesson 30. It was a lesson about the song "We Are the World," which was written and composed by Michael Jackson and Lionel Richie. Every student was listening attentively to the song, except me.

　　I was dozing off and having a dream. In my dream, the date on the blackboard changed from January 15, 2005, to January 15, 2025. I was teaching English grammar to my students. The whole class was entirely quiet, except for the teacher blabbering about the nuts and bolts. So you would guess that all of my students were dozing off in class.

　　I was in such a rage that I banged my hand on the desk in front of me. "Wake up!" I roared. All at once, I heard Mr. Wang saying, "Wake up!" Much to my embarrassment, I realized that everybody had been watching me dozing off.

Step 4　寫句實戰分析 Analyzing Sentences

第一段

　1. In the English class last week, Mr. Wang was teaching Lesson 30.
　　上禮拜的英文課，王老師在上第三十課。

> ⚠文法句型　・注意：本篇屬敘事文，全篇動詞用過去式。

2. It was a lesson about the song "We Are the World," which was written and composed by Michael Jackson and Lionel Richie.

那是關於「四海一家」這首歌的一課，這首歌是由麥克傑克森 (Michael Jackson) 和萊諾李奇 (Lionel Richie) 所譜寫的。

> ⚠字詞提示　・compose *v.* 編寫，作曲

3. Every student was listening attentively to the song, except me.

每個學生都很專注地聽這首歌，除了我之外。

> ⚠字詞提示　・attentively *adv.* 專注地

> ⚠文法句型　・except (for)　除了⋯之外

第二段

1. I was dozing off and having a dream.

我當時正在打瞌睡，並且在做夢。

> ⚠文法句型
> ・doze off　打瞌睡
> ・注意：and 二邊連接對等的詞組。

2. In my dream, the date on the blackboard changed from January 15, 2005, to January 15, 2025.

在我的夢境裡，黑板上的日期從二〇〇五年一月十五日變成了二〇二五年一月十五日。

> ⚠文法句型
> ・change from A to B　從 A 的情形轉變為 B
> ・注意：一般英文日期的寫法，例：February 15, 2008

3. I was teaching English grammar to my students.

我正在教我的學生英文文法。

> ⚠文法句型　・注意：teach 可當授與動詞，後加直接受詞 + to + 間接受詞。

4. The whole class was entirely quiet, except for the teacher blabbering about the nuts and bolts.

UNIT
1
UNIT
2
UNIT
3
UNIT
4
UNIT
5
UNIT
6
UNIT
7
UNIT
8
UNIT
9
UNIT
10
UNIT
11
UNIT
12
UNIT
13
UNIT
14
UNIT
15
UNIT
16
UNIT
17
UNIT
18
UNIT
19
UNIT
20

全班都很安靜，只有老師一個人喋喋不休地講授細節。

⚠️ **字詞提示**
- blabber *v.* 喋喋不休
- the nuts and bolts *n.* (事物的) 基本要素，具體細節

5. So you would guess that all of my students were dozing off in class.

所以你可以猜的到，我所有的學生都在打瞌睡。

第三段

1. I was in such a rage that I banged my hand on the desk in front of me.

我勃然大怒，很用力地用手敲我前面的桌子。

⚠️ **文法句型**
- in a rage　勃然大怒
- such + 名詞 (詞組) + that + S + V　如此⋯以致於⋯
- bang + 身體部位 + on sth.　用身體某部位重擊某物

2. "Wake up!" I roared.

我大吼：「醒醒吧！」

⚠️ **字詞提示**
- roar *v.* 大吼

⚠️ **文法句型**
- 注意：引句後面的主詞若為代名詞，則不倒裝，置於動詞之前。

3. All at once, I heard Mr. Wang saying, "Wake up!"

突然間，我聽見王老師說：「醒醒吧！」

⚠️ **文法句型**
- all at once　突然
- 感官動詞 hear/watch/see... + O + V/V-ing....

4. Much to my embarrassment, I realized that everybody had been watching me dozing off.

令我尷尬的是，我這才知道原來每個人都在看我打瞌睡。

⚠️ **文法句型**
- to one's + 情緒性 N　令人感到⋯
- 注意：過去完成式比過去式發生的時間早。

Step 5

用字遣詞 Words → Sentences

1. compose [kəm`poz] *v.* 編寫，作曲

   Mozart composed hundreds of musical works in his short life of 35 years.

   莫札特在短短 35 年的壽命當中創作了數以百計的音樂作品。

2. attentively [ə`tɛntɪvlɪ] *adv.* 專注地

   The audience listened attentively to the speech.

   觀眾們專注地聽著演講。

3. blabber [`blæbɚ] *v.* 喋喋不休

   What was Grandpa blabbering on about?　爺爺為了什麼事情喋喋不休？

4. the nuts and bolts [`nʌtz ən `boltz] *n.* (事物的) 基本要素，具體細節

   Dad taught me about the nuts and bolts of running a business, but I was not interested at all.　爸爸教我經營一家公司的細節，但是我一點興趣也沒有。

5. roar [ror] *v.* 大吼

   "Stand back!" the firefighter roared at the crowd.

   消防員對群眾大吼：「退後一點！」

文法句型 Grammar Points → Sentences

1. except (for)　除了…之外

   My friends all came to my birthday party, except (for) Jane.

   除了 Jane 之外，我的朋友都來參加我的生日派對。

2. doze off　打瞌睡

   John usually dozes off in class.　John 上課常常打瞌睡。

3. change from A to B　從 A 的情形轉變為 B

   The traffic lights changed from red to green.　交通號誌從紅燈轉為綠燈。

4. in a rage　勃然大怒

   Sue went out of the room in a rage.　Sue 勃然大怒地衝出了房間。

5. such + 名詞 (詞組) + that + S + V　如此…以致於…

   Jeff had put on such a large amount of weight that he couldn't put on his pants.

   Jeff 胖了好多，所以他的褲子都穿不下了。

6. bang + 身體部位 + on sth.　用身體某部位重擊某物

   Peter tripped and banged his knee on the ground.

   Peter 絆了一跤，膝蓋撞到地板。

all at once　突然

　　All at once, there was a loud crushing sound.　突然間，有陣巨響。

8. 感官動詞 hear/watch/see... + O + V/V-ing....

　　Paul heard someone calling his name.　Paul 聽到有人在叫他的名字。

9. to one's + 情緒性 N　令人感到…

　　The new dramatist's work, to my surprise, was quite good.

　　令我驚訝的是，這個新生代劇作家的作品還挺精采的。

UNIT 5

Narrative Writing 敘事文

A Fender-Bender 小擦撞

北區公立高中 95 年第二次學測模擬考

根據下列三張連環圖畫的內容，將圖中男子與女子所發生的事件，作一合理的敘述。文長 120 個英文字左右。

Reasonably narrate the events happening to the man and the woman through the following three-frame comic strip. Write your essay in 120 words or so.

Step 1 看圖聯想 Association　依人、事、時、地、物、原因和方法聯想與題目相關的事項

Step 2 組織大綱提示 Organization　依照想到的事項，定出寫作優先順序及細節

圖 1

1. 主題句：Smith 先生去車商那兒取新車。

2. 付完錢他便開著新車離開。

3. 他在馬路上開得很慢，試圖把車速保持在時速三十公里左右。

圖 2

4. 主題句：新車發生小擦撞，撞上了超市的購物手推車。

5. 他聽見手推車的主人尖叫。

6. 他的汽車和那台手推車都有受損，手推車主人的雜貨也散落在馬路上。

圖 3

7. 主題句：他和這位女士開始指責對方。

8. 結論：兩個教訓

第一，過馬路之前，一定要記得先看一下。

第二，事實一旦造成，便無法復原了。

Step 3 範文 Model Composition

A Fender-Bender

On a clear morning, Mr. Smith was extremely excited to go to Speedy Car Dealership to pick up his new car, which was priced at US$28,000. Right after paying a down payment of twenty percent, he drove his new car away from the car dealer. He drove slowly on the road, trying to keep the speed at around thirty kilometers per hour. But, unfortunately, as he was driving by a supermarket, his car collided with a shopping cart being pushed by a lady and then came to a stop on the roadside near the supermarket. At the moment, he heard the lady screaming. No sooner had he got out of the car than he saw damage to both his car and the shopping cart, and her groceries scattering across the road. He and the lady started accusing each other of being rude and irresponsible. From the story, we learn two things: first, we must always remember to be careful when crossing the road; second, what is done cannot be undone.

Step 4 寫句實戰分析 Analyzing Sentences

1. On a clear morning, Mr. Smith was extremely excited to go to Speedy Car Dealership to pick up his new car, which was priced at US$28,000.

   某個晴朗的上午，Smith 先生興致勃勃地到 Speedy 車商那兒取他的新車，那輛車定價兩萬八千美元。

   ⚠ 字詞提示
   - extremely *adv.* 極端地，非常
   - price *v.* 給…定價

   ⚠ 文法句型
   - pick up sth. 拿取

UNIT 1
UNIT 2
UNIT 3
UNIT 4
UNIT 5
UNIT 6
UNIT 7
UNIT 8
UNIT 9
UNIT 10
UNIT 11
UNIT 12
UNIT 13
UNIT 14
UNIT 15
UNIT 16
UNIT 17
UNIT 18
UNIT 19
UNIT 20

2. Right after paying a down payment of twenty percent, he drove his new car away from the car dealer.

付完百分之二十的頭期款之後，他就開著他的新車離開了那家車商。

> !字詞提示
> • down payment *n.* 分期付款的頭期款；訂金
> • dealer *n.* 經銷商，業者

3. He drove slowly on the road, trying to keep the speed at around thirty kilometers per hour.

他在馬路上開得很慢，試圖將車速保持在時速三十公里左右。

> !文法句型
> • S + V$_1$..., V$_2$-ing.... = S + V$_1$..., and V$_2$....　分詞構句

4. But, unfortunately, as he was driving by a supermarket, his car collided with a shopping cart being pushed by a lady and then came to a stop on the roadside near the supermarket.

但是，不幸地，當他開車經過一家超市時，他的車子撞上了一位女士推著的購物手推車，然後停在超市附近的馬路邊。

> !字詞提示
> • collide *v.* 相撞
> • shopping cart *n.* 購物手推車

> !文法句型
> • come to a stop　停止
> • 請注意過去進行式 was + V-ing 與進行被動的用法 (which was) being + V-en。

5. At the moment, he heard the lady screaming.

當時，他聽見這位女士尖叫。

> !字詞提示
> • scream *v.* 尖叫，呼嘯

> !文法句型
> • 注意：本句為感官動詞 + O + V-ing 的用法。

6. No sooner had he got out of the car than he saw damage to both his car and the shopping cart, and her groceries scattering across the road.

他一下車就看到他的車和那台手推車都有受損，而她買的雜貨也散落在馬路上。

UNIT 1
UNIT 2
UNIT 3
UNIT 4
UNIT 5
UNIT 6
UNIT 7
UNIT 8
UNIT 9
UNIT 10
UNIT 11
UNIT 12
UNIT 13
UNIT 14
UNIT 15
UNIT 16
UNIT 17
UNIT 18
UNIT 19
UNIT 20

ⓘ 字詞
提示
- damage *n.* 損壞
- scatter *v.* 散落，分散

ⓘ 文法
句型
- no sooner...than....　一…就…

7. He and the lady started accusing each other of being rude and irresponsible.

他和這位女士開始互控對方無禮和不負責任。

ⓘ 字詞
提示
- irresponsible *adj.* 不負責任的

ⓘ 文法
句型
- accuse sb. of + 罪行　指控某人犯下某罪行

8. From the story, we learn two things: first, we must always remember to be careful when crossing the road; second, what is done cannot be undone.

從這則故事我們學到兩件事：第一，過馬路時一定要記得小心為上；第二，事實一旦造成，便無法復原了。

ⓘ 字詞
提示
- undo *v.* 使復原

Step 5

用字遣詞 Words → Sentences

1. extremely [ɪk`strimlɪ] *adv.* 極端地，非常

   The girl is extremely beautiful.　這位女孩漂亮極了。

2. price [praɪs] *v.* 給…定價

   The bike was priced at two thousand dollars.　這輛腳踏車定價兩千塊。

3. down payment [`daʊn `pemənt] *n.* 分期付款的頭期款；訂金

   Lisa has made a down payment on a new computer.

   Lisa 已經付了一台新電腦的頭期款。

4. dealer [`dilɚ] *n.* 經銷商，業者

   Matt bought a used car from a second-hand car dealer.

   Matt 從一個二手車商那兒買了一輛中古車。

5. collide [kə`laɪd] *v.* 相撞

   The two cars collided at the crossroads.　這兩輛車在十字路口相撞。

6. shopping cart [`ʃɑpɪŋ ˌkɑrt] *n.* 購物手推車

Be sure to put your shopping cart back to where you got it.

記得把購物手推車放回原處。

7. scream [skrim] *v.* 尖叫，呼嘯

The firefighters could hear people screaming for help.

消防人員可以聽見人們呼叫求救的聲音。

8. damage [`dæmɪdʒ] *n.* 損壞

Last night, strong winds caused serious damage to the windows.

昨晚，強風造成窗戶嚴重受損。

9. scatter [`skætɚ] *v.* 散落，分散

The scared crowd scattered at the sound of gunshots.

聽到槍聲，受驚嚇的群眾四散逃開。

10. irresponsible [ˌɪrɪ`spɑnsəbl] *adj.* 不負責任的

It was irresponsible of a mother to leave her kid alone in the house.

媽媽把小孩單獨留在家裡是不負責任的。

11. undo [ʌn`du] *v.* 使復原

It will be very hard to undo the damage. 要把損害恢復將非常困難。

文法句型 Grammar Points → Sentences

1. pick up sth. 拿取

Could you help me pick up the books I ordered?

你可以幫我拿我訂的書嗎？

2. S + V₁..., V₂ing.... = S + V₁..., and V₂.... 分詞構句

分詞構句的動詞和主要子句動詞同時發生。

They speed up, trying to beat the light before it changes.

他們加速，試圖搶在變燈之前通過。

3. come to a stop 停止

A taxi came to a stop in front of the hotel. 一輛計程車停在飯店門口。

4. no sooner...than.... 一…就…

No sooner had my dad started washing the car than it started raining.

我爸爸才剛開始洗車，就開始下雨了。

5. accuse sb. of + 罪行 指控某人犯下某罪行

My teacher accused me of lying. 老師指控我說謊。

UNIT
1
UNIT
2
UNIT
3
UNIT
4
UNIT
5
UNIT
6
UNIT
7
UNIT
8
UNIT
9
UNIT
10
UNIT
11
UNIT
12
UNIT
13
UNIT
14
UNIT
15
UNIT
16
UNIT
17
UNIT
18
UNIT
19
UNIT
20

UNIT 6

Narrative Writing　敘事文

A Misunderstanding　誤解

95 年指定科目考試

　　人的生活中，難免有遭人誤解因而感到委屈的時候。請以此為主題，寫一篇至少 120 字的英文作文；文分兩段，第一段描述個人被誤解的經驗，第二段談這段經驗對個人的影響與啟示。

　　In our lifetime, we can scarcely avoid feeling wronged because of being misunderstood by others. Use no less than 120 words to write a two-paragraph composition on a misunderstanding that happened to you. In paragraph one, describe your experience of being misunderstood; in paragraph two, write about how this experience influenced you and what it meant to you.

✎ **Step 1** 聯想提示 Association　依人、事、時、地、物、原因和方法聯想與題目相關的事項

- 誰誤會我？　Who misunderstood me?
- 這件事是在哪裡發生？　Where did it happen?
- 這件事是在什麼時候發生的？　When did it happen?
- 她／他如何誤會我？　How did she/he misunderstand me?
- 誤會的內容是什麼？　What was it about?
- 我的感受如何？　How did I feel about it?

✎ **Step 2** 組織大綱提示 Organization　依照想到的事項，定出寫作優先順序及細節

第一段

1. 主題句：同班同學考試作弊被檢舉。

2. 支持句：細節

　a. 他懷疑我打小報告。

　b. 我受不了他對我的不實指控。

　c. 我努力證明我的清白，並希望他明白他冤枉我了。

第二段

1. 主題句：那是好朋友對我最嚴重的侮辱之一。

2. 支持句：細節

　　a. 對我來說，告密幾乎跟犯罪同義。

　　b. 我覺得很不好受，因為他對我的指控不公平。

　　c. 但只能逆來順受。

　　d. 現在還是因為這個誤會感到難過。

Step 3 範文 Model Composition

A Misunderstanding

　　Once in junior high school, one of my classmates was reported for cheating on an exam. He suspected that I was the one who snitched on him because I sat right behind him and could see whether he was cheating or not. I was sensitive and couldn't take his groundless accusation against me. I tried all I could to convince him of my innocence and wished he understood that he had done me a great wrong.

　　That was one of the gravest insults I had ever received from someone who I thought was a better friend than that. To me, being a snitch is akin to crime itself. It makes me feel sick to my stomach. I really felt hurt because what he accused me of was not fair. However, I could do nothing but grin and bear it. Right now I am still confused and a little upset with him for misunderstanding me.

Step 4 寫句實戰分析 Analyzing Sentences

第一段

1. Once in junior high school, one of my classmates was reported for cheating on an exam. 唸國中時，有一次我的同班同學考試作弊被檢舉。

　　!字詞提示 ・report v. 檢舉

UNIT
1

UNIT
2

UNIT
3

UNIT
4

UNIT
5

UNIT
6

UNIT
7

UNIT
8

UNIT
9

UNIT
10

UNIT
11

UNIT
12

UNIT
13

UNIT
14

UNIT
15

UNIT
16

UNIT
17

UNIT
18

UNIT
19

UNIT
20

⚠ **文法句型** · be reported for + V-ing　被檢舉做了…

2. He suspected that I was the one who snitched on him because I sat right behind him and could see whether he was cheating or not.

他懷疑是我打小報告，因為我就坐在他的正後方，可以看到他有沒有作弊。

⚠ **字詞提示** · suspect *v.* 懷疑
· snitch *v.* 告密

⚠ **文法句型** · snitch on sb. (to sb.)　(向某人) 打某人的小報告

3. I was sensitive and couldn't take his groundless accusation against me.

我很敏感，而且受不了他對我毫無根據的指控。

⚠ **字詞提示** · groundless *adj.* 沒有根據的
· accusation *n.* 指控

4. I tried all I could to convince him of my innocence and wished he understood that he had done me wrong.

我盡我所能使他相信我的清白，並希望他明白他使我蒙受了冤屈。

⚠ **字詞提示** · innocence *n.* 清白

⚠ **文法句型** · convince sb. of sth.　使某人相信某事
· A do B wrong　A 冤枉 B
· 注意：過去完成式比過去式發生的時間更早。

第二段

1. That was one of the gravest insults I had ever received from someone who I thought was a better friend than that.

那是我所受到過最嚴重的侮辱之一，而它來自於某個我認為不會這樣對我的好朋友。

⚠ **字詞提示** · grave *adj.* 嚴重的
· insult *n.* 侮辱

⚠ **文法句型** · 注意：副詞 ever 搭配完成式及前面的最高級形容詞。

2. To me, being a snitch is akin to crime itself.

對我來說，告密幾乎跟犯罪沒什麼兩樣。

① 字詞
提示
· snitch *n.* 告密者

① 文法
句型
· be akin to 相似的，同類的

3. It makes me feel sick to my stomach.

它讓我覺得很不好受。

① 文法
句型
· feel sick to one's stomach 覺得很不好受
· 注意：本句的動詞用現在式來表示一種目前仍存在的狀態。

4. I really felt hurt because what he accused me of was not fair.

我真的感到很受傷，因為他對我的指控是不公平的。

① 文法
句型
· accuse sb. of sth. 指控某人做了某事
· 注意：以 what 引導的子句當主詞時，動詞用單數。

5. However, I could do nothing but grin and bear it.

然而，我只能逆來順受。

① 文法
句型
· can/could do nothing but + 原型 V 只能
· grin and bear it 逆來順受

6. Right now I am still confused and a little upset with him for misunderstanding me.

此刻，我還是因為他對我的誤解而感到困惑並且有些難過。

① 文法
句型
· be upset with sb. for + V-ing 針對某人做某事而感到不悅或難過

Step 5

用字遣詞 Words → Sentences

1. report [rɪ`port] *v.* 檢舉

The young lady was reported to the police for drunk driving.

這位年輕女子遭人向警方檢舉她酒醉駕車。

2. suspect [sə`spɛkt] *v.* 懷疑

I suspect that the student might be lying. 我懷疑這個學生可能在說謊。

3. snitch [snɪtʃ] *v.*; *n.* 告密；告密者

    My brother always snitches on me to my mom when I watch TV before finishing my homework. 我哥哥總是向媽媽告密，說我還沒有做完家庭作業就看電視。

4. groundless [ˈgraʊndlɪs] *adj.* 沒有根據的

    Their fears of their daughter's marriage being broken proved groundless.
    他們害怕女兒婚姻破裂的憂慮已被證明是沒有根據的。

5. accusation [ˌækjəˈzeʃən] *n.* 指控

    No one believed Michael's wild accusations against his wife.
    沒有人相信 Michael 對他太太的胡亂指控。

6. innocence [ˈɪnəsns̩] *n.* 清白

    We are sure of Jack's innocence. 我們確信 Jack 的清白。

7. grave [grev] *adj.* 嚴重的

    The villagers in the mountain were in grave danger when the typhoon hit.
    颱風來襲時，山上村民的情況危急。

8. insult [ˈɪnsʌlt] *n.* 侮辱

    Their comments were seen as an insult to our country.
    他們的言論被視為是對我國的一種侮辱。

文法句型 Grammar Points → Sentences

1. convince sb. of sth. 使某人相信某事

    You have to convince your boss of your enthusiasm for the job.
    你必須讓你的老闆相信你對這份工作的熱忱。

2. A do B wrong A 冤枉 B

    Mom has done us wrong. 媽媽錯怪我們了。

3. be akin to 相似的，同類的

    Your music taste is akin to mine. 你的音樂品味和我的差不多。

4. feel sick to one's stomach 覺得很不好受

    My boss's harsh sarcasm made me feel sick to my stomach.
    我老闆的嚴厲諷刺讓我覺得很不好受。

5. accuse sb. of sth. 指控某人做了某事

    The bookstore owner accused the boy of stealing a comic book.
    書店老闆指控那男孩偷了一本漫畫書。

6. can/could do nothing but + 原型 V 只能

UNIT 1
UNIT 2
UNIT 3
UNIT 4
UNIT 5
UNIT 6
UNIT 7
UNIT 8
UNIT 9
UNIT 10
UNIT 11
UNIT 12
UNIT 13
UNIT 14
UNIT 15
UNIT 16
UNIT 17
UNIT 18
UNIT 19
UNIT 20

It's raining hard. We can do nothing but wait now.

雨下的很大。我們現在也只能等了。

7. grin and bear it　逆來順受

Please don't just grin and bear it. Do something to help yourself with the situation.　請不要逆來順受。做點事來幫助自己應付這種處境。

8. be upset with sb. for + V-ing　針對某人做某事而感到不悅或難過

I am upset with you for not telling me that you are getting married.

我生你的氣是因為你沒有告訴我你要結婚了。

UNIT
1

UNIT
2

UNIT
3

UNIT
4

UNIT
5

UNIT
6

UNIT
7

UNIT
8

UNIT
9

UNIT
10

UNIT
11

UNIT
12

UNIT
13

UNIT
14

UNIT
15

UNIT
16

UNIT
17

UNIT
18

UNIT
19

UNIT
20

UNIT 7

Narrative Writing　敘事文

A Picnic at the Beach　海灘野餐

　　寫一篇有關你曾經度過的一次家庭野餐，文長不得少於 120 個英文字。你可能在公園裡、在湖邊或在海灘享受那次野餐。

　　Use no less than 120 words to write about a family picnic that you have had. You may have enjoyed the picnic in the park, by the lake, or at the beach.

Step 1　聯想提示 Association　依人、事、時、地、物、原因和方法聯想與題目相關的事項

- 我跟誰去野餐？　Who did I go on a picnic with?
- 我們在哪裡野餐？　Where did we have a picnic?
- 我們怎麼去？　How did we get there?
- 我們在那裡看到了什麼？　What did we see there?
- 我們帶了什麼食物？　What specific foods did we bring?
- 我們在那裡做了什麼？　What specific things did we do there?

Step 2　組織大綱提示 Organization　依照想到的事項，定出寫作優先順序及細節

第一段

1. 主題句：我們全家人到淡水附近的一個海灘去野餐。
2. 細節：
   a. 我們開車去，旅途中很開心。
   b. 約花了四十分鐘抵達目的地。
   c. 一到了海灘，我們都變得很興奮。
   d. 海灘上有很多人，從事各種活動。

第二段

1. 享受野餐的經過：
   a. 我們找到了一個空位，把塑膠墊子攤開在沙灘上。
   b. 我們把食物拿出來。
2. 結論：我們一起在海邊享受野餐。

第三段

1.享受海灘遊玩的經過：

　　a.在沙灘上玩飛盤、在海裡游泳、沿著海灘漫步。

　　b.最精采的部份之一就是堆沙堡。

　　c.沿著海岸拍了許多美麗的風景照。

第四段

1.主題句：整整玩了一個下午。

2.支持句：我們玩得很累，收拾好東西準備回家。

3.結論：我們真的玩得很愉快。

Step 3　範文 Model Composition

A Picnic at the Beach

One wonderful summer day, all my family had a picnic at the beach near Danshui. We went there by car. We were singing, chatting and laughing on our way to the beach. It took us forty minutes or so to get to the destination. On arriving at the beach, we all got so excited. The beach was swarming with tourists. There we saw many people fishing, swimming, going surfing and scuba diving.

We found a vacant place to spread out a plastic mat on the sand. We took out the foods we had packed in airtight plastic containers and put them on the mat, including sandwiches, fried chicken, crackers, soft drinks, salad and fruit. We enjoyed our picnic together by the ocean.

Besides, we played Frisbee on the sand, swam in the ocean, and strolled leisurely along the beach. One of the highlights of the trip was building sand castles. We also took lots of pictures of the views along the beautiful seashore, such as ocean waves, boats, and mountains.

The picnic lasted all afternoon. We got so tired that we packed our things and were ready to go home. Really, we all had a good time.

UNIT
1

UNIT
2

UNIT
3

UNIT
4

UNIT
5

UNIT
6

UNIT
7

UNIT
8

UNIT
9

UNIT
10

UNIT
11

UNIT
12

UNIT
13

UNIT
14

UNIT
15

UNIT
16

UNIT
17

UNIT
18

UNIT
19

UNIT
20

✒ Step 4 寫句實戰分析 Analyzing Sentences

第一段

1. One wonderful summer day, all my family had a picnic at the beach near Danshui.

   在一個美好的夏日，我們全家人到淡水附近的一個海灘去野餐。

   ⚠ **文法句型** ・注意：表小地方的副詞片語 (at the beach) 置於表大地方的副詞片語 (near Danshui) 之前。

2. We went there by car. We were singing, chatting and laughing on our way to the beach.

   我們開車去那裡，在往海灘的路上我們唱歌、聊天和歡笑。

   ⚠ **文法句型**
   ・ by + 交通工具　搭乘…
   ・ on one's way to + 地方　在往…的途中
   ・注意：過去進行式表示過去一段時間全程的持續動作。

3. It took us forty minutes or so to get to the destination.

   我們大約花了四十分鐘抵達目的地。

   ⚠ **字詞提示** ・ destination n. 目的地

   ⚠ **文法句型**
   ・ It takes sb. + 時間 + to + V　某人花多少時間做了某事
   ・注意：It 是虛主詞，真正主詞為不定詞片語 to get to the destination。

4. On arriving at the beach, we all got so excited.

   一到了海灘，我們都變得很興奮。

   ⚠ **文法句型** ・ On + V-ing..., S +V....　一…，就…

5. The beach was swarming with tourists.

   海灘擠滿了觀光客。

   ⚠ **字詞提示**
   ・ swarm v. 擠滿，群集
   ・ tourist n. 遊客，觀光客

6. There we saw many people fishing, swimming, going surfing and scuba diving.

在那裡我們看見有很多人釣魚、游泳、衝浪以及做水肺潛水。

> **字詞提示**
> • scuba diving *n.* 水肺潛水

> **文法句型**
> • 感官動詞 see/watch/hear... ＋ O ＋ V/V-ing

第二段

1. We found a vacant place to spread out a plastic mat on the sand.
   我們找到了一個空位，把塑膠墊子攤開在沙灘上。

> **字詞提示**
> • vacant *adj.* 空著的，未被佔用的

> **文法句型**
> • spread out　把…攤開

2. We took out the foods we had packed in airtight plastic containers and put them on the mat, including sandwiches, fried chicken, crackers, soft drinks, salad and fruit.
   我們把原先裝在密封塑膠容器中的食物拿出來擺在墊子上，包括三明治、炸雞、餅乾、飲料、沙拉和水果。

> **字詞提示**
> • pack *v.* 包裝
> • airtight *adj.* 密封的

3. We enjoyed our picnic together by the ocean.
   我們一起在海邊享受野餐。

> **文法句型**
> • 注意：「在…的旁邊」用介系詞 by 表達。

第三段

1. Besides, we played Frisbee on the sand, swam in the ocean, and strolled leisurely along the beach.
   此外，我們也在沙灘上玩飛盤、在海裡游泳、悠閒地沿著海灘漫步。

> **字詞提示**
> • Frisbee *n.* 飛盤

2. One of the highlights of the trip was building sand castles.

UNIT
1
UNIT
2
UNIT
3
UNIT
4
UNIT
5
UNIT
6
UNIT
7
UNIT
8
UNIT
9
UNIT
10
UNIT
11
UNIT
12
UNIT
13
UNIT
14
UNIT
15
UNIT
16
UNIT
17
UNIT
18
UNIT
19
UNIT
20

這趟旅遊最精采的部份之一就是堆沙堡。

① 字詞
提示　· highlight *n.* 最精采的部份

3. We also took lots of pictures of the views along the beautiful seashore, such as ocean waves, boats, and mountains.

我們也沿著美麗的海岸拍了許多風景照，例如：海浪、船隻和山脈。

① 文法
句型　· 注意：舉例時可用 "for example"，"such as"，"..., and so on,"，"..., etc." 等等。

第四段

1. The picnic lasted all afternoon.

這次的野餐持續了一整個下午。

① 文法
句型　· last (for) + 一段期間　持續

2. We got so tired that we packed our things and were ready to go home.

我們玩得很累，收拾好東西準備回家。

① 文法
句型　· so...that....　如此…以致於…

3. Really, we all had a good time.

我們真的都玩得很愉快。

① 文法
句型　· 注意：Really 放在句首，用以強調語氣。

Step 5

用字遣詞 Words → Sentences

1. destination [ˌdɛstə`neʃən] *n.* 目的地

At noon they arrived at the destination.　中午他們抵達了目的地。

2. swarm [swɔrm] *v.* 擠滿，群集

The museum is swarming with visitors.　博物館擠滿了參觀者。

3. tourist [`turɪst] *n.* 遊客，觀光客

The plane was packed with Taiwanese tourists.

這架飛機滿載台灣的遊客。

4. scuba diving [`skubə͵daɪvɪŋ] *n.* 水肺潛水

There are more and more people learning scuba diving.

有愈來愈多人在學習水肺潛水。

5. vacant [`vekənt] *adj.* 空著的，未被佔用的

The seat next to her was vacant. 她隔壁的座位是空著的。

6. pack [pæk] *v.* 包裝

When Ann was leaving the company, she packed a few things into a bag.

Ann 離開公司時，將一些東西打包到一個袋子裡。

7. airtight [`ɛr`taɪt] *adj.* 密封的

You must store the cake in an airtight container.

你必須把這個蛋糕儲存在密閉的容器中。

8. Frisbee [`frɪzbi] *n.* 飛盤

Doug is trying to teach his dog to catch Frisbee.

Doug 正試著想教他的狗接飛盤。

9. highlight [`haɪ͵laɪt] *n.* 最精采的部份

The highlights of the match will be broadcast later this evening.

這場比賽最精采的部分將在今晚稍後播出。

文法句型 Grammar Points → Sentences

1. by + 交通工具　搭乘

My friends and I traveled around the island by train.

我跟朋友搭火車環島旅遊。

2. on one's way to + 地方　在往…的途中

Dan came across an old friend on his way to the office.

Dan 在前往辦公室的途中遇到一個老朋友。

3. It takes sb. + 時間 + to + V　某人花多少時間做了某事

It took the workers ten years to complete the bridge.

工人們花了十年的時間才完成這座橋樑。

4. On + V-ing..., S +V....　一…，就…

On arriving at school, Joy found that it was Sunday.

一到學校，Joy 就發現那天是星期天。

5. 感官動詞 see/watch/hear... + O + V/V-ing

I heard a dog barking. 我聽到一隻狗在叫。

6. spread out　把…攤開

My sister and I spread the map out on the floor.

我跟妹妹把這幅地圖攤開在地板上。

7. last (for) + 一段期間　持續

The meeting lasted (for) two hours.　這個會議持續了兩個小時。

8. so...that....　如此…以致於…

Bob spoke so quietly that I could hardly hear him.

Bob 講話好小聲，以致於我幾乎聽不到。

UNIT 1
UNIT 2
UNIT 3
UNIT 4
UNIT 5
UNIT 6
UNIT 7
UNIT 8
UNIT 9
UNIT 10
UNIT 11
UNIT 12
UNIT 13
UNIT 14
UNIT 15
UNIT 16
UNIT 17
UNIT 18
UNIT 19
UNIT 20

UNIT 8

Narrative Writing 敘事文

A Special Day to Remember 一個特別值得回憶的日子

北區公立高中 94 年度第一次學測模擬考

以 "A Special Day to Remember" 為題，敘述你所記得的一個特別的日子，並說明這個日子為什麼會特別令你懷念。文長至少 120 個英文字。

Write an essay entitled "A Special Day to Remember." Write about a special day you remember and explain why. Write your essay in no less than 120 words.

Step 1　聯想提示 Association　依人、事、時、地、物、原因和方法聯想與題目相關的事項

- 這個日子是哪一天？　What day was it?
- 那一天為什麼特別？　Why was it special?
- 我那一天去了哪裡？　Where did I go on that day?
- 誰跟我一起去？　Who went there with me?
- 在那裡發生了什麼事？　What happened there?
- 我的感覺如何？　How did I feel about it?

Step 2　組織大綱提示 Organization　依照想到的事項，定出寫作優先順序及細節

第一段

1. 時間：好幾年前的一個星期天上午。

   身份：國二學生。

   事件：生平第一次造訪育幼院。

   目的：和可愛的小朋友們同樂。

2. 經過：

   a. 我們帶了好多禮物給他們。

   b. 我們從事各式各樣的餘興活動。

   c. 我們唱感恩歌結束了這次的造訪。

第二段

1. 下午，我們又去了陽明山國家公園。

2. 我們在山上健行，途中：

UNIT 1
UNIT 2
UNIT 3
UNIT 4
UNIT 5
UNIT 6
UNIT 7
UNIT 8
UNIT 9
UNIT 10
UNIT 11
UNIT 12
UNIT 13
UNIT 14
UNIT 15
UNIT 16
UNIT 17
UNIT 18
UNIT 19
UNIT 20

a. 對當地豐富的野生生物感到驚嘆。

b. 停下來休息並觀賞地形和景觀之美。

3. 結論：玩得很開心，真是特別值得回憶的一天。

Step 3　範文 Model Composition

A Special Day to Remember

One Sunday morning many years ago, when I was a second-grade student at Ger-Jyh Middle School in Sanchong, I visited an orphanage in Taipei for the first time in my life. I went there with my classmates under the leadership of our English teacher, Mr. Liu. The reason for our visit to the orphanage was to have fun with the lovely children living there. We brought them a lot of gifts, including comic books, candies, and fruit. We engaged in various activities, such as a blindfold game, a treasure hunt, singing, and dancing. We ended the visit with a song of gratitude to God.

In the afternoon, we went to Yangmingshan National Park, located at the northern edge of the Taipei basin. During our journey through the mountains, we hiked and marveled at the rich wildlife in the region—thousands of species of animals and plants. We paused every once in a while to rest and enjoy the beauty of the terrain and landscape. We spent a wonderful afternoon there. It was really a special day to remember.

Step 4　寫句實戰分析 Analyzing Sentences

第一段

1. One Sunday morning many years ago, when I was a second-grade student at Ger-Jyh Middle School in Sanchong, I visited an orphanage in Taipei for the first time in my life.

好幾年前的一個星期天上午，當我還是三重格致中學二年級生時，我生平第一次造訪一家位於台北的育幼院。

⏺**字詞提示** ・ orphanage *n.* 孤兒院，育幼院

⏺**文法句型** ・ for the first time　第一次

2. I went there with my classmates under the leadership of our English teacher, Mr. Liu.

在我們的英文老師劉老師的帶領下，我和同班同學一起造訪該育幼院。

⏺**字詞提示** ・ leadership *n.* 領導

3. The reason for our visit to the orphanage was to have fun with the lovely children living there.

我們造訪該育幼院，是為了要和住在那邊的可愛小朋友們同樂。

⏺**文法句型** ・注意：with 後接名詞詞組，詞組中的動詞要用分詞的形式。

4. We brought them a lot of gifts, including comic books, candies, and fruit.

我們帶了好多禮物給他們，有漫畫書、糖果、以及水果。

⏺**文法句型**
・ bring sb. sth. = bring sth. to/for sb.　(授與動詞) 帶某物給某人
・ including A, B, and C　包括了 A，B，和 C (舉例時)

5. We engaged in various activities, such as a blindfold game, a treasure hunt, singing, and dancing.

我們從事各式各樣的餘興活動，我們玩矇眼遊戲、尋寶遊戲、還有唱歌和跳舞。

⏺**字詞提示** ・ blindfold *n.* 眼罩，遮眼之物 (布或繃帶)

⏺**文法句型** ・ engage in　參與，從事

6. We ended the visit with a song of gratitude to God.

我們以一首感謝上帝的歌結束了這次的造訪。

⏺**字詞提示** ・ gratitude *n.* 感恩，感激

UNIT 1
UNIT 2
UNIT 3
UNIT 4
UNIT 5
UNIT 6
UNIT 7
UNIT 8
UNIT 9
UNIT 10
UNIT 11
UNIT 12
UNIT 13
UNIT 14
UNIT 15
UNIT 16
UNIT 17
UNIT 18
UNIT 19
UNIT 20

⚠ 文法句型 ・ end...with...　以⋯結束⋯

第二段

1. In the afternoon, we went to Yangmingshan National Park, located at the northern edge of the Taipei basin.

下午，我們又去了陽明山國家公園，它就位於台北盆地的北方邊緣地帶。

⚠ 文法句型 ・注意：句中的關係代名詞 + be 動詞可以一起省略，原句為 ..., (which is) located at....

2. During our journey through the mountains, we hiked and marveled at the rich wildlife in the region—thousands of species of animals and plants.

在翻山越嶺的途中，我們一直健行，並對當地豐富的野生生物感到驚嘆——有數千種動植物。

⚠ 字詞提示 ・ journey *n.* 旅程；行程

⚠ 文法句型 ・ marvel at　對⋯感到驚嘆

3. We paused every once in a while to rest and enjoy the beauty of the terrain and landscape.

偶爾我們會停下來休息並觀賞地形和景觀之美。

⚠ 字詞提示 ・ terrain *n.* 地形

⚠ 文法句型 ・ (every) once in a while　有時候，偶爾

4. We spent a wonderful afternoon there. It was really a special day to remember.

我們在那邊度過了一個美妙的下午。那真是特別值得回憶的一天。

⚠ 文法句型 ・注意：句尾的不定詞 to remember 當形容詞用，修飾前面的名詞 day。

✎ Step 5

用字遣詞 Words → Sentences

1. orphanage [ˋɔrfənɪdʒ] *n.* 孤兒院，育幼院

An orphanage is a place for children who don't have parents to take care of them to live. 孤兒院是一個讓沒有父母照顧的孩子們住的地方。

2. leadership [ˈlidəˌʃɪp] *n.* 領導

Under Mr. Johnson's leadership, the party would remain united.

在 Johnson 先生的領導之下，該黨將維持團結。

3. blindfold [ˈblaɪndˌfold] *n.* 眼罩，遮眼之物 (布或繃帶)

Billy likes to practice kung fu with a blindfold on.

Billy 喜歡戴著眼罩練習功夫。

4. gratitude [ˈgrætəˌtjud] *n.* 感恩，感激

Judy expressed immense gratitude to Mr. Thompson.

Judy 對 Thompson 先生表達深深的感謝。

5. journey [ˈdʒɝnɪ] *n.* 旅程，行程

My parents went on a long train journey across Russia.

我爸媽進行了一趟橫跨俄羅斯的漫長火車之旅。

6. terrain [ˈtɛren] *n.* 地形

We looked down at the terrain from the cliff. 我們從懸崖上俯瞰地形。

文法句型 Grammar Points → Sentences

1. for the first time　第一次

Last summer, I took a trip to Japan for the first time and took a lot of pictures there. 去年夏天，我第一次到日本旅遊，並在那裡拍了很多照片。

2. bring sb. sth. = bring sth. to/for sb. (授與動詞) 帶某物給某人

Please bring Mary a cup of coffee. = Please bring a cup of coffee to Mary.

請拿一杯咖啡給 Mary。

3. including A, B, and C　包括了 A，B，和 C (舉例時)

I bought several kinds of fruits at the market, including apples, oranges, and bananas.

我在市場買了好幾種水果，包括蘋果、柳橙以及香蕉。

4. engage in　參與，從事

The two companies have agreed to engage in a comprehensive discussion to resolve the problem.

這兩家公司已經同意參與全面性的討論，以解決這個問題。

5. end...with....　以…結束…

The students ended the ceremony with a song dedicated to their parents.

這些學生以一首獻給他們父母的歌曲作為典禮的結束。

6. marvel at 對⋯感到驚嘆

We marveled at the architecture of the Forbidden City.

我們對紫禁城的建築構造感到驚奇。

7. (every) once in a while 有時候，偶爾

I go to the beach every once in a while. 我有時候會去海邊。

UNIT 9

Narrative Writing　敘事文

A Taxi Ride　搭乘計程車的經驗

請以 A Taxi Ride 為題目,寫一篇 120 到 150 個字左右的英文作文,敘述你搭乘計程車的一次經驗。

Please write an essay with the title "A Taxi Ride" in 120 to 150 words, in which you describe one of your experiences of riding a taxi.

Step 1　聯想提示 Association　依人、事、時、地、物、原因和方法聯想與題目相關的事項

• 我在哪裡上下車?　Where did I get in and off the taxi?
• 這輛計程車有什麼特色?　What was special about the taxi?
• 這位計程車司機有什麼特色?　What was special about the taxi driver?
• 我在車上做什麼?　What did I do in the taxi?
• 我在途中看到了什麼?　What did I see on the way?

Step 2　組織大綱提示 Organization　依照想到的事項,定出寫作優先順序及細節

1. 主題句:說明搭計程車的時間、地點及目的地。
2. 支持句:搭乘的細節
   a. 描寫計程車的外觀。
   b. 告知司機目的地。
   c. 描寫計程車司機:①司機的年齡、身高。
   　　　　　　　　　②司機令我尊敬,因為他很優秀。
   　　　　　　　　　③舉證 1:他開車很小心並且遵守交通規則。
   　　　　　　　　　④舉證 2:他從不闖紅燈。
3. 在車上做的事情:
   a. 與司機閒聊。
   b. 沿途景物盡收眼底。
4. 抵達目的地,花了 40 分鐘。
5. 結果:付車資和小費並互道再見。

UNIT
1
UNIT
2
UNIT
3
UNIT
4
UNIT
5
UNIT
6
UNIT
7
UNIT
8
UNIT
9
UNIT
10
UNIT
11
UNIT
12
UNIT
13
UNIT
14
UNIT
15
UNIT
16
UNIT
17
UNIT
18
UNIT
19
UNIT
20

Step 3 範文 Model Composition

A Taxi Ride

One morning, I took a taxi from Guandu to downtown Taipei. The taxi, bright yellow in color, looked as if it were brand-new. As soon as I got in, I told the driver where I was going. The driver, who looked young, was of average height. He was such a good driver that I respected him. He drove with care and followed the traffic rules all the way to the destination. He never ran a red light. As the car moved along, we chitchatted about this and that. At times, I looked out of the window, interesting sights, such as a wide plain, conspicuous buildings, and vehicles of all sorts, coming into view, one after another. About forty minutes later, we got to Taipei. I paid three hundred and fifty dollars to the driver and told him to keep the change. Then, we said goodbye to each other.

Step 4 寫句實戰分析 Analyzing Sentences

1. One morning, I took a taxi from Guandu to downtown Taipei.
   一天早上，我從關渡搭了一輛計程車要到台北市區。

   ⚠字詞提示
   • downtown *adj.* 位於商業區的；位於市中心的

2. The taxi, bright yellow in color, looked as if it were brand-new. As soon as I got in, I told the driver where I was going.
   這輛計程車是亮黃色的，看起來像全新的。我一上車，就告訴司機我要去哪裡。

   ⚠字詞提示
   • brand-new *adj.* 嶄新的，全新的

   ⚠文法句型
   • as if = as though　似乎，好像。as if 後面用假設法動詞 were。
   • as soon as　一…就…
   • 疑問詞 who/what/when/where/how + S + V 構成名詞子句。本句中 where 引導的名詞子句做直接受詞。

51

3. The driver, who looked young, was of average height. He was such a good driver that I respected him.

這位司機看起來很年輕,身高普通。他是一位非常好的司機,所以我尊敬他。

ⓘ **字詞提示**
- average *adj.* 一般的;普通的

ⓘ **文法句型**
- 連綴動詞 look/sound/smell/taste/feel + adj.
- such + N. + that + S + V 如此…以致於…
- 注意:of + 狀態名詞相當於形容詞。例:of great importance = very important。

4. He drove with care and followed the traffic rules all the way to the destination. He never ran a red light.

他在開往目的地的一路上都小心駕駛,並遵守交通規則。他從不闖紅燈。

ⓘ **字詞提示**
- destination *n.* 目的地

ⓘ **文法句型**
- with care = carefully 小心地
- all the way 一路上
- run a red light 闖紅燈

5. As the car moved along, we chitchatted about this and that.

隨著車子一邊行進,我們聊東聊西的。

ⓘ **字詞提示**
- chitchat *v.* 閒談

ⓘ **文法句型**
- this and that = this, that, and the other 這些那些 (指各種事)

6. At times, I looked out of the window, interesting sights, such as a wide plain, conspicuous buildings, and vehicles of all sorts, coming into view, one after another.

偶爾,我看著窗外。寬闊的平原、醒目的建築物、各式各樣的車輛等有趣的景象都一一映入眼簾。

ⓘ **字詞提示**
- conspicuous *adj.* 引人注目的,醒目的

UNIT 1
UNIT 2
UNIT 3
UNIT 4
UNIT 5
UNIT 6
UNIT 7
UNIT 8
UNIT 9
UNIT 10
UNIT 11
UNIT 12
UNIT 13
UNIT 14
UNIT 15
UNIT 16
UNIT 17
UNIT 18
UNIT 19
UNIT 20

ⓘ 文法
句型
· S₁ + V-ing, S₂ + V....　獨立分詞構句
· come into view　進入視線
· one after another　一個接著一個，陸陸續續地

7. About forty minutes later, we got to Taipei. I paid three hundred and fifty dollars to the driver and told him to keep the change. Then, we said goodbye to each other.

大約四十分鐘之後，我們到了台北。我付給司機三百五十塊錢並告訴他零錢不用找了。之後，我們互道再見。

ⓘ 文法
句型
· keep the change　不用找錢，零錢當作小費

Step 5

用字遣詞 Words → Sentences

1. downtown [daʊn`taʊn] *adj.* 位於商業區的；位於市中心的
   My uncle owns an apartment in downtown Los Angeles.
   我叔叔在洛杉磯市中心擁有一棟公寓。

2. brand-new [`brænd`nju] *adj.* 嶄新的，全新的
   Judy's coat looks as if it is brand-new. I haven't seen it before.
   Judy 的外套看起來好像全新的。我之前從沒有看過。

3. average [`ævrɪdʒ] *adj.* 一般的；普通的
   Tom is a student of average ability. He doesn't perform extraordinarily well in any of the subjects.
   Tom 是個能力普通的學生。他沒有哪一個科目表現特別優異。

4. destination [,dɛstə`neʃən] *n.* 目的地
   Our luggage was checked all the way to our final destination.
   我們的行李被一路託運到我們最後的目的地。

5. chitchat [`tʃɪt,tʃæt] *v.* 閒談
   I was just chitchatting about this and that with Joanna. We didn't talk about anything serious.
   我只是在和 Joanna 聊東聊西的。沒有講什麼嚴肅的話題。

6. conspicuous [kən`spɪkjʊəs] *adj.* 引人注目的，醒目的
   The advertisements were all posted in a conspicuous place so that a lot of people would see them.

這些廣告都被登在一個醒目的地方，所以很多人都會看到。

文法句型 Grammar Points → Sentences

1. as if = as though　似乎；好像

   It sounds as if you had a good time.　聽起來你好像玩得很開心。

2. as soon as　一⋯就⋯

   As soon as we saw our teacher, we knew there was something wrong.

   一看到我們的老師，我們就知道有事不對勁。

3. 疑問詞 who/what/when/where/how + S + V　名詞子句

   Dad asked me what I was doing.　我爸問我在做什麼。

   Could you tell me where my coat is?　你可以告訴我我的外套在哪裡嗎？

4. 連綴動詞 look/sound/smell/taste/feel + adj.

   連綴動詞後接形容詞，作主詞補語，修飾主詞。

   Your idea sounds great.　你的主意聽起來很棒。

   These oranges taste nice.　這些柳橙嚐起來不錯。

5. such + N. + that + S + V　如此⋯以致於⋯

   Pauline told us such a funny story that we all laughed.

   Pauline 跟我們說了一個這麼好笑的故事，以致於我們都笑了。

6. with care = carefully　小心地

   Cross the road with care. = Cross the road carefully.　過馬路要小心。

7. all the way　一路上

   Mom didn't speak a word to me all the way back home.

   在回家的一路上，媽媽一句話都沒有跟我說。

8. run a red light　闖紅燈

   Whoever runs a red light will be fined.　任何人闖紅燈都會被處以罰鍰。

9. this and that = this, that, and the other　這些那些 (指各種事)

   They were sitting there talking about this, that, and the other.

   他們正坐在那兒天南地北什麼都聊。

10. S_1 + V-ing, S_2 + V....　獨立分詞構句

    將副詞子句改為獨立分詞構句的步驟：去掉連接詞→保留不同的主詞→動詞改為分詞

    If the weather permits, we can go to the zoo.

    → The weather permitting, we can go to the zoo.

    如果天氣許可，我們就可以去動物園。

    If time permits, I'll go fishing with you this Sunday.

→ Time permitting, I'll go fishing with you this Sunday.

如果時間允許，這個禮拜天我會跟你一起去釣魚。

11. come into view　進入視線

The clouds lifted and the tops of the mountains suddenly came into view.

雲消散了，群山的山頂突然間映入眼簾。

12. one after another　一個接著一個，陸陸續續地

The bills kept coming in, one after another.　帳單接二連三地寄來。

13. keep the change　不用找錢，零錢當作小費

Here's a $100 bill. You can keep the change.

這是一百元鈔票。零錢不用找了。

UNIT 1
UNIT 2
UNIT 3
UNIT 4
UNIT 5
UNIT 6
UNIT 7
UNIT 8
UNIT 9
UNIT 10
UNIT 11
UNIT 12
UNIT 13
UNIT 14
UNIT 15
UNIT 16
UNIT 17
UNIT 18
UNIT 19
UNIT 20

UNIT 10

Narrative Writing　敘事文

A Ten-Minute Break　下課休息十分鐘

　　請以 "A Ten-Minute Break" 為題，描述一次在學校下課休息十分鐘的情景，段落不拘。

　　Please use "A Ten-Minute Break" as the title to describe a ten-minute break at school in one or more paragraphs.

Step 1　聯想提示 Association　依人、事、時、地、物、原因和方法聯想與題目相關的事項

- 誰宣布下課？　Who announced the break?
- 休息時間發生了什麼事？　What happened during the break?
- 我們在哪裡度過下課休息時間？　Where did we spend the break?
- 我們如何運用這個下課休息時間？　How did we use the break?
- 誰讓這次下課變得別具意義？　Who made the break special?

Step 2　組織大綱提示 Organization　依照想到的事項，定出寫作優先順序及細節

第一段

1. 揭示事件開端：下課鐘聲響了，老師宣布下課休息十分鐘。
2. 事件：為同學慶生，是 Johnny 的十七歲生日。

第二段

1. 主題句：我們對 Johnny 惡作劇，藉此慶祝他的生日。
2. 事件經過：
   a. 我們抓住他、把他抬起來，並且拋到半空中。
   b. 端出生日蛋糕，一起唱「生日快樂歌」。
3. 事件高潮：
   a. 別班一位漂亮的女生突然出現，勇敢地走進教室。
   b. Johnny 朝她走過去，給她一個擁抱並親了她一下。
   c. 這位女孩說：「生日快樂」，把禮物塞到他手上，然後轉身離去。

第三段

4. 上課鐘響，慶生活動落幕。

UNIT
1

UNIT
2

UNIT
3

UNIT
4

UNIT
5

UNIT
6

UNIT
7

UNIT
8

UNIT
9

UNIT
10

UNIT
11

UNIT
12

UNIT
13

UNIT
14

UNIT
15

UNIT
16

UNIT
17

UNIT
18

UNIT
19

UNIT
20

Step 3 範文 Model Composition

A Ten-Minute Break

"Class dismissed," announced our chemistry teacher as the bell rang. The class arose and bowed, and there was a ten-minute break. We used this chance to celebrate one of our classmates' birthday. It was Johnny's seventeenth birthday, which most of us were not aware of until it was revealed by Johnny's best friend Ray.

We celebrated Johnny's birthday in the classroom by playing a trick on him. We took hold of him, lifted him up, and threw him up into the air. Then, some of us brought a cake for him, and we all sang "Happy Birthday to You" to him. While we were sharing the cake, a pretty girl from another class suddenly appeared at the door of our classroom and fearlessly entered the room with her hands behind her back. Much to our amazement, Johnny stood up, walked over and gave her a hug and a kiss on the cheek. The girl said, "Happy Birthday," thrusting a delicately wrapped package into his hands, and then turned around and walked away.

All too soon, the bell rang again, signaling the end of the break. Although the break only took ten minutes, it gave us a precious memory.

Step 4 寫句實戰分析 Analyzing Sentences

第一段

1. "Class dismissed," announced our chemistry teacher as the bell rang. The class arose and bowed, and there was a ten-minute break.

   鐘響時，我們的化學老師宣佈「下課」。全班起立、鞠躬敬禮，然後下課十分鐘。

   ⓘ字詞
   提示
   • dismiss v. 解散
   • announce v. 宣佈
   • arise v. 起立

> ① **文法句型**
> ・複合形容詞：數字-單位。例：a two-hour lesson　一堂兩小時的課
> ・注意："S$_1$ + V$_1$...," V$_2$ + S$_2$.... 為引用句型，" " 中為引用的句子。S$_2$ 若為代名詞，則不可倒裝。

2. We used this chance to celebrate one of our classmates' birthday.

   我們利用這個機會為一個同學慶生。

> ① **文法句型**
> ・注意：use + O + to + V　利用…來…

3. It was Johnny's seventeenth birthday, which most of us were not aware of until it was revealed by Johnny's best friend Ray.

   那天是 Johnny 的十七歲生日，大部份同學一直到 Johnny 最好的朋友 Ray 透露才知道。

> ① **字詞提示**
> ・reveal v. 揭露，透露

> ① **文法句型**
> ・not...until...　直到…才…
> ・be aware of　知道

第二段

4. We celebrated Johnny's birthday in the classroom by playing a trick on him.

   我們在教室裡對 Johnny 惡作劇，藉此來慶祝他的生日。

> ① **字詞提示**
> ・celebrate v. 慶祝

> ① **文法句型**
> ・play a trick on sb.　跟某人開玩笑或惡作劇

5. We took hold of him, lifted him up, and threw him up into the air.

   我們抓住他，把他抬起來，並且把他拋到半空中。

> ① **文法句型**
> ・take hold of　抓住

6. Then, some of us brought a cake for him, and we all sang "Happy Birthday to You" to him. While we were sharing the cake, a pretty girl from another class suddenly appeared at the door of our classroom and fearlessly entered the room with her hands behind her back.

   接下來，有人把蛋糕端出來給他，我們還一起對他唱「祝你生日快樂」。當我們在分蛋糕的

時候，別班一位漂亮的女生突然出現在我們教室的門口，而且雙手放在背後，勇敢地走進教室。

· fearlessly *adv.* 無畏地，勇敢地

7. Much to our amazement, Johnny stood up, walked over and gave her a hug and a kiss on the cheek.

令我們驚奇的是，Johnny 站了起來，走過去給她一個擁抱並親了她的臉頰。

· amazement *n.* 驚奇

· to sb's surprise/amazement, ... 令某人感到驚訝／奇的是
· 介系詞 + the/sb's + 身體部位 表接觸身體某部位

8. The girl said, "Happy Birthday," thrusting a delicately wrapped package into his hands, and then turned around and walked away.

那女生說：「生日快樂」，並把一份包裝精美的禮物塞到他手上，然後轉身離去。

· delicately *adv.* 精緻地，細緻地
· wrap *v.* 包裝
· thrust *v.* 塞
· turn around 轉身

· S + V₁..., V₂-ing.... 分詞構句，表示 V₁ 和 V₂ 幾乎同時發生。

第三段

9. All too soon, the bell rang again, signaling the end of the break.

時間過得真快，鐘聲再次響起，表示下課時間結束了。

· signal *v.* 顯示，發出信號

· all too + adj. 表否定強調
· S + V₁..., V₂-ing.... 表示 V₁ 和 V₂ 幾乎同時發生。

10. Although the break only took ten minutes, it gave us precious memory.

雖然那次下課只有短短十分鐘，但它卻給了我們一段珍貴的回憶。

① 字詞提示　· precious *adj.* 珍貴的；貴重的

Step 5

用字遣詞 Words → Sentences

1. dismiss [dɪsˋmɪs] *v.* 解散

   The class was dismissed at 12 o'clock.　這堂課於十二點下課。

2. announce [əˋnaʊns] *v.* 宣佈

   The government announced a tax cut.　政府宣布減稅。

3. arise [əˋraɪz] *v.* 起立

   The whole audience arose and applauded when the performance ended.

   表演結束時，全體觀眾都起立鼓掌。

4. reveal [rɪˋvil] *v.* 揭露，透露

   The doctor did not reveal the truth to Tom.　醫生並未對 Tom 透露實情。

5. celebrate [ˋsɛlə͵bret] *v.* 慶祝

   Joe's friends held a party in his place to celebrate his birthday.

   Joe 的朋友在他家辦了一場派對，以慶祝他的生日。

6. fearlessly [ˋfɪrlɪslɪ] *adv.* 無畏地，勇敢地

   The soldiers fought fearlessly against their enemies.　士兵們勇敢地對抗敵人。

7. amazement [əˋmezmənt] *n.* 吃驚，訝異

   Susan stared at the stranger in amazement when he asked her to marry him.

   當那位陌生人向 Susan 求婚時，她訝異地瞪著他。

8. delicately [ˋdɛləkətlɪ] *adv.* 精緻地，細緻地

   The products are delicately made by hand.　這些產品是用手工精製而成的。

9. wrap [ræp] *v.* 包裝

   The old man wrapped the yam in a sheet of newspaper and gave it to me.

   那位老先生把番薯包裝在一張報紙裡並把它遞給我。

10. thrust [θrʌst] *v.* 塞

    Ben's mother thrust a thousand-dollar bill in his hand before he went out.

    在 Ben 出門前，他的媽媽塞了張千元大鈔到他手中。

11. signal [ˋsɪgnl̩] *v.* 顯示，發出信號

    Rain in early June could signal the arrival of the rainy season.

    六月初的降雨可能顯示雨季的來臨。

UNIT
1
UNIT
2
UNIT
3
UNIT
4
UNIT
5
UNIT
6
UNIT
7
UNIT
8
UNIT
9
UNIT
10
UNIT
11
UNIT
12
UNIT
13
UNIT
14
UNIT
15
UNIT
16
UNIT
17
UNIT
18
UNIT
19
UNIT
20

12. precious [ˋprɛʃəs] *adj.* 珍貴的；貴重的

This photo with his wife is the soldier's most precious treasure.

這張與他妻子的合照是那名士兵最珍貴的寶物。

文法句型 Grammar Points → Sentences

1. 複合形容詞：數字-單位

Here are a few pictures of my three-day trip.

這裡有幾張我去旅遊三天的照片。

The winner of the women's 100-meter race was Sara.

女子一百公尺賽跑由 Sara 贏得冠軍。

2. not...until....　直到…才…

I did not read your letter until yesterday.　我直到昨天才看了你的信。

3. be aware of　知道

They were all aware of the difficulty of this research.

他們都知道這項研究的困難度。

4. play a trick on sb.　跟某人開個玩笑或惡作劇

The kids are always playing tricks on their teacher.

這些小孩總是對他們的老師惡作劇。

5. take hold of　抓住

The teacher took hold of Brian's hands to stop him from continuing to fight with another boy.　老師抓住 Brian 的雙手，阻止他繼續和另一個男孩打鬥。

6. to sb's surprise/amazement　令某人感到驚訝／奇的是

Much to Jane's surprise, there is a crowd of friends waiting for her!

令 Jane 十分驚訝的是，有一群朋友正在等她！

7. 介系詞 + the/sb's + 身體部位　表接觸身體某部位

Zoe caught the thief by the hand.　Zoe 抓住小偷的手。

Tim hit the burglar on the nose.　Tim 打了竊賊的鼻子。

Don't pat the dog on the head.　別拍打狗的頭。

8. turn around　轉身

You should face the music, but not just turn around and pretend it never happened.　你該勇敢承擔後果，而非轉身並假裝這件事從未發生過。

9. all too + adj.　表否定強調

All too often we take the love from our parents for granted.

我們太常把父母的愛視為理所當然。

10. S + V$_1$..., V$_2$-ing....　分詞構句表「伴隨情況」

The girl ran out of the classroom, and she carried her schoolbag.

→ The girl ran out of the classroom, carrying her schoolbag.

那女孩背著她的書包跑出了教室。

UNIT
1
UNIT
2
UNIT
3
UNIT
4
UNIT
5
UNIT
6
UNIT
7
UNIT
8
UNIT
9
UNIT
10
UNIT
11
UNIT
12
UNIT
13
UNIT
14
UNIT
15
UNIT
16
UNIT
17
UNIT
18
UNIT
19
UNIT
20

UNIT 11

Narrative Writing　敘事文

A Trip to Yangmingshan　陽明山之旅

寫一篇大約一百二十個英文字的短文，描述你某次旅行的經驗。

Use 120 words or so to write an essay about one of your trips.

Step 1　聯想提示 Association　依人、事、時、地、物、原因和方法聯想與題目相關的事項

- 我什麼時候去陽明山？　When did I go to Yangmingshan?
- 我是跟誰去的？　Who did I go with?
- 我怎麼去的？　How did I go there?
- 途中發生了什麼事？　What happened on the way?
- 我在那邊做了什麼？　What did I do there?
- 我對這次旅遊的感想如何？　How did I feel about it?

Step 2　組織大綱提示 Organization　依照想到的事項，定出寫作優先順序及細節

1. 主題句：昨天我們一家人開車到陽明山國家公園。
2. 支持句：經過
   a. 因為山路蜿蜒，我暈車並且想吐。
   b. 一抵達目的地，我們就進入一家咖啡館用餐。
   c. 午餐後，我們沿著咖啡館附近散步，欣賞風景。
   d. 我們看見了綠樹、白雲還有美麗的花朵。
   e. 在山裡健行時，我們也聽見了蟬鳴鳥叫此起彼落。
   f. 我們在公園裡度過大約四小時，玩得很開心。
3. 結論：這真是一次美好的經驗。

Step 3　範文 Model Composition

A Trip to Yangmingshan

Yesterday, my family went to Yangmingshan National Park by car. We all felt so excited. But, riding in the car made me feel unwell owing to the winding roads in the mountains. I got carsick and felt like vomiting. As soon as we got to the destination, we went into a coffee shop, where we ordered our lunch and waited patiently for our order to come. After lunch, we took a walk around the coffee shop, viewing the beautiful scenery. The scenery there was poetic. We saw high mountains with green trees, white clouds and a wide array of beautiful blossoms. Hiking in the mountains, we also heard birds singing and cicadas buzzing here and there. We had a good time together for about four hours in the park. It was really a nice experience.

Step 4 寫句實戰分析 Analyzing Sentences

1. Yesterday, my family went to Yangmingshan National Park by car. We all felt so excited. 昨天我們一家人開車到陽明山國家公園，大家都很興奮。

> **文法句型**
> - by + car/bus/train/plane 搭乘車子／巴士／火車／飛機

2. But, riding in the car made me feel unwell owing to the winding roads in the mountains. I got carsick and felt like vomiting.

然而，因為山路蜿蜒，搭車讓我覺得不舒服，我暈車而且覺得想吐。

> **字詞提示**
> - unwell *adj.* 不舒服的
> - winding *adj.* 曲折的，彎曲的
> - vomit *v.* 嘔吐

> **文法句型**
> - ride in the car 搭乘汽車
> - make + O + V 使人或物…
> - owing to 因為，由於

3. As soon as we got to the destination, we went into a coffee shop, where we

ordered our lunch and waited patiently for our order to come.

一抵達目的地，我們就進入了一家咖啡館；我們點了午餐並且耐心地等候上菜。

⚠ 字詞 提示
- destination *n.* 目的地

⚠ 文法 句型
- As soon as + S + V, S + V.... 一…就…
- S + V..., where/when + S + V.... 關係副詞的非限定用法
- wait for + O + to come 等候…來

4. After lunch, we took a walk around the coffee shop, viewing the beautiful scenery. The scenery there was poetic.

午餐後，我們在咖啡館附近散步，觀賞美麗的風景，那兒的景色如詩。

⚠ 字詞 提示
- view *v.* 觀看
- scenery *n.* 風景
- poetic *adj.* 富有詩意的

⚠ 文法 句型
- S + V..., V-ing.... 分詞構句

5. We saw high mountains with green trees, white clouds and a wide array of beautiful blossoms.

我們看見了高山上的綠樹、白雲還有各式各樣的美麗花朵。

⚠ 文法 句型
- a wide array of 各式各樣的，琳瑯滿目的

6. Hiking in the mountains, we also heard birds singing and cicadas buzzing here and there. 在山裡健行時，我們也聽見了蟬鳴鳥叫聲此起彼落。

⚠ 字詞 提示
- hike *v.* 健行
- cicada *n.* 蟬

⚠ 文法 句型
- V-ing..., S + V.... 分詞構句
- 感官動詞 + O + V-ing/V/V-en

7. We had a good time together for about four hours in the park. It was really a nice experience.

我們在公園裡度過大約四小時，玩得很開心。這真是一次美好的經驗。

Step 5

1. unwell [ʌn`wɛl] *adj.* 不舒服的

   Mary said she was feeling unwell and went home.

   Mary 說她覺得不舒服，然後就回家了。

2. winding [`waɪndɪŋ] *adj.* 曲折的，彎曲的

   Driving along a long and winding road doesn't appeal to her.

   在漫長曲折的道路上開車並不吸引她。

3. vomit [`vɑmɪt] *v.* 嘔吐

   The bad smell made her sick, and she began to vomit.

   這難聞的臭味讓她覺得噁心，並開始嘔吐。

4. destination [ˌdɛstə`neʃən] *n.* 目的地

   It took us three hours to reach the destination.

   我們花了三小時才抵達目的地。

5. view [vju] *v.* 觀看

   People from all over the world come to the museum to view Van Gogh's works.

   來自世界各地的人們到這個博物館觀看梵谷的作品。

6. scenery [`sinərɪ] *n.* 風景

   The mountain scenery is magnificent.　這山上的風景很壯觀。

7. poetic [po`ɛtɪk] *adj.* 富有詩意的

   There is a poetic quality in the dancer's performance.

   這位舞者的表演當中有種如詩般的特質。

8. hike [haɪk] *v.* 健行

   If the weather's fine, we'll go hiking this weekend.

   如果天氣好的話，我們這個週末會去健行。

9. cicada [sɪ`kedə] *n.* 蟬

   You can hear cicadas hum all the time during summer in Taiwan.

   在台灣，整個夏天都可以聽見蟬鳴。

1. by + car/bus/train/plane　搭乘車子／巴士／火車／飛機

   Bruce often travels by plane.　Bruce 常搭飛機旅遊。

2. ride in the car　搭乘汽車

When I rode in the car with John, he showed me where the Central Park is.

當我跟 John 一起搭車時，他告訴我中央公園在哪裡。

3. make + O + V　使人或物⋯

Sally told us a sad story, which made us all cry.

Sally 跟我們說了一個悲傷的故事，讓我們全都哭了。

4. owing to　因為，由於

The game was canceled owing to the rain.　這場比賽因為下雨而取消。

5. As soon as + S + V, S + V....　一⋯就⋯

As soon as I got home, I called Dad.　我一到家，就打電話給爸爸。

6. S + V..., where/when + S + V....　關係副詞的非限定用法

關係副詞的非限定用法，主要是用來補述前面主要子句的不足，關係副詞的前面必須加逗點。

Dan went to Kaohsiung, where he stayed for a week.

= Dan went to Kaohsiung, in which he stayed for a week.

= Dan went to Kaohsiung, and he stayed there for a week.

Dan 去了高雄，並在那裡停留了一個禮拜。

7. wait for + O + to come　等候⋯來

I'm waiting for my aunt to come.　我正在等我阿姨來。

8. S + V..., V-ing.... 或 V-ing..., S + V....　分詞構句

分詞構句通常相當於簡化的副詞子句，或與主要子句的動作同時發生的動作，其作用為補充說明主要子句。

Sandy said goodbye, waving her hand.

→ Sandy said goodbye and waved her hand.
　　　　　　　　　　　對等子句

Sandy 說了再見並揮揮她的手。

When the minister arrived at the hotel, he met two secret agents.

→ Arriving at the hotel, the minister met two secret agents.

抵達飯店之後，這位部長與兩名特務會面。

9. a wide array of　各式各樣的，琳瑯滿目的

We can find a wide array of jewels available at this store.

在這家店裡我們可以找到琳瑯滿目的珠寶。

10. 感官動詞 + O + V-ing/V/V-en

I could hear a dog barking.　我可以聽到一隻狗在吠。

（感官動詞後接現在分詞，強調動作正在進行的過程或狀態。）

Jenny heard her husband go out.　Jenny 聽到她先生出去了。

（感官動詞後接原形動詞，強調事實。）

Kiki saw a vase broken on the floor. Kiki 看見一只花瓶被摔破在地上。

（感官動詞後接過去分詞，分詞作為受詞補語，強調受詞的狀態。）

UNIT
1

UNIT
2

UNIT
3

UNIT
4

UNIT
5

UNIT
6

UNIT
7

UNIT
8

UNIT
9

UNIT
10

UNIT
11

**UNIT
12**

UNIT
13

UNIT
14

UNIT
15

UNIT
16

UNIT
17

UNIT
18

UNIT
19

UNIT
20

UNIT 12

A World Without Electricity　沒有電的世界

96 年大學指定科目考試

你能想像一個沒有電 (electricity) 的世界嗎？請寫一篇文章，文長至少 120 個英文字。第一段描述我們的世界沒有了電以後，會是什麼樣子，第二段說明這樣的世界是好是壞，並舉例解釋原因。

Can you imagine a world without electricity? Please write an essay in no less than 120 words. In the first paragraph, describe what our world would be like if we had no electricity. In the second paragraph, explain whether such a world is good or bad by giving examples.

Step 1　聯想提示 Association　依人、事、時、地、物、原因和方法聯想與題目相關的事項

- 沒有電的世界會是什麼樣子？　What would a world without electricity be like?
- 可能會發生什麼事？　What could happen?
- 它會如何影響我們的生活？　How would it affect our lives?
- 我們可以做什麼？　What could we do?

Step 2　組織大綱提示 Organization　依照想到的事項，定出寫作優先順序及細節

第一段

1. 主題句：若我們住在一個沒有電的世界，會怎麼樣呢？

2. 支持句：所有電器用品都會運作失常。

3. 結論：我們只能焦急地等待，而我們的世界亦將陷入困境。

第二段

1. 主題句：如果電力中斷的時間很長，情況可能會不堪設想。

2. 支持句：舉例

　a. 搭電梯的人會被困在電梯裡。

　b. 交通號誌燈會失靈，造成交通癱瘓。

　c. 正在接受手術的病人會喪命。

　d. 儲藏在冰箱裡的食物會腐壞。

e. 水將無法抽到屋頂的水塔裡。

3. 結論：百業蕭條，日常生活陷入混亂。

Step 3 範文 Model Composition

A World Without Electricity

What if we live in a world without electricity? All electrical appliances, such as air-conditioners, refrigerators, washing machines, dish washers, and vacuum cleaners, might malfunction. Then we could do nothing but wait anxiously and our world would be mired in difficulties.

It could be deadly if there were no electricity for a prolonged period. The people taking elevators would be stuck inside. Traffic lights would fail to work, causing traffic jam and paralyzing railway systems. Patients might die because the operations being performed would be interrupted. The food kept in refrigerators would spoil and emit a putrid smell. Water could not be pumped up to rooftop tanks. Thus, all business would be languished and everyday life would be plunged into chaos.

Step 4 寫句實戰分析 Analyzing Sentences

第一段

1. What if we live in a world without electricity?

若是我們住在一個沒有電的世界，會怎麼樣呢？

文法句型
- what if + S + V...? 如果，假使

2. All electrical appliances, such as air-conditioners, refrigerators, washing machines, dish washers, vacuum cleaners, might malfunction.

像冷氣、冰箱、洗衣機、洗碗機、吸塵器等所有電器用品都會運作失常。

字詞提示
- appliance *n.* 用具，設備
- malfunction *v.* 發生故障

3. Then we could do nothing but wait anxiously and our world would be mired in difficulties.

我們除了焦急地等待別無他法，而我們的世界亦將陷入困境。

⚠️ **文法 句型**
- do nothing but + V　除了…什麼都沒做
- be mired in　陷入 (困境)

第二段

1. It could be deadly if there were no electricity for a prolonged period.

如果電力中斷時間很長，情況可能不堪設想。

⚠️ **字詞 提示**
- prolonged *adj.* 特別長的，延長的

⚠️ **文法 句型**
注意：S + could + V..., if + S + were...　與現在事實相反的假設語氣

2. The people taking elevators would be stuck inside.

搭電梯的人會被困在電梯裡。

⚠️ **文法 句型**
- be stuck in　被困在…裡

3. Traffic lights would fail to work, causing traffic jam and paralyzing railway systems.　交通號誌燈會失靈，造成塞車並癱瘓鐵路系統。

⚠️ **字詞 提示**
- paralyze *v.* 使癱瘓

4. Patients might die because the operations being performed would be interrupted.　正在接受手術的病人會因手術中斷而喪命。

⚠️ **字詞 提示**
- interrupt *v.* 打斷，使中斷

5. The food kept in refrigerators would spoil and emit a putrid smell.

儲藏在冰箱裡的食物會腐壞並發出惡臭。

⚠️ **字詞 提示**
- putrid *adj.* 惡臭的，腐敗的

6. Water could not be pumped up to rooftop tanks.

水將無法抽到屋頂的水塔裡。

UNIT 1
UNIT 2
UNIT 3
UNIT 4
UNIT 5
UNIT 6
UNIT 7
UNIT 8
UNIT 9
UNIT 10
UNIT 11
UNIT 12
UNIT 13
UNIT 14
UNIT 15
UNIT 16
UNIT 17
UNIT 18
UNIT 19
UNIT 20

> ! 字詞提示
>
> • pump *v.* 使用幫浦打水、打氣

7. Thus, all business would be languished and everyday life would be plunged into chaos.　如此一來，百業蕭條，而日常生活亦將陷入混亂。

> ! 字詞提示
>
> • languish *v.* 變得沒有生氣，變得憔悴
> • chaos *n.* 混亂

> ! 文法句型
>
> • be plunged into　陷入⋯

Step 5

用字遣詞 Words → Sentences

1. appliance [ə`plaɪəns] *n.* 用具，設備

   The kitchen is equipped with modern appliances.

   這廚房配有現代化的設備。

2. malfunction [mæl`fʌŋʃən] *v.* 發生故障

   The soldier was killed when his parachute malfunctioned.

   這名士兵因降落傘發生故障而喪命。

3. prolonged [prə`lɔŋd] *adj.* 特別長的，延長的

   Reservoir levels were greatly lowered after a prolonged period of dry weather.

   經過特別漫長的乾季之後，水庫的水位大幅下降。

4. paralyze [`pærə͵laɪz] *v.* 使癱瘓

   The airport was paralyzed by the strike.　機場因為罷工而癱瘓。

5. interrupt [͵ɪntə`rʌpt] *v.* 打斷，使中斷

   I am sorry to interrupt, but Mr. Anderson would like to talk to you on the phone.

   很抱歉打擾了，不過 Anderson 先生來電，想跟你講話。

6. putrid [`pjutrɪd] *adj.* 惡臭的，腐敗的

   There is a putrid smell of burnt rubber in the car.

   車裡有一股橡皮燒焦的惡臭味。

7. pump [pʌmp] *v.* 使用幫浦打水、打氣

   After the typhoon, our house is flooded. We need to pump the water out of our house.　颱風過後，我們家淹水了。我們必須用幫浦把水打出我們家。

8. languish [`læŋgwɪʃ] *v.* 變得沒有生氣，變得憔悴

Johnson has become languished in jail for the past twelve years.

過去十二年來 Johnson 在獄中變得很憔悴。

9. chaos [`keɑs] *n.* 混亂

The room was in chaos after the party.　派對結束後房間一團混亂。

文法句型 Grammar Points → Sentences

1. what if + S + V...?　如果，假使

What if the plane arrives late?　如果飛機誤點怎麼辦？

2. do nothing but + V　除了⋯什麼都沒做

My brother did nothing but watch TV all night.

我弟弟一整晚除了看電視，什麼事都沒做。

3. be mired in　陷入 (困境)

Our country's economy was mired in recession.

我國的經濟陷入了蕭條的困境。

4. be stuck in　被困在⋯裡

Many of the commuters are stuck in traffic on the way home from the office.

有許多通勤者在下班回家途中被困在車陣裡。

5. be plunged into　陷入⋯

The area was plunged into darkness because of a power cut.

這個區域因停電而陷入黑暗。

UNIT 1
UNIT 2
UNIT 3
UNIT 4
UNIT 5
UNIT 6
UNIT 7
UNIT 8
UNIT 9
UNIT 10
UNIT 11
UNIT 12
UNIT 13
UNIT 14
UNIT 15
UNIT 16
UNIT 17
UNIT 18
UNIT 19
UNIT 20

UNIT 13

An Unbearable Thing　一件難以容忍的事情

以 "An Unbearable Thing" 為題，寫一篇約 120 到 150 個英文字的短文，描述個人生活中一件難以容忍的事情。

Write a short essay entitled "An Unbearable Thing" in about 120 to 150 words, in which you narrate one thing that is unbearable to you in life.

Step 1　聯想提示 Association　依人、事、時、地、物、原因和方法聯想與題目相關的事項

- 什麼事情令我難以容忍？　What was it?
- 我在哪裡經歷這件事？　Where did I experience it?
- 這件事情發生的時間？　When did it happen?
- 這件事情發生的經過？　How did it happen?
- 誰與這件事情有關？　Who was involved?
- 它為什麼難以容忍？　Why was it unbearable?

Step 2　組織大綱提示 Organization　依照想到的事項，定出寫作優先順序及細節

1. 主題句：某天，我和朋友到學校附近的一家自助餐館吃午飯。
2. 支持句：經過
   a. 朋友先去找座位，我去櫃檯排隊，當時已有十位客人在等候點餐。
   b. 一開始，大家一個接一個依序等候；過了一會兒，從外面突然進來兩個人插隊。
   c. 因為他們插隊，其他人必須等很久才能點餐，秩序因此被擾亂了。
3. 結論：他們無禮的行為真是一件令人難以容忍的事情。

Step 3　範文 Model Composition

An Unbearable Thing

One day I went with my friend to a cafeteria in the vicinity of our school for lunch. As soon as we entered the crowded room, I told her to seek a vacant table for us to sit down. I went without delay to the counter, where a group of approximately ten customers lined up and were ready to order their meals. At first, everyone followed one after another in an orderly way. After a while, I suddenly saw two people coming in from outside and going directly to the cashier, bypassing the waiting customers to order their dishes. Obviously, they caused the others to have a long wait for their lunches. The existing orderliness of the room, as a result, was disrupted. Their lack of manners proved to be an unbearable thing.

Step 4　寫句實戰分析 Analyzing Sentences

1. One day I went with my friend to a cafeteria in the vicinity of our school for lunch. 有一天，我和朋友到學校附近的一家自助餐館吃午飯。

   字詞提示
   • cafeteria *n.* 自助餐廳

   文法句型
   • in the vicinity of　在⋯的附近

2. As soon as we entered the crowded room, I told her to seek a vacant table for us to sit down. 我們一進到擁擠的餐館，我就叫她先去找一個空位給我們坐。

   字詞提示
   • crowded *adj.* 擁擠的，擠滿人群的
   • vacant *adj.* 空著的

   文法句型
   • as soon as S + V..., S + V....　一⋯就⋯

3. I went without delay to the counter, where a group of approximately ten customers lined up and were ready to order their meals.
   我立刻到櫃檯去，在那裡大約有十位客人在排隊準備點餐。

   字詞提示
   • counter *n.* 櫃檯
   • approximately *adv.* 大約地，概略地
   • customer *n.* 顧客

文法句型
- without delay = immediately 立刻地
- line up 排隊

4. At first, everyone followed one after another in an orderly way.

一開始，大家都依序一個接著一個排隊。

文法句型
- one after another 一個接著一個
- 注意：at first = in the beginning 起初，一開始

5. After a while, I suddenly saw two people coming in from outside and going directly to the cashier, bypassing the waiting customers to order their dishes.

過了一會兒，我突然看到兩個人從外面走進來，繞過等候的顧客，直接到櫃檯收銀員那裡點餐。

字詞提示
- cashier n. 櫃台收銀員
- bypass v. 迴避，繞道而過

文法句型
- 感官動詞 see/hear/watch + O + V/V-ing

6. Obviously, they caused the others to have a long wait for their lunches.

顯然，他們讓其他人等很久才能吃午餐。

文法句型
- 注意 cause 的用法：cause sb. to V

7. The existing orderliness of the room, as a result, was disrupted.

餐館裡原有的秩序因此被打亂了。

字詞提示
- existing adj. 目前的，現存的
- disrupt v. 擾亂，干擾

文法句型
- as a result 因此 (= therefore)

8. Their lack of manners proved to be an unbearable thing.

他們缺乏禮貌的行為的確是一件令人難以容忍的事情。

文法句型
- prove to be sth. 證實是…，的確是…

UNIT
1

UNIT
2

UNIT
3

UNIT
4

UNIT
5

UNIT
6

UNIT
7

UNIT
8

UNIT
9

UNIT
10

UNIT
11

UNIT
12

UNIT
13

UNIT
14

UNIT
15

UNIT
16

UNIT
17

UNIT
18

UNIT
19

UNIT
20

Step 5

用字遣詞 Words → Sentences

1. cafeteria [ˌkæfəˈtɪrɪə] *n.* 自助餐廳

   There is a cafeteria at the campus, where you can have your lunch.

   校園內有自助餐廳，你可以在那邊吃午餐。

2. crowded [ˈkraʊdɪd] *adj.* 擁擠的，擠滿人群的

   This Italian restaurant is always crowded because their food is the best in town.

   這家義大利餐廳總是擠滿了人，因為他們的食物是城裡最棒的。

3. vacant [ˈvekənt] *adj.* 空著的

   The hospital has no vacant beds.　這家醫院沒有空床。

4. counter [ˈkaʊntɚ] *n.* 櫃檯

   There was nobody behind the counter when I went into the hotel.

   當我進到那家旅館的時候，櫃檯後面沒有人。

5. approximately [əˈprɑksəmɪtlɪ] *adv.* 大約地，概略地

   The job will take approximately three weeks.

   這個工作大約會花上三個星期的時間。

6. customer [ˈkʌstəmɚ] *n.* 顧客

   Mr. Wilson is one of our regular customers.

   Wilson 先生是我們的常客之一。

7. cashier [kæˈʃɪr] *n.* 櫃檯收銀員

   A cashier works in a shop, checking customers' purchase and receiving the payment.　櫃檯收銀員在商店工作，查看顧客購買的物品及結帳。

8. bypass [ˈbaɪˌpæs] *v.* 迴避，繞道而過

   The President bypassed the security checks and entered the building directly.

   總統繞過安全檢查，直接進入了大樓。

9. existing [ɪgˈzɪstɪŋ] *adj.* 目前的，現存的

   New laws will soon replace existing ones.

   新的法律將很快取代現有的法令。

10. disrupt [dɪsˈrʌpt] *v.* 擾亂，干擾

    The building construction disrupted our class.

    建築工程干擾了我們上課。

文法句型 Grammar Points → Sentences

1. in the vicinity of　在…的附近

   There are several hotels in the immediate vicinity of the station.

   緊鄰著車站就有好幾家飯店。

2. as soon as S + V..., S + V....　一…就…

   As soon as we arrived at the hotel, we went to the swimming pool.

   我們一到飯店，就去了游泳池。

3. without delay = immediately　立刻地

   We must report it to the police without delay.

   我們必須立刻向警方報案。

4. line up　排隊

   People lined up and were ready to board the ship.

   人們排好隊，準備登船。

5. one after another　一個接著一個

   The bills kept coming in, one after another.　帳單一張接一張不斷湧進。

6. 感官動詞 see/hear/watch + O + V/V-ing

   I saw the man running away from the scene of the crime.

   我看到這名男子逃離犯罪現場。

7. as a result　因此 (= therefore)

   Jack made one big mistake. As a result, he lost his job.

   Jack 犯了一個大錯。因此，他丟了飯碗。

8. prove to be sth.　證實是…，的確是…

   The new treatment has proved to be a disaster.

   這個新療法證實是項徹底的失敗。

UNIT
1
UNIT
2
UNIT
3
UNIT
4
UNIT
5
UNIT
6
UNIT
7
UNIT
8
UNIT
9
UNIT
10
UNIT
11
UNIT
12
UNIT
13
UNIT
14
UNIT
15
UNIT
16
UNIT
17
UNIT
18
UNIT
19
UNIT
20

UNIT 14

Persuasive Writing　説理文

Fighting Pollution　防制污染

　　請以防制污染為題寫一篇 120 到 150 個英文字的短文。短文分成兩段：第一段分類列舉說明有哪些環境污染的來源；第二段提出防制污染的措施。

　　Write an essay with the title "Fighting Pollution" in 120 to 150 words. Describe sources of pollutions in the first paragraph; list ways to fight pollution in the second paragraph.

Step 1　聯想提示 Association　依人、事、時、地、物、原因和方法聯想與題目相關的事項

- 我們面臨什麼樣的污染？　What kinds of pollution do we face?
- 我們可以如何防制污染？　How can we fight pollution?
- 政府應該做什麼？　What should the government do?
- 什麼造成了污染？　What causes the pollution?
- 防制污染的具體訣竅為何？　What are the specific tips on fighting pollution?
- 誰應該防制污染？　Who should fight pollution?

Step 2　組織大綱提示 Organization　依照想到的事項，定出寫作優先順序及細節

第一段

1. 主題句：當誇耀快速的經濟成長時，我們也要對環境污染保持警覺。

2. 支持句：三種污染來源

　　a. 空氣污染：汽車的濫用是主要的空氣污染來源。

　　b. 水污染：來自工廠的化學和有毒物質嚴重污染了水。

　　c. 噪音污染：人口稠密的城市居民飽受噪音之苦。

第二段

1. 主題句：列舉防制污染的訣竅。

2. 支持句：

　　a. 通勤者儘量使用大眾運輸來代替開車上班。

　　b. 政府對任意傾倒工業廢料，並因此污染空氣和水的工廠嚴加取締。

　　c. 有關當局應更嚴格地執行噪音防治法，嚇阻製造噪音者。

3. 結論：創造零污染的環境，人人有責。

Step 3 範文 Model Composition

Fighting Pollution

In boasting of the rapid growth of economy, we must also stay alert for environmental pollution. Our overuse of motor vehicles is the main source of air pollution. Our water is heavily polluted because of chemicals and toxins from factories. Residents who live in densely populated cities suffer from excess noise.

Here are several tips to help fight pollution. First, commuters should use mass transit instead of driving to work in an effort to promote clean air and reduce noise pollution. Second, it is time for all levels of government to take tougher measures to crack down on factories that pollute our air and water by discharging untreated industrial waste. Third, the proper authorities should enforce the anti-noise laws more strictly to provide a sufficient deterrent to noise polluters. In short, it is everybody's business to create a pollution-free environment.

Step 4 寫句實戰分析 Analyzing Sentences

第一段

1. In boasting of the rapid growth economy, we must also stay alert for environmental pollution.

   在誇耀快速經濟成長的同時，我們也必須對環境污染保持警覺。

   字詞提示
   • growth n. 成長

   文法句型
   • boast of　自誇
   • stay alert　保持警覺

UNIT 1
UNIT 2
UNIT 3
UNIT 4
UNIT 5
UNIT 6
UNIT 7
UNIT 8
UNIT 9
UNIT 10
UNIT 11
UNIT 12
UNIT 13
UNIT 14
UNIT 15
UNIT 16
UNIT 17
UNIT 18
UNIT 19
UNIT 20

2. Our overuse of motor vehicles is the main source of air pollution.

我們對汽車的濫用是主要的空氣污染來源。

⚠️ 字詞提示　• source *n.* 來源

3. Our water is heavily polluted because of chemicals and toxins from factories.

我們的用水因為來自工廠的化學和有毒物質而受到嚴重污染。

⚠️ 字詞提示　• toxin *n.* 有毒物質

⚠️ 文法句型　• 注意：被動語態句型 be + V-en

4. Residents who live in densely populated cities suffer from excess noise.

居住在人口稠密的城市中的居民則飽受過量噪音之苦。

⚠️ 字詞提示　• densely *adv.* 稠密地
　　　　　　• populated *adj.* 有人居住的
　　　　　　• excess *adj.* 過多的，額外的

第二段

1. Here are several tips to help fight pollution.

這裡是幾個有助於防制污染的訣竅。

⚠️ 文法句型　• 注意：在本句中，以不定詞 to help 為首的片語當形容詞用，修飾名詞 tips。

2. First, commuters should use mass transit instead of driving to work in an effort to promote clean air and reduce noise pollution.

首先，通勤者應使用大眾運輸代替開車上班，以促進空氣清新並減少噪音污染。

⚠️ 字詞提示　• commuter *n.* 通勤者
　　　　　　• mass transit *n.* 大眾運輸
　　　　　　• promote *v.* 促進，推動

⚠️ 文法句型　• in an effort to + V　是為了要…

3. Second, it is time for all levels of government to take tougher measures to crack down on factories that pollute our air and water by discharging untreated

industrial waste.

第二，各級政府是時候該採取更嚴厲的措施取締工廠，以禁止其排放未經處理的工業廢料，進而污染我們的空氣和水。

Ⓘ 字詞提示
- tough *adj.* 強硬的，嚴厲的
- measure *n.* 措施
- discharge *v.* 排出，排放

Ⓘ 文法句型
- it is time for sb. to + V　該是某人做…的時候
- crack down on　強力取締

4. Third, the proper authorities should enforce the anti-noise laws more strictly to provide a sufficient deterrent to noise polluters.

第三，有關當局應更嚴格地執行噪音防治法，以對噪音污染製造者提供足夠的嚇阻。

Ⓘ 字詞提示
- authority *n.* 當局；官方
- enforce *v.* 力行，實施
- sufficient *adj.* 足夠的
- deterrent *n.* 嚇阻的力量

5. In short, it is everybody's business to create a pollution-free environment.

簡言之，創造一個零污染的環境是每一個人的責任。

Ⓘ 字詞提示
- N.-free *adj.* 不含…的

Ⓘ 文法句型
- 注意：it 為虛主詞，真正的主詞為 to create...environment。

✐ Step 5

用字遣詞 Words → Sentences

1. growth [groθ] *n.* 成長

   The famous author's new book describes the rapid growth in violent crime.

   這位著名作家的新書描寫暴力犯罪的急速成長。

2. source [sors] *n.* 來源

   Our local library is a useful source of information.

   我們本地的圖書館是個有用的資訊來源。

3. toxin [ˋtɑksɪn] *n.* 有毒物質

Many of the toxins come from environmental pollutants.

許多有毒物質來自環境的污染物。

4. densely [`dɛnslɪ] *adv.* 稠密地

The hills have been densely planted with fruit trees.

山丘上稠密地栽種了果樹。

5. populated [`pɑpjəˌletɪd] *adj.* 有人居住的

New York might be the most densely populated city in the world.

紐約可能是世界上人口最稠密的城市。

6. excess [ɪk`sɛs] *adj.* 過多的，額外的

Driving with excess alcohol in the blood is a serious offense.

開車時血液中酒精濃度過高是嚴重犯法的行為。

7. commuter [kə`mjutɚ] *n.* 通勤者

If you take the train in the morning, you have to travel with a lot of commuters.

如果你早上搭火車，就必須跟許多通勤族一起坐車。

8. mass transit [`mæs `trænsɪt] *n.* 大眾運輸

It is convenient to travel around Taipei by using its mass transit system.

利用大眾運輸系統漫遊台北是很方便的。

9. promote [prə`mote] *v.* 促進，推動

I support the candidate because she devotes herself to promoting the public's awareness of environmental issues.

我支持那位候選人，因為她致力於推動大眾對環保議題的認知。

10. tough [tʌf] *adj.* 強硬的，嚴厲的

The public would like to see tougher punishment for murder.

社會大眾希望見到對謀殺罪有更嚴厲的懲罰。

11. measure [`mɛʒɚ] *n.* 措施

The police are imposing new measures to prevent crime.

警方正採行新措施來預防犯罪。

12. discharge [dɪs`tʃɑrdʒ] *v.* 排出，排放

Those who discharge untreated industrial waste water into the river will be fined 50,000 to 150,000 dollars.

那些將未經處理的工業廢水排放至河裡的人，將會被罰款五萬到十五萬元。

13. authority [ə`θɔrətɪ] *n.* 當局；官方

The health authorities are investigating the spreading of the epidemic.

衛生當局正在調查這個傳染病的擴散。

UNIT 1
UNIT 2
UNIT 3
UNIT 4
UNIT 5
UNIT 6
UNIT 7
UNIT 8
UNIT 9
UNIT 10
UNIT 11
UNIT 12
UNIT 13
UNIT 14
UNIT 15
UNIT 16
UNIT 17
UNIT 18
UNIT 19
UNIT 20

14. enforce [ɪn`fors] *v.* 力行，實施

    The police are the people who enforce the law. 警察是執行法律的人。

15. sufficient [sə`fɪʃənt] *adj.* 足夠的

    Is ten thousand dollars sufficient for your expenses for a month?

    一萬元足夠你一個月的花費嗎？

16. deterrent [dɪ`tɝrənt] *n.* 嚇阻的力量

    Hopefully Harry's punishment will act as a deterrent to others.

    希望 Harry 的處罰會對其他人形成嚇阻的作用。

17. N.-free *adj.* 不含…的

    a duty-free shop 免稅店　　a smoke-free restaurant 無菸餐廳

文法句型 Grammar Points → Sentences

1. boast of 自誇

   Jeffery openly boasted of his skill as a burglar.

   Jeffery 公開地誇耀自己當小偷的伎倆。

2. stay alert 保持警覺

   The Department of Health is urging the public to stay alert for dengue fever.

   衛生署呼籲社會大眾對登革熱保持警戒。

3. in an effort to + V 是為了要…

   The company hired 30 workers in an effort to start a new department.

   這家公司為了新部門開始營運，請了三十名員工。

4. it is time for sb. to + V 該是某人做…的時候

   After a day's hard work, it is time for Dad to take a rest.

   忙了一天之後，該是爸爸休息的時候了。

5. crack down on 強力取締

   The police are cracking down on drug dealers. 警方正在強力取締毒販。

UNIT
1

UNIT
2

UNIT
3

UNIT
4

UNIT
5

UNIT
6

UNIT
7

UNIT
8

UNIT
9

UNIT
10

UNIT
11

UNIT
12

UNIT
13

UNIT
14

UNIT
15

UNIT
16

UNIT
17

UNIT
18

UNIT
19

UNIT
20

UNIT 15

Getting the Wrong Gift　拿錯禮物

北區公立高中95年第一次學測模擬考

　　根據下列三張連環圖畫的內容，將圖中所發生的事件作一合理的敘述。文長 120 個英文字左右。

　　Reasonably narrate a whole series of events through the following three-frame comic strip. Write your essay in 120 words or so.

Step 1 看圖聯想 Association 依人、事、時、地、物、原因和方法聯想與題目相關的事項

Step 2 組織大綱提示 Organization 依照想到的事項，定出寫作優先順序及細節

圖一：在珠寶店裡

1.事件：John 去珠寶店買禮物給女友 Mary。

2.細節：

　　a.他仔細端詳一串珍珠項鍊。

　　b.他覺得那條項鍊很好，決定買下來。

　　c.他讓這條項鍊被包裝在盒子裡。

3.小結論：付錢離開之後，他高興地前往附近的公園，Mary 正等著他。

圖二：在街角

4.事件：當在街角轉彎時，他撞到一位也拿著盒子的紳士。

5.經過：他們都摔跤了，兩人的盒子都掉在人行道上。

6.結論：John 撿起他腳邊的盒子，並匆忙地向公園走去。

圖三：在公園裡

7.事件：Mary 打開盒子，結果盒子裡裝的是一條領帶。

8.結論：John 在街角拿到別人的盒子了。

Step 3 範文 Model Composition

Getting the Wrong Gift

One afternoon, John went alone to a jewel store to buy a gift for his girlfriend, Mary. He picked up a string of pearl necklace, looking carefully at it for a while. It was such a nice necklace that he decided to take it. He had it wrapped in a box. After paying the money, he left the store and happily headed for a nearby park, where Mary was waiting. When walking around a street corner, he bumped into a gentleman wearing a suit and tie and also carrying a box. Both of them fell down on the ground, their boxes dropping on the sidewalk. John picked up the box by his feet and walked hurriedly to the park. Not until Mary opened the box did John find what was in the box was a necktie instead of a necklace. Obviously, he had got the wrong box by mistake at the street corner.

Step 4 寫句實戰分析 Analyzing Sentences

1. One afternoon, John went alone to a jewel store to buy a gift for his girlfriend, Mary.

   某個下午，John 獨自去一家珠寶店買一份禮物給他的女友 Mary。

   字詞提示
   • alone *adv.* 獨自地
   • jewel *n.* 珠寶

2. He picked up a string of pearl necklace, looking carefully at it for a while.

   他拿起了一串珍珠項鍊，並仔細地端詳了一會兒。

UNIT
1

UNIT
2

UNIT
3

UNIT
4

UNIT
5

UNIT
6

UNIT
7

UNIT
8

UNIT
9

UNIT
10

UNIT
11

UNIT
12

UNIT
13

UNIT
14

UNIT
15

UNIT
16

UNIT
17

UNIT
18

UNIT
19

UNIT
20

⚠️**字詞提示**
- string *n.* 一串
- pearl *n.* 珍珠
- necklace *n.* 項鍊

3. It was such a nice necklace that he decided to take it.

那真的是一條很好的項鍊，所以他決定把它買下來。

⚠️**文法句型**
- such...that....　如此…以致於…

4. He had it wrapped in a box.　他把這條項鍊裝到盒子裡。

⚠️**字詞提示**
- wrap *v.* 包裝

⚠️**文法句型**
- have sth. V-en　使…被… (使役動詞)

5. After paying the money, he left the store and happily headed for a nearby park, where Mary was waiting.

付了錢之後，他離開這家店，並高興地前往附近的公園，Mary 正在那裡等著。

⚠️**字詞提示**
- head *v.* 前往

⚠️**文法句型**
- S + V..., where S + V....　關係副詞 where 的非限定用法
- After + V-ing..., S + V.... = After + S + V..., S + V....　分詞構句

6. When walking around a street corner, he bumped into a gentleman wearing a suit and tie and also carrying a box.

當走到一個街口轉角時，他撞到一位穿西裝打領帶、手上也拿著盒子的紳士。

⚠️**字詞提示**
- bump *v.* 撞到

⚠️**文法句型**
- 注意：主要子句裡的 wearing...and also carrying... 是由關係子句 who wore...and also carried... 改寫而來。

7. Both of them fell down on the ground, their boxes dropping on the sidewalk.

他們兩個都摔倒在地上，他們的盒子也掉在人行道上。

> ⚠️ **文法句型**
> - $S_1 + V_1..., S_2 + V_2\text{-ing}.... = S_1 + V_1..., \text{and } S_2 + V_2....$　獨立分詞構句

8. John picked up the box by his feet and walked hurriedly to the park.

John 撿起他腳邊的盒子，並匆忙地向公園走去。

> ⚠️ **文法句型**
> - pick up　拿起，撿起

9. Not until Mary opened the box did John find what was in the box was a necktie instead of a necklace.

直到 Mary 打開盒子，John 才發現盒子裡裝的是一條領帶，而不是項鍊。

> ⚠️ **文法句型**
> - Not until + S + V + did + S + V....　倒裝句：直到…才…
> - instead of　而不是

10. Obviously, he had got the wrong box by mistake at the street corner.

顯然地，他之前在街角誤拿了錯的盒子。

> ⚠️ **文法句型**
> - by mistake　錯誤地
> - 注意：本句的過去完成式 had + V-en 比前句的過去式動詞發生的時間更早。

✒ Step 5

用字遣詞 Words → Sentences

1. alone [ə`lon] *adv.* 獨自地

Sharon likes to go shopping alone. She doesn't need anyone to keep her company.　Sharon 喜歡一個人逛街。她不需要任何人陪她。

2. jewel [`dʒuəl] *n.* 珠寶

These precious jewels should be kept in a safe.

這些珍貴的珠寶應該被放在保險箱裡。

3. string [strɪŋ] *n.* 一串

The businessman bought his wife a string of pearls.

這個商人買給他太太一串珍珠。

4. pearl [pɝl] *n.* 珍珠

I like pearls better than diamonds. Pearls look warm to me, while diamonds look sharp and cold.

我喜歡珍珠勝過鑽石。我覺得珍珠看起來很溫暖，但鑽石看起來鋒利又冰冷。

5. necklace [`nɛklɪs] *n.* 項鍊

The necklace around Jenny's neck caught my attention. I guess it's a birthday gift from Eddie.

Jenny 戴在脖子上的項鍊引起了我的注意。我想那是 Eddie 送她的生日禮物。

6. wrap [ræp] *v.* 包裝

The clerk wrapped the present with beautiful wrapping paper.

這名店員用漂亮的包裝紙把這個禮物包了起來。

7. head [hɛd] *v.* 前往

I headed home directly after school.　我放學後直接回家。

8. bump [bʌmp] *v.* 撞到

The bus bumped into the taxi in front of it.

這輛巴士撞到它前面的計程車。

文法句型 Grammar Points → Sentences

1. such...that.... 如此…以致於…

Sun Moon Lake is such a beautiful place that I want to visit it again and again.

日月潭是個如此美麗的地方，以致於我想要一再造訪。

2. have sth. V-en 使…被… (使役動詞)

Jamie had the wall in her room painted green.

Jamie 將她房間的牆漆成綠色的。

3. S + V..., where S + V.... 關係副詞 where 的非限定用法

Ken went to Taipei, where he stayed for a week.

= Ken went to Taipei, in which he stayed for a week.

= Ken went to Taipei, and he stayed there for a week.

Ken 去了台北，並在那裡待了一個禮拜。

4. After + V-ing..., S + V.... = After + S + V..., S + V.... 分詞構句

　a. 副詞子句的主詞和主要子句相同時，則省略副詞子句的主詞。

　b. 省略連接詞。(為了使句意清楚，有時會保留連接詞。)

　c. 將副詞子句的動詞改為分詞。

After paying the money, John left the store and happily headed for a nearby park....

→ After John paid the money, he left the store and happily headed for a nearby park....

付了錢之後，John 離開這家店，並高興地前往附近的公園…

UNIT 1
UNIT 2
UNIT 3
UNIT 4
UNIT 5
UNIT 6
UNIT 7
UNIT 8
UNIT 9
UNIT 10
UNIT 11
UNIT 12
UNIT 13
UNIT 14
UNIT 15
UNIT 16
UNIT 17
UNIT 18
UNIT 19
UNIT 20

After I arrived home, I took a shower immediately.

→ After arriving home, I took a shower immediately.

→ Arriving home, I took a shower immediately.

　　我到家後，就馬上洗了個澡。

5. $S_1 + V_1..., S_2 + V_2$-ing.... = $S_1 + V_1...,$ and $S_2 + V_2....$　　獨立分詞構句

　　a. 對等子句的主詞和主要子句不同時，要保留對等子句的主詞。

　　b. 省略連接詞。

　　c. 將對等子句的動詞改為分詞。

Both of them fell down on the ground, and their boxes dropped on the sidewalk.

→ Both of them fell down on the ground, their boxes dropping on the sidewalk.

　　他們兩個都摔倒在地上，他們的盒子也掉在人行道上。

John entered the classroom, and Julie followed him.

→ John entered the classroom, Julie following him.

　　John 走進教室，Julie 也跟在他後面。

6. pick up　拿起，撿起

They picked up the trash before leaving the park.

他們在離開公園之前把垃圾撿起來。

7. Not until + S + V + did + S + V....　倒裝句：直到…才…

Not until Sam arrived the train station did he find that he forgot his ticket.

直到 Sam 到了車站，他才發現他忘了帶車票。

8. instead of　而不是

Tanya believes in love instead of money.　Tanya 相信愛，而不是錢。

9. by mistake　錯誤地

Jim took my bag by mistake because our bags are much alike.

Jim 誤拿了我的袋子，因為我們的袋子看起來太像了。

UNIT
1
UNIT
2
UNIT
3
UNIT
4
UNIT
5
UNIT
6
UNIT
7
UNIT
8
UNIT
9
UNIT
10
UNIT
11
UNIT
12
UNIT
13
UNIT
14
UNIT
15
UNIT
16
UNIT
17
UNIT
18
UNIT
19
UNIT
20

UNIT 16

Informative Writing 訊息文

How I Prepare for the College Entrance Exams

我如何準備大學入學考試

北區公立高中 94 年第三次指考模擬考

　　你在高三這一年是如何準備應考大學入學考試的呢?請以 "How I Prepare for the College Entrance Exams" 為題，寫一篇 120 個英文字左右的作文，與學弟妹分享你高三這一年成功或失敗的經驗吧！

　　How have you prepared for the College Entrance Exams since the beginning of your third year in senior high school? Write an essay entitled "How I Prepare for the College Entrance Exams" in 120 words or so in order to share with your junior schoolmates your success or failure in exams.

Step 1 　聯想提示 Association 　依人、事、時、地、物、原因和方法聯想與題目相關的事項

- 為什麼我要準備大學入學考試？ Why do I have to prepare for the college entrance exams?
- 我如何準備？ How do I prepare for them?
- 考試成功的關鍵是什麼？ What is the key to success?
- 有哪些具體的方法？ Give specific examples.

Step 2 　組織大綱提示 Organization 　依照想到的事項，定出寫作優先順序及細節

第一段

1. 主題句：上了高三就忙著準備大學入學考試。

2. 原因：想進入理想大學。

3. 轉折：只要遵守一些原則，我就會是一位很有效率的考生。(以下段落舉出例子)

第二段

1. 主題句：考試成敗取決於是否充分準備。

2. 支持句：

　a. 預先熟悉考試的題材內容。

　b. 用功、問問題並溫習學過的東西。

第三段

1. 主題句：應試需要好體力，因為在考試時需要大量思考。

2. 支持句：考前要睡個好覺、早餐要吃得好。

第四段

1. 主題句：要擅於考試就必須勤加練習。

2. 支持句：成績要進步，多做模擬考是最有效的。

Step 3 範文 Model Composition

How I Prepare for the College Entrance Exams

Since the beginning of my third year in high school, I have been busy preparing for this year's college entrance exams. It is because I wish to enter an ideal university. I believe I am most effective as an examinee when I abide by the following principles.

Whether I succeed or fail in an exam depends on whether I am well-prepared for it. I must, in advance, be familiar with the materials to be tested. Therefore, to get good grades in an exam, I have to study, ask questions and, most importantly, brush up on lessons learned in the past.

In addition, good stamina is needed in taking an exam, when I will do a lot of thinking about the test questions and their answers. So, it is important that I have a good night's sleep before the exam and a good breakfast on the morning of the exam.

Last but not least, it takes practice for me to be good at exams. So there is no more effective way to raise scores than taking lots and lots of mock exams.

Step 4 寫句實戰分析 Analyzing Sentences

第一段

1. Since the beginning of my third year in high school, I have been busy preparing for this year's college entrance exams.

UNIT 1

UNIT 2

UNIT 3

UNIT 4

UNIT 5

UNIT 6

UNIT 7

UNIT 8

UNIT 9

UNIT 10

UNIT 11

UNIT 12

UNIT 13

UNIT 14

UNIT 15

UNIT 16

UNIT 17

UNIT 18

UNIT 19

UNIT 20

自從上了高三，我就一直忙著準備今年的大學入學考試。

文法句型
- Since + 過去時間 ..., S + has/have + V-en....　自從…，…就一直…
- busy + V-ing　忙著…

2. It is because I wish to enter an ideal university.

那是因為我想進入一所理想的大學。

字詞提示
- ideal *adj.* 理想的

3. I believe I am most effective as an examinee when I abide by the following principles.

我相信身為一個考生，只要我遵守下列幾個原則，我就會是最有效率的。

字詞提示
- examinee *n.* 應試者
- principle *n.* 原則

文法句型
- abide by　遵守
- 注意：as 表示「身為…」。

第二段

1. Whether I succeed or fail in an exam depends on whether I am well-prepared for it.　考試成功或失敗要看我考前是否準備充分。

文法句型
- depend on　取決於…
- 注意：「whether + S + V」是名詞子句，在本句中做主詞也做受詞。

2. I must, in advance, be familiar with the materials to be tested.

我必須預先熟悉要測驗的內容。

字詞提示
- material *n.* 材料，內容

文法句型
- in advance　預先
- be familiar with　熟悉
- 注意：不定詞 to be + V-en 作形容詞片語用，修飾前面的名詞。

3. Therefore, to get good grades in an exam, I have to study, ask questions and, most importantly, brush up on lessons learned in the past.

因此，為了要在考試中得高分，我必須用功、問問題，而且最重要的是，溫習以前學過的課業。

⚠️ 文法句型 ・ brush up on 溫習

第三段

1. In addition, good stamina is needed in taking an exam, when I will do a lot of thinking about the test questions and their answers.

此外，應試需要好體力，因為在考試時我會對試題及答案做很多的思考。

⚠️ 字詞提示 ・ stamina *n.* 體力

⚠️ 文法句型 ・ in addition 此外

2. So, it is important that I have a good night's sleep before the exam and a good breakfast on the morning of the exam.

所以，考前睡好覺，並在考試當天早上吃頓豐盛的早餐是很重要的。

⚠️ 文法句型 ・ 注意：It is/was + adj. + that + S + V.... 中的 It 為虛主詞，真正主詞為 that 所引導的子句。

第四段

1. Last but not least, it takes practice for me to be good at exams.

最後但並非最不重要的一點就是：我要擅於考試就必須靠練習。

⚠️ 文法句型 ・ it takes...to + V 做…需要…

2. So there is no more effective way to raise scores than taking lots and lots of mock exams.

所以，要提高分數，沒有任何其他方法比做大量的模擬考來得更有效。

⚠️ 字詞提示
・ raise *v.* 提高
・ score *n.* 分數

✒ Step 5

用字遣詞 Words → Sentences

1. ideal [ar`diəl] *adj.* 理想的

Matthew's the ideal candidate for the class leader.

UNIT 1
UNIT 2
UNIT 3
UNIT 4
UNIT 5
UNIT 6
UNIT 7
UNIT 8
UNIT 9
UNIT 10
UNIT 11
UNIT 12
UNIT 13
UNIT 14
UNIT 15
UNIT 16
UNIT 17
UNIT 18
UNIT 19
UNIT 20

Matthew 是班長的理想人選。

2. examinee [ɪg͵zæməˋni] *n.* 應試者

While answering an essay question, examinees have to write down their opinion about the question.

回答申論題時，應試者必須寫下他們對該問題的意見。

3. principle [ˋprɪnsəpl̩] *n.* 原則

The most important principle that my parents taught me is honesty.

我父母教過我最重要的原則就是誠實。

4. material [məˋtɪrɪəl] *n.* 材料，內容

The teacher asked us to preview the reading materials for the class next week.

老師要我們預習下個禮拜上課的閱讀材料。

5. stamina [ˋstæmənə] *n.* 體力

It takes a lot of stamina to run a marathon.　跑馬拉松需要耗費很多體力。

6. raise [rez] *v.* 提高

Bread becomes more expensive because the price of flour has been raised.

麵包變貴是因為麵粉的價格提高了。

7. score [skor] *n.* 分數

If you want to go to a public university, you have to get higher test scores.

如果你想念公立大學，你必須考更高分。

文法句型 Grammar Points → Sentences

1. Since + 過去時間 ..., S + has/have + V-en....　自從…，…就一直…

Since the beginning of this year, I've been very busy.

從今年初開始，我就一直很忙。

2. busy + V-ing　忙著…

Joan is busy practicing for the school concert.

Joan 正忙著為學校的音樂會做練習。

3. abide by　遵守

Every citizen should abide by the law.　每個公民都應該守法。

4. depend on　取決於…

Choosing where to live depends on where I work.

選擇住在哪裡取決於我在哪裡工作。

5. in advance　預先

It will be cheaper if you book the hotel in advance.

如果你預先訂旅館會比較便宜。

6. be familiar with　熟悉

Since you were born here, you must be very familiar with the city.

既然你是在這裡出生的，必定對這個城市相當熟悉。

7. brush up on　溫習

You have to brush up on your French before going to Paris.

去巴黎之前，你必須先溫習一下你的法文。

8. in addition　此外

Maggie can speak both Chinese and English. In addition, she can speak Japanese.

Maggie 會說中文和英文，此外，她還能說日文。

9. it takes...to + V　做…需要…

It takes great effort to educate those boys.

教育那些男孩需要費很大的功夫。

UNIT
1

UNIT
2

UNIT
3

UNIT
4

UNIT
5

UNIT
6

UNIT
7

UNIT
8

UNIT
9

UNIT
10

UNIT
11

UNIT
12

UNIT
13

UNIT
14

UNIT
15

UNIT
16

UNIT
17

UNIT
18

UNIT
19

UNIT
20

UNIT 17

Expository Writing　說明文

How the Weather Affects My Mood　天氣如何影響我的心情

談談不同天氣對你的心情所造成的影響。

Write about how the weather might affect your mood.

Step 1　聯想提示 Association　依人、事、時、地、物、原因和方法聯想與題目相關的事項

- 天氣會影響我的心情嗎？　Does the weather affect my mood?
- 我討厭什麼樣的天氣？　What kinds of weather do I hate?
- 我為什麼討厭它們？　Why do I hate them?
- 我喜歡什麼樣的天氣？　What kinds of weather do I like?
- 我為什麼喜歡它們？　Why do I like them?
- 我對不同天氣的感受如何？　How do I feel about different kinds of weather?

Step 2　組織大綱提示 Organization　依照想到的事項，定出寫作優先順序及細節

1. 主題句：天氣對我的心情影響很大。
2. 我討厭下雨天，因為心情會不好。
3. 下雨時，我會把自己悶在房間裡。
4. 天冷的時候，身體血液循環不良，四肢動作緩慢，只想在家裡冬眠。
5. 天氣炎熱潮濕的時候，我會比較容易發脾氣。
6. 我喜歡怡人乾爽的好天氣，心情會比較好。
7. 結論：天氣好，心情就好；天氣不好，就覺得不舒服。

Step 3　範文 Model Composition

How the Weather Affects My Mood

Weather affects my mood a lot. I hate rainy days because the rain always puts me in a bad mood. I might not do anything but hide myself away in my room when it is rainy and moist. When the weather is cold, my blood circulates so slowly that my limbs become clumsy, which makes me want to just hibernate at home. When it is hot and humid, I get so cranky and irritable that the slightest thing might set me off. I prefer lovely, dry, cool and sunny weather, which always makes me feel uplifted and usually triggers my desire to travel. In a word, I actually feel happier when the weather is fine, whereas discomfort typically occurs when the weather becomes bad.

Step 4 寫句實戰分析 Analyzing Sentences

1. Weather affects my mood a lot.
   天氣對我的心情影響很大。

   ①字詞提示
   · affect *v.* 影響
   · mood *n.* 心情

   ①文法句型
   · 注意：a lot = very much　很大；非常

2. I hate rainy days because the rain always puts me in a bad mood.
   我討厭下雨天，因為下雨總是會讓我心情不好。

   ①文法句型
   · S + V + 附屬連接詞 + S + V.... = 附屬連接詞 + S + V, S + V....
   · in a bad mood　心情不好

3. I might not do anything but hide myself away in my room when it is rainy and moist.
   多雨潮濕的時候，我會自己躲在房間裡，什麼事也不做。

   ①字詞提示
   · moist *adj.* 潮濕的

   ①文法句型
   · not do anything but + V = do nothing but + V　除了…之外什麼都不做

4. When the weather is cold, my blood circulates so slowly that my limbs become clumsy, which makes me want to just hibernate at home.

天冷時，我的血液循環很慢，因而使我的四肢變得笨拙，讓我只想待在家裡冬眠。

字詞提示
- circulate *v.* 循環
- clumsy *adj.* 笨拙的
- hibernate *v.* 冬眠

文法句型
- so adj./adv. that + S + V　如此…以致於

5. When it is hot and humid, I get so cranky and irritable that the slightest thing might set me off.

在炎熱潮溼的天氣裡，我會變得暴躁易怒，往往一點最輕微的小事就會引爆我。

字詞提示
- cranky *adj.* 暴躁不安的
- irritable *adj.* 易怒的，煩躁的

文法句型
- set off　使…爆炸

6. I prefer lovely, dry, cool and sunny weather, which always makes me feel uplifted and usually triggers my desire to travel.

我比較喜歡怡人、乾爽、涼快、晴朗的天氣，這會讓我的心情振奮，而且經常會激發我想去旅行的慾望。

字詞提示
- uplifted *adj.* 感到振奮的
- trigger *v.* 觸發，引起

文法句型
- 關係代名詞的非限定用法，僅作補述之用，不用以限定先行詞。

7. In a word, I actually feel happier when the weather is fine, whereas discomfort typically occurs when the weather becomes bad.

總而言之，天氣好時我真的會感到比較快樂，而當天氣變壞時，不舒服的情況通常會發生。

文法句型
- in a word　總而言之
- S + V, whereas + S + V....　而，卻
- feel + adj.　連綴 v. 後加 adj.，為主詞補語，修飾主詞。

UNIT 1
UNIT 2
UNIT 3
UNIT 4
UNIT 5
UNIT 6
UNIT 7
UNIT 8
UNIT 9
UNIT 10
UNIT 11
UNIT 12
UNIT 13
UNIT 14
UNIT 15
UNIT 16
UNIT 17
UNIT 18
UNIT 19
UNIT 20

Step 5

1. affect [ə`fɛkt] *v.* 影響

    Paul's opinion will not affect my decision.

    Paul 的意見不會影響我的決定。

2. mood [mud] *n.* 心情

    Mary's just not in the mood for a party tonight.

    Mary 今晚根本沒心情參加派對。

3. moist [mɔɪst] *adj.* 潮濕的

    The path was moist with dew.　這條小徑因露水而潮濕。

4. circulate [`sɝkjə,let] *v.* 循環

    The disease prevents the blood from circulating normally.

    這種疾病讓血液無法正常循環。

5. clumsy [`klʌmzɪ] *adj.* 笨拙的

    Cindy's clumsy fingers couldn't untie the knot.

    Cindy 笨拙的手指沒辦法解開這個結。

6. hibernate [`haɪbə,net] *v.* 冬眠

    Some bears hibernate in winter.　有些熊冬天會冬眠。

7. cranky [`kræŋkɪ] *adj.* 暴躁不安的

    Ivy's mother has been cranky recently. She yelled at Ivy sometimes.

    Ivy 的媽媽最近情緒暴躁不安。她有時會對著 Ivy 咆哮。

8. irritable [`ɪrətəbl] *adj.* 易怒的，煩躁的

    Be careful about what you say—John is irritable today.

    說話小心點—John 今天很暴躁。

9. uplifted [ʌp`lɪftɪd] *adj.* 感到振奮的

    Nancy felt very uplifted when she listened to the music.

    當 Nancy 聽到音樂時，她感到很振奮。

10. trigger [`trɪgɚ] *v.* 觸發，引起

    Seconds later, a spark triggered an explosion.

    幾秒鐘後，一個火花引發了爆炸。

1. S + V + 附屬連接詞 + S + V.... → 附屬連接詞 + S + V, S + V....

I will buy a villa for my parents if I become rich.

→ If I become rich, I will buy a villa for my parents.

如果我變得很有錢，我會買一棟別墅給我的父母。

2. in a bad mood　心情不好

Jerry was just scolded by the teacher for his poor grades. He must be in a bad mood now.

Jerry 剛剛才因為他的爛成績被老師罵。他現在心情一定不好。

3. not do anything but + V = do nothing but + V　除了…之外，什麼事都不做

We didn't do anything/did nothing but watch movies yesterday.

我們昨天除了看電影之外，什麼都沒做。

4. so adj./adv. that + S + V　如此…以致於

Betty spoke so quietly that I couldn't hear her.

Betty 講得很小聲，所以我聽不到她說了什麼。

5. set off　使…生氣；使…爆炸

The terrorists set off the bomb in the Madrid Subway yesterday.

恐怖份子昨天在馬德里地下鐵引爆了炸彈。

6. 關係代名詞的非限定用法

a. 關係子句僅作補述之用，而不用以限定先行詞時，關係代名詞前面一定要有逗號。

b. 補述用法的關係子句常可以和對等子句或副詞子句替換。

Barry said nothing, which made me angry.

→ Barry said nothing, and this made me angry.

Barry 什麼都沒說，這一點讓我很生氣。

I hired this man, who can speak English.

= I hired this man, for he can speak English.

我雇用了這個人，因為他會講英文。

7. in a word　總而言之

Bad things happened to Laura. In a word, she was in bad luck.

壞事總發生在 Laura 身上。總而言之，她運氣不好。

8. S + V, whereas + S + V....　而，卻

Some people like fatty meat, whereas others dislike it.

有些人喜歡肥肉，而其他人則不喜歡。

9. feel + adj.　連綴 V 後加 adj.，為主詞補語，修飾主詞。

Tammi said she felt cold and moved closer to me.

Tammi 說她覺得冷，往我這兒靠了過來。

UNIT 1
UNIT 2
UNIT 3
UNIT 4
UNIT 5
UNIT 6
UNIT 7
UNIT 8
UNIT 9
UNIT 10
UNIT 11
UNIT 12
UNIT 13
UNIT 14
UNIT 15
UNIT 16
UNIT 17
UNIT 18
UNIT 19
UNIT 20

UNIT 18

Narrative/Persuasive Writing　敘事文／說理文

How to Get a Good Night's Sleep　如何才能睡一個好覺

　　很多人常因睡眠不足而誤事。寫一篇大約 120 個英文字的短文。請把文章分成兩段：第一段敘述因為睡眠不足而造成的不愉快經驗；第二段舉例說明如何才能睡一個好覺。

　　Many people often bungle matters due to a lack of sleep. Write an essay of two paragraphs in 120 words or so. Depict an unhappy experience resulting from a lack of sleep in paragraph one; list several examples to demonstrate how to get a good night's sleep in paragraph two.

Step 1　聯想提示 Association　依人、事、時、地、物、原因和方法聯想與題目相關的事項

• 為什麼睡眠很重要？　Why is sleep important?

• 你可以向誰求助？　Who can you ask for help?

• 要是你缺乏睡眠會怎麼樣？　What if you lack sleep?

• 你要如何改善睡眠？　How to improve your sleep?

Step 2　組織大綱提示 Organization　依照想到的事項，定出寫作優先順序及細節

第一段

1. 主題句：嚴重缺乏睡眠會給個人帶來困擾。

2. 舉例：睡過頭

　　a. 某天早上搭公車上學時，由於在車上打瞌睡，不知不覺睡過站。

　　b. 真後悔不該熬夜看漫畫，不過知道的時候已經太遲了。

第二段

1. 主題句：為準備第二天而睡一個好覺是必要的。

2. 舉例：幫助睡眠的秘訣

　　a. 養成每晚固定時間就寢的習慣。

　　b. 不要在床上做與睡覺無關的事情。

　　c. 挑一張好床，使身體得到完全放鬆。

　　d. 如有必要可以請教醫師。

UNIT
1

UNIT
2

UNIT
3

UNIT
4

UNIT
5

UNIT
6

UNIT
7

UNIT
8

UNIT
9

UNIT
10

UNIT
11

UNIT
12

UNIT
13

UNIT
14

UNIT
15

UNIT
16

UNIT
17

UNIT
18

UNIT
19

UNIT
20

✒ Step 3　範文 Model Composition

How to Get a Good Night's Sleep

A severe lack of sleep may lead to personal trouble. One morning, I took a bus to school. Feeling tired on the bus, I dozed off and didn't realize that I had missed my stop. Suddenly I awoke to find myself in the bus terminal. I shouldn't have stayed up in bed reading comic books, and it was too late to regret what I had done.

One thing is clear: a good night's sleep is needed to prepare for the next day. Here are several tips to help you get to sleep. First, get into a regular routine of going to bed at the same time each night. Second, keep your bed a place for sleep, but not one for reading, watching TV, or anything irrelevant to sleep. Third, sleep on a good firm bed, which will give your whole body the support it needs to totally relax. Last but not least, consult your doctor if necessary.

✒ Step 4　寫句實戰分析 Analyzing Sentences

第一段

1. A severe lack of sleep may lead to personal trouble.
嚴重缺乏睡眠會給個人帶來困擾。

⊙字詞
提示　· lack *n.* 缺乏

⊙文法
句型　· lead to + N/V-ing　導致

2. One morning, I took a bus to school.　一天早上，我搭公車上學。

⊙文法
句型　· 注意：搭乘交通工具的動詞用 take。

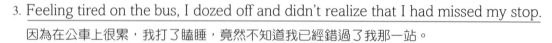

3. Feeling tired on the bus, I dozed off and didn't realize that I had missed my stop.

因為在公車上很累，我打了瞌睡，竟然不知道我已經錯過了我那一站。

⏻ 字詞
提示
· realize *v.* 了解

⏻ 文法
句型
· 過去完成式比過去式發生的時間更早。
· 注意：Feeling tired.... = As/Because I felt tired....

4. Suddenly I awoke to find myself in the bus terminal.

忽然間，我醒來發現自己已在公車總站了。

⏻ 字詞
提示
· terminal *n.* 終點站，總站

⏻ 文法
句型
· 本句的不定詞片語 to V 表結果，用以修飾前面的動詞。

5. I shouldn't have stayed up in bed reading comic books, and it was too late to regret what I had done.

我不該在床上熬夜看漫畫，但當時對我的所作所為感到後悔已經太遲了。

⏻ 字詞
提示
· regret *v.* 後悔

⏻ 文法
句型
· should not have + V-en　過去不應該發生，而事實上卻發生了
· too + adj./adv. + to + V　太…而不能…

第二段

1. One thing is clear: a good night's sleep is needed to prepare for the next day. Here are several tips to help you get to sleep.　有件事是很清楚的：要為第二天做好準備，睡一個好覺是必要的。這裡有幾個幫助你睡眠的秘訣。

⏻ 字詞
提示
· tip *n.* 竅門，秘訣

⏻ 文法
句型
· get to sleep (= start sleeping)　睡著

2. First, get into a regular routine of going to bed at the same time each night.

首先，養成每晚相同時間上床的規律習慣。

UNIT
1
UNIT
2
UNIT
3
UNIT
4
UNIT
5
UNIT
6
UNIT
7
UNIT
8
UNIT
9
UNIT
10
UNIT
11
UNIT
12
UNIT
13
UNIT
14
UNIT
15
UNIT
16
UNIT
17
UNIT
18
UNIT
19
UNIT
20

ⓘ字詞提示　• routine *n.* 慣例，常規

ⓘ文法句型
　• get into a routine of　養成⋯的習慣
　• 注意：祈使句句首以原形動詞開頭。

3. Second, keep your bed a place for sleep, but not one for reading, watching TV, or anything irrelevant to sleep.　第二，把你的床鋪保持為用來睡覺的地方，而不要用來閱讀、看電視、或做任何與睡覺無關的事情。

ⓘ字詞提示　• irrelevant *adj.* 不相干的，無關的

4. Third, sleep on a good firm bed, which will give your whole body the support it needs to totally relax.

第三，睡在一張堅固的床上，它可以提供足以讓你全身完全放鬆所需的支撐力。

ⓘ字詞提示
　• support *n.* 支撐
　• relax *v.* 放鬆

5. Last but not least, consult your doctor if necessary.

最後但並非最不重要的一點就是，如果有必要，可以請教你的醫生。

ⓘ字詞提示　• consult *v.* 請教，與⋯商量

ⓘ文法句型　• if necessary　如果有必要

Step 5

用字遣詞 Words → Sentences

1. lack [læk] *n.* 缺乏

Jenny is afraid of speaking in front of the public because of lack of confidence.

因為缺乏自信，Jenny 不敢在大家面前講話。

2. realize [ˋrɪəˌlaɪz] *v.* 了解

Carl realized that he was wrong when Julie told him the truth.

當 Julie 向 Carl 說出實情時，他才了解到他錯了。

3. terminal [ˋtɝmənl] *n.* 終點站，總站

I live near the bus terminal, so it's convenient for me to go anywhere.

我住在公車總站附近，所以要去哪裡都很方便。

4. regret [rɪ`grɛt] *v.* 後悔

Once you've made the decision, don't regret it.　一旦下了決定，就不要後悔。

5. tip [tɪp] *n.* 竅門，秘訣

Here are two tips to stay healthy. First, exercise regularly. Second, go to bed on time.　以下是兩個保持健康的小秘訣。第一，規律運動。第二，準時睡覺。

6. routine [ru`tin] *n.* 慣例，常規

Make exercise part of your daily routine.

讓運動變成你每天日常作息的一部份。

7. irrelevant [ɪ`rɛləvənt] *adj.* 不相干的，無關的

Joan's working ability is irrelevant to her educational background.

Joan 的工作能力與她的教育背景無關。

8. support [sə`port] *n.* 支撐

The nurse put pillows behind the patient's back to give extra support to his body when he wanted to sit up.

當病人想坐起來時，護士將枕頭墊在他背後，給予身體額外的支撐。

9. relax [rɪ`læks] *v.* 放鬆

After working all day, I need a nice hot bath to relax myself.

在工作一整天後，我需要好好洗個熱水澡來讓自己放鬆一下。

10. consult [kən`sʌlt] *v.* 請教，與…商量

Did you consult your doctor about your illness?

你有跟你的醫生請教你的病情嗎？

文法句型 Grammar Points → Sentences

1. lead to + N/V-ing　導致

Having too much sugar can lead to health problems.

吃太多糖可能導致健康問題。

2. 過去完成式 V.S. 過去式　同一句中的過去完成式比過去式發生的時間更早

I didn't remember that I had met Mr. Johnson before.

我不記得我之前見過 Johnson 先生。

3. 不定詞片語當副詞用時，可依其功能分為以下幾種用法：

I awoke to find myself in the police station.

我醒來發現自己在警察局裡。(表結果)

The manager was determined to carry out this project.

經理已下定決心要實行這項企劃。(表目的)

I'm sorry to hear about your decision.

我因聽到你的決定而感到遺憾。(表原因)

4. should not have + V-en　過去不應該發生，而事實上卻發生了

   You should not have eaten the ice cream, but you did.

   你不應該吃冰淇淋的，但是你吃了。

   should have + V-en　過去應該發生，而事實上卻沒有發生

   The train should have arrived ten minutes ago, but it didn't.

   火車應該在十分鐘前就到的，但它沒有到。

5. too + adj./adv. + to + V　太…而不能…

   My grandpa is too old to play basketball.

   我的爺爺太老以致於不能打籃球。

6. get to sleep (= start sleeping)　睡著

   Counting sheep helps me get to sleep.　數羊幫助我入睡。

7. get into a routine of　養成…的習慣

   If you want to lose weight, you should get into a routine of exercising every day.

   如果你想要減重，就該養成每天運動的習慣。

8. if necessary　如果有必要

   If necessary, you can contact me by telephone.

   如果有必要，你可以打電話找我。

UNIT 1
UNIT 2
UNIT 3
UNIT 4
UNIT 5
UNIT 6
UNIT 7
UNIT 8
UNIT 9
UNIT 10
UNIT 11
UNIT 12
UNIT 13
UNIT 14
UNIT 15
UNIT 16
UNIT 17
UNIT 18
UNIT 19
UNIT 20

UNIT 19

Making Decisions　做決定

　　寫一篇大約 120 至 150 個字的英文作文，分成兩段，題目是 "Making Decisions"。第一段的第一句必須是主題句 "Growing up means making my own decisions."。第二段的第一句必須是主題句 "The hardest decision that I ever made was _____."。同時在空格中填入自己所做的決定。

　　Write a two-paragraph essay with the title "Making Decisions" in about 120 to 150 words. Paragraph one should begin with the topic sentence "Growing up means making my own decisions." Paragraph two should begin with the topic sentence "The hardest decision that I ever made was _____." And fill in the blank with the decision you made on your own.

Step 1　聯想提示 Association　依人、事、時、地、物、原因和方法聯想與題目相關的事項

- 我對做決定的看法是什麼？　What do I think about making decisions?
- 我做過了什麼決定？　What specific decision did I make?
- 我什麼時候做了這個決定？　When did I make the decision?
- 這個決定是關於什麼？　What was the decision about?
- 我為什麼做這個決定？　Why did I make the decision?
- 我做這個決定的經過？　How did I make the decision?

Step 2　組織大綱提示 Organization　依照想到的事項，定出寫作優先順序及細節

第一段

1. 主題句：長大表示為自己做決定。

2. 支持句：

　　a. 十八歲已經夠大，可以對自己做的任何決定負責。

　　b. 已經不再是天真無邪的小女生了，變得比較獨立。

3. 結論：應該開始學會為自己做決定。

第二段

1. 主題句：我所做過最困難的決定，就是幾天前決定和男友分手。

2. 支持句：我們因為意見分歧導致關係不和諧而分開。

2. 支持句：我們因為意見分歧導致關係不和諧而分開。

3. 細節：相遇到分手

    a. 在兩年前的一次聖誕派對中相遇並交往。

    b. 剛開始有趣，後來變得乏味。

    c. 後來發現無法相處，因為意見不同。

4. 結論：

    a. 爭論是誰的錯已經沒有用了，一切已經過去。

    b. 我絕不後悔我幾天前所做的那個決定。

Step 3　範文 Model Composition

Making Decisions

Growing up means making my own decisions. Being an eighteen-year-old girl, I know I am old enough to be responsible for whatever decisions I make. That is, I am no longer the dependent girl I once was; I become more self-reliant and independent. Therefore, I should start learning to decide for myself.

The hardest decision that I ever made was deciding to break up with my boyfriend the other day. We parted on difficult terms because of differences of opinion. I first met him during a Christmas party two years ago and we had been dating ever since. It was fun at first, but things began to get dull in our relationship. I later found we could not get along because we were opposite to each other in every way. There is no use arguing about who was more to blame —it's all history after all. However, one thing is for sure—I'll never regret the decision I made.

Step 4　寫句實戰分析 Analyzing Sentences

第一段

1. <u>Growing up means making my own decisions.</u>　長大表示為自己做決定。

109

> ⚠️ **文法句型**　· V-ing... + V....　動名詞當主詞的句型

2. Being an eighteen-year-old girl, I know I am old enough to be responsible for whatever decisions I make.

身為十八歲的女孩，我知道我的年紀夠大，可以對自己做的任何決定負責。

> ⚠️ **文法句型**
> · be + adj. + enough to V　夠…去做某事
> · 注意：whatever + N. + S + V = any + N. + that + S + V

3. That is, I am no longer the dependent girl I once was; I become more self-reliant and independent. Therefore, I should start learning to decide for myself.

換言之，我已經不再是以前那個依賴別人的小女生了；我開始變得更不依賴他人也更加獨立。因此，我應該開始學會為自己做決定。

> ⚠️ **字詞提示**
> · self-reliant *adj.* 不依賴他人的
> · independent *adj.* 獨立自主的

> ⚠️ **文法句型**
> · that is (= that is to say)　換言之
> · no longer　不再

第二段

1. The hardest decision that I ever made was deciding to break up with my boyfriend the other day.

我所做過最困難的決定，就是幾天前決定和男友分手。

> ⚠️ **文法句型**
> · break up with　和…分手
> · the other day = a few days ago　幾天前

2. We parted on difficult terms because of differences of opinion.

我們因為意見分歧導致關係不和諧而分開。

> ⚠️ **文法句型**　· on + adj. + terms (with sb.)　(與某人) 有…的關係

3. I first met him during a Christmas party two years ago and we had been dating ever since.

我在兩年前的一個聖誕派對中第一次遇見他，之後就一直交往。

> ⚠️ **字詞提示**　· date *v.* 約會，交往

UNIT 1
UNIT 2
UNIT 3
UNIT 4
UNIT 5
UNIT 6
UNIT 7
UNIT 8
UNIT 9
UNIT 10
UNIT 11
UNIT 12
UNIT 13
UNIT 14
UNIT 15
UNIT 16
UNIT 17
UNIT 18
UNIT 19
UNIT 20

ⓘ **文法句型**
- ever since　自從那時候起

4. It was fun at first, but things began to get dull in our relationship.

　剛開始還滿好玩的，後來我們感情的狀況開始變得乏味。

ⓘ **字詞提示**
- things *n.* (生活中事件的) 情況
- dull *adj.* 無聊，無趣
- relationship *n.* (戀愛) 關係

5. I later found we could not get along because we were opposite to each other in every way.

　我後來發現我們無法和睦相處，因為我們在每個方面都和對方意見相反。

ⓘ **文法句型**
- get along　和睦相處
- be opposite to　與…相對立

6. There is no use arguing about who was more to blame—it's all history after all.

　爭論誰錯的比較多已經沒有用了——畢竟一切都已是過去的事了。

ⓘ **文法句型**
- There is no use + (in) + V-ing　…是沒有用的
- be to blame　…應受譴責，歸咎於…

7. However, one thing is for sure—I'll never regret the decision I made.

　然而，有件事是確定的——我絕不後悔我所做的決定。

ⓘ **文法句型**
- one thing is for sure　有件事是確定的
- 注意：regret 是及物動詞，後面直接接受詞。

Step 5

用字遣詞 Words → Sentences

1. self-reliant [ˌsɛlfrɪˋlaɪənt] *adj.* 不依賴他人的

　I become more self-reliant after I moved out from home.

　我從家裡搬出來之後，變的比較不依賴他人。

2. independent [ˌɪndɪˋpɛndənt] *adj.* 獨立自主的

　Jewel has always been financially independent since she was a college student.

　Jewel 自從大學以來一直都在財務上獨立自主。

3. date [det] *v.* 約會，交往

Jason and Phoebe have been dating for months.

Jason 和 Phoebe 已經交往好幾個月了。

4. things [θɪŋz] *n.* (生活中事件的) 情況

Things are getting better between Ben and Lily.

Ben 和 Lily 之間的情況愈來愈好了。

5. dull [dʌl] *adj.* 無聊，無趣

Things never get dull when I am with Liz.

我跟 Liz 在一起時，從不覺得無聊。

6. relationship [rɪˋleʃən͵ʃɪp] *n.* (戀愛) 關係

I like Rick a lot, but I have already been in a relationship with Henry.

我很喜歡 Rick，但是我已經跟 Henry 在一起了。

文法句型 Grammar Points → Sentences

1. V-ing... + V....　動名詞當主詞的句型

動名詞可以在句子中當作主詞，其後使用單數動詞。

Being polite means being kind to others.　有禮貌的意思是對別人親切。

2. be + adj. + enough to V　夠…去做某事

Henna is tall enough to reach the book on the shelf, so I ask her to get it for me.

Henna 夠高，可以拿到架子上的書，所以我請她幫我拿。

3. that is (= that is to say)　換言之

I have no money left; that is, I can't pay my rent.

我沒有錢了；也就是說，我付不出房租。

4. no longer　不再

The typewriter is no longer used.　打字機已經不再被使用了。

5. break up with　和…分手

Sean just broke up with his girlfriend; he felt his heart torn apart.

Sean 才剛和他的女朋友分手；他覺得他的心被撕裂了。

6. the other day = a few days ago　幾天前

I ran into my teacher from elementary school in the post office the other day.

我幾天前在郵局裡碰到我的國小老師。

7. on + adj. + terms (with sb.)　(與某人) 有…的關係

Lucy and Vera have been on bad terms since they had a fight.

Lucy 和 Vera 爭吵之後關係很不和諧。

8. ever since　自從那時候起

Jason came to Taipei two years ago and has lived here ever since.

Jason 兩年前來到台北，並從那時候起就住在這裡。

9. get along 和睦相處

Elijah got along well with his aunt. Elijah 跟他的阿姨相處得很好。

10. be opposite to 與⋯相對立

Nina's opinion is completely opposite to mine. We don't agree with each other.

Nina 的意見跟我的完全相反。我們不同意彼此的想法。

11. There is no use + (in) + V-ing ⋯是沒有用的

There is no use arguing anymore. 再繼續爭論下去是沒有用的。

12. be to blame ⋯應受譴責，歸咎於⋯

Television is partly to blame for kids' violent behavior.

兒童的暴力行為有一部份可歸咎於電視節目。

13. one thing is for sure 有一件事是確定的

One thing is for sure—I'll never go to that restaurant again.

有件事是確定的——我再也不會去那家餐廳了。

UNIT 1
UNIT 2
UNIT 3
UNIT 4
UNIT 5
UNIT 6
UNIT 7
UNIT 8
UNIT 9
UNIT 10
UNIT 11
UNIT 12
UNIT 13
UNIT 14
UNIT 15
UNIT 16
UNIT 17
UNIT 18
UNIT 19
UNIT 20

UNIT 20

My Advice on How to Make Good Use of High School Life

我對如何善用高中生活的建議

　　高中生活將接近尾聲，想必充滿酸甜苦辣、有歡笑、有榮耀、或有些遺憾。請你依自身的經驗，以 "My Advice on How to Make Good Use of High School Life" 為題，寫一篇約 120 到 150 個字的英文短文，鼓勵學弟妹能善用高中生活。短文分為兩段：第一段描述個人高中生活的成就與憾事；第二段依據自己失敗的經驗，提出建言。

　　Your high school life is coming to an end and must have been full of feelings of various sorts, like joy, glory, or some regret. Please write a short essay in your own experience with the title "My Advice on How to Make Good Use of High School Life" in 120 to 150 words to encourage junior schoolmates to make good use of their high school life. Divide the essay into two paragraphs. Describe something proud and something regretful in paragraph one; give suggestions according to your own experiences in failure.

Step 1　聯想提示 Association　依人、事、時、地、物、原因和方法聯想與題目相關的事項

- 我對自己的高中生活感想如何？How do I feel about my high school life?
- 為什麼我那樣覺得？Why do I feel that way?
- 這段時間我在做什麼？What have I been doing during the period?
- 我建議高中生做什麼？What do I suggest a high school student do?
- 高中生可採取什麼具體的措施？What specific steps can a high school student take?

Step 2　組織大綱提示 Organization　依照想到的事項，定出寫作優先順序及細節

第一段

1. 主題句：我的高中生活充滿了喜怒哀樂。
2. 支持句：
   a. 積極參與社團活動，從中得到滿足。
   b. 但學業成績每況愈下。
3. 結論：高中生活期間最大的遺憾——沒有花心思在課業上。

UNIT
1

UNIT
2

UNIT
3

UNIT
4

UNIT
5

UNIT
6

UNIT
7

UNIT
8

UNIT
9

UNIT
10

UNIT
11

UNIT
12

UNIT
13

UNIT
14

UNIT
15

UNIT
16

UNIT
17

UNIT
18

UNIT
19

UNIT
20

第二段

1. 主題句：建議高中生應該要善用高中生活。

2. 支持句：實際的方法

  a. 為自己定一份合理的進度表，聰明地運用時間。

  b. 上課時做筆記，保持積極和警覺。

3. 結論：大量投入心力將讓高中生活多采多姿。

Step 3　範文 Model Composition

My Advice on How to Make Good Use of High School Life

In my experience, high school life is full of joy, sorrow, fun, and frustration. I have been actively participating in club activities because I find contentment in them. However, I feel sorry about a continuing decline in my academic achievement. The reason is that I put little effort into my schoolwork, which is my greatest regret during my high school life.

A high school student, I suggest, should make good use of high school life. As an efficient student, you need to spend your time wisely by setting yourself a reasonable schedule, which will allow sufficient time for study and adequate time for recreation. It is also necessary for you to take notes when the teacher goes over the material in class, for note taking will keep you active and alert. In summary, a tremendous amount of dedication will guarantee you a great high school life.

Step 4　寫句實戰分析 Analyzing Sentences

第一段

1. In my experience, high school life is full of joy, sorrow, fun, and frustration.

 在我的經驗中，高中生活充滿了歡笑、悲傷、樂趣和挫折。

 ⚠字詞提示　· frustration n. 挫折

文法句型
- in my experience　在我的經驗中
- be full of　充滿

2. I have been actively participating in club activities because I find contentment in them.　我一直積極參與社團活動，因為我從中得到滿足。

！字詞提示
- participate *v.* 參加
- contentment *n.* 滿足

3. However, I feel sorry about a continuing decline in my academic achievement.
但是，我卻對學業成績每況愈下感到遺憾。

！字詞提示
- decline *n.* 減少，衰退
- academic *adj.* 學術上的
- achievement *n.* 成就

4. The reason is that I put little effort into my schoolwork, which is my greatest regret during my high school life.
原因在於我沒有放什麼心力在我的課業上，這是我高中生活期間最大的遺憾。

！文法句型
- put little/great/a lot of effort into　放很少／很多／許多的心力在…

第二段

1. A high school student, I suggest, should make good use of high school life.
我建議，一個高中生應該要善用高中生活。

！文法句型
- make good use of　善用
- 注意：原句為 I suggest that a high school student should make....

2. As an efficient student, you need to spend your time wisely by setting yourself a reasonable schedule, which will allow sufficient time for study and adequate time for recreation.
身為一個有效率的學生，你需要藉由為自己定一份合理的進度表，來聰明地運用你的時間，它會讓你有充分的時間唸書，也有足夠的時間休閒。

！字詞提示
- efficient *adj.* 有效率的
- schedule *n.* 進度表
- allow *v.* 容許，提供

3. It is also necessary for you to take notes when the teacher goes over the material in class, for note taking will keep you active and alert.

當老師在課堂上講解上課資料時，做筆記對你來說也是必要的，因為做筆記可以讓你保持積極和警覺。

ⓘ 字詞提示
- alert *adj.* 警覺的，警醒的

ⓘ 文法句型
- keep + sb./sth. + adj. 使…維持… (狀態)
- 注意：for + S + V 表原因或理由。

4. In summary, a tremendous amount of dedication will guarantee you a great high school life.

總而言之，大量投入心力將保證你的高中生活多采多姿。

ⓘ 字詞提示
- dedication *n.* 獻身，奉獻心力
- guarantee *v.* 承諾，保證

ⓘ 文法句型
- in summary 總而言之

✎ Step 5

用字遣詞 Words → Sentences

1. frustration [frʌs`treʃən] *n.* 挫折

   Mrs. Brown couldn't stand the frustration of not being able to help.

   Brown 女士無法忍受幫不上忙的挫敗感。

2. participate [pɑr`tɪsə,pet] *v.* 參加

   Greg never participated in any of our discussions.

   Greg 從未參加我們的任何討論。

3. contentment [kən`tɛntmənt] *n.* 滿足

   The mother looked at her baby with a look of contentment on her face.

   這個媽媽看著她的小孩，臉上帶著滿足的表情。

4. decline [dɪ`klaɪn] *n.* 減少，衰退

   The superpower is suffering from a major economic decline.

   這個世界強國正因經濟大衰退而苦。

5. academic [,ækə`dɛmɪk] *adj.* 學術上的

UNIT 1
UNIT 2
UNIT 3
UNIT 4
UNIT 5
UNIT 6
UNIT 7
UNIT 8
UNIT 9
UNIT 10
UNIT 11
UNIT 12
UNIT 13
UNIT 14
UNIT 15
UNIT 16
UNIT 17
UNIT 18
UNIT 19
UNIT 20

Schools in Taiwan focus a lot on students' academic performance.

台灣的學校非常注重學生在學術上的表現。

6. achievement [ə`tʃivmənt] *n.* 成就

My parents are very proud of my achievements.

我的父母對我的成就感到非常驕傲。

7. efficient [ɪ`fɪʃənt] *adj.* 有效率的

Rachel is the most efficient employee in my department. She does her job well and never wastes time.

Rachel 是我這個部門裡最有效率的員工。她把工作做的很好,又從不浪費時間。

8. schedule [`skɛdʒul] *n.* 進度表

My boss has a very busy schedule this week; I don't think he can spare any time to see you.

我老闆這個禮拜的行程很忙;我不覺得他能夠空出時間見你。

9. allow [ə`lau] *v.* 容許,提供

Taking a vacation once in a while allows me some time for relaxing and refreshing. 偶爾放個假讓我有時間可以放鬆及重振精神。

10. alert [ə`lɝt] *adj.* 警覺的,警醒的

Stay alert while driving at night. 晚上開車的時候要保持警覺。

11. dedication [ˌdɛdə`keʃən] *n.* 獻身,奉獻心力

Michael's dedication to work impressed the boss.

Michael 對工作的奉獻讓老闆印象深刻。

12. guarantee [ˌgærən`ti] *v.* 承諾,保證

The ticket guarantees you free entry. 這張票可保證你免費入場。

文法句型 Grammar Points → Sentences

1. in my experience 在我的經驗中

In my experience, college life is exciting and full of opportunities to learn.

在我的經驗中,大學生活很刺激,而且充滿了學習機會。

2. be full of 充滿

Life is full of surprises. 生命充滿了驚奇。

3. put little/great/a lot of effort into 放很少／很多／許多的心力在…

Jack put a lot of effort into his work. Jack 在工作上投注很大的心力。

4. make good use of 善用

We should make good use of the earth's precious resources.

我們應該善用地球的珍貴資源。

5. keep + sb./sth. + adj.　使…維持… (狀態)

The nurse tried to keep the patient calm.　護士試圖讓病人保持冷靜。

6. in summary　總而言之

The dancers' moves were so beautiful, and the music was touching. In summary, this was a very successful performance.

舞者的動作非常優美，音樂也很感人。總之，這是一場非常成功的表演。

UNIT 1
UNIT 2
UNIT 3
UNIT 4
UNIT 5
UNIT 6
UNIT 7
UNIT 8
UNIT 9
UNIT 10
UNIT 11
UNIT 12
UNIT 13
UNIT 14
UNIT 15
UNIT 16
UNIT 17
UNIT 18
UNIT 19
UNIT 20

UNIT 21

My Ambition　我的志向

　　寫一篇 120 到 150 字的英文作文，來談談你的志向。文章分成兩段：第一段寫出你的志向，並且說明志向的內容及其重要性；第二段寫你的志向是如何形成的，並簡單說明如何達成。

　　Write an essay about your ambition in 120 to 150 words. Organize the essay into two paragraphs. In paragraph one, write out your ambition and explain what it is about and its importance; in paragraph two, describe how your ambition has been formed and concisely explain how you can carry it out.

Step 1　聯想提示 Association　依人、事、時、地、物、原因和方法聯想與題目相關的事項

- 我的志向是什麼？　What is my ambition?
- 為什麼是這個志向？　Reasons to do it?
- 我的志向有什麼重要性和意義？　What is it about?
- 這個志向是如何形成的？　How did it develop?
- 實現這個志向的機會有多少？　The chance of realizing it?

Step 2　組織大綱提示 Organization　依照想到的事項，定出寫作優先順序及細節

第一段

1. 主題句：點出自己的志向——我一直很想當一位精神治療師。

2. 支持句：說明志向的內容

　a. 我想要協助人們解決情緒問題、從精神疾病中康復、恢復自信心。

　b. 近年來，越來越多人因承受很大的工作壓力而一直很沮喪。

3. 結論：因此，要營造一個強健的社會，精神治療師扮演了重要的角色。

第二段

1. 說明志向形成的背景之一：從小學開始，我就一直很喜歡觀察同班同學如何處理在學校遭遇的日常壓力。

2. 說明志向形成的背景之二：我也很樂於協助他們克服每天例行活動中所遭遇的障礙。

3. 我對實現夢想有旺盛的企圖心和強烈的自信心。

UNIT
21

UNIT
22

UNIT
23

UNIT
24

UNIT
25

UNIT
26

UNIT
27

UNIT
28

UNIT
29

UNIT
30

UNIT
31

UNIT
32

UNIT
33

UNIT
34

UNIT
35

UNIT
36

UNIT
37

UNIT
38

UNIT
39

UNIT
40

4.結論：終有一天，我可以成為一位出色的精神治療師。

Step 3 範文 Model Composition

My Ambition

I have always had a burning ambition to be a psychotherapist. I want to help people solve their emotional problem, recover from mental illnesses and regain their self-confidence. In recent years, an increasing number of people have gotten deeply depressed under a great deal of pressure at work. Therefore, the role of a psychotherapist in keeping our society strong and healthy is getting more and more important.

Since elementary school, I have really enjoyed observing how my classmates coped with daily stresses they encountered at school. I have also enjoyed giving them help to overcome barriers to normal day-to-day activities. Being a highly self-motivated person, I feel confident about my ability to make my dream come true. As the well-known saying goes, "Where there's a will, there's a way." I believe that I will become an outstanding psychotherapist some day.

Step 4 寫句實戰分析 Analyzing Sentences

第一段

1. I have always had a burning ambition to be a psychotherapist.

我一直有個強烈的志向，那就是希望能成為一名精神治療師。

- 字詞提示
  - burning *adj.* (情感) 強烈的
  - psychotherapist *n.* 精神治療師

- 文法句型
  - 注意：have always + V-en 一直

2. I want to help people solve their emotional problem, recover from mental

121

illnesses and regain their self-confidence.

我想要幫助人們解決情緒上的問題、從精神疾病中康復並重拾自信。

⊕字詞提示
- recover *v.* 康復、復原
- mental *adj.* 精神的，心理的
- regain *v.* 恢復，重新獲得
- self-confidence *n.* 自信

⊕文法句型
- help + O + (to) + V.... 協助…做…
- 注意：and 連接三個原形 V，即 solve、recover 以及 regain。

3. In recent years, an increasing number of people have gotten deeply depressed under a great deal of pressure at work.

近年來，有越來越多人因承受龐大的工作壓力而極度沮喪。

⊕字詞提示
- increasing *adj.* 日益增多的

⊕文法句型
- in recent years　近年來 (通常與現在完成式搭配使用)
- 注意：an increasing number of + 複數 N　越來越多的
　　　　a great deal of + 不可數 N　龐大的，大量的

4. Therefore, the role of a psychotherapist in keeping our society strong and healthy is getting more and more important.

因此，精神治療師在扮演強化並健全社會的角色上變得越來越重要。

⊕文法句型
- keep + O + adj.　使…保持在某一狀態
- be getting + adj.-er and adj.-er/more and more + adj.　變得越來越…

第二段

5. Since elementary school, I have really enjoyed observing how my classmates coped with daily stresses they encountered at school.

從小學開始，我就很喜歡觀察同學們如何處理每天在學校裡所遭遇到的壓力。

⊕字詞提示
- observe *v.* 觀察
- encounter *v.* 遭遇

⊕文法句型
- cope with　應付 (困難)
- Since + 過去時間 , S + have/has + V-en....　自…以來，…就一直…

UNIT
21
UNIT
22
UNIT
23
UNIT
24
UNIT
25
UNIT
26
UNIT
27
UNIT
28
UNIT
29
UNIT
30
UNIT
31
UNIT
32
UNIT
33
UNIT
34
UNIT
35
UNIT
36
UNIT
37
UNIT
38
UNIT
39
UNIT
40

· S + V + how/what/when/where/why + S + V.... 名詞子句

6. I have also enjoyed giving them help to overcome barriers to normal day-to-day activities.

我也很樂於提供他們所需要的協助，以克服每天日常活動中所遭遇到的障礙。

!字詞
提示
· barrier *n.* 障礙
· day-to-day *adj.* 每天的

!文法
句型
·注意：第一個 to 是接不定詞片語，第二個 to 是介系詞。

7. Being a highly self-motivated person, I feel confident about my ability to make my dream come true.

身為一個主動積極的人，我對於實現夢想感到很有自信。

!字詞
提示
· motivated *adj.* 有積極性的

!文法
句型
· feel confident about　對…有信心
· ability to + V　做…的能力
· make + O + 原形 V　使役動詞後接原形動詞

8. As the well-known saying goes, "Where there's a will, there's a way."

正如大家所熟知的諺語所說的：「有志者，事竟成。」

!字詞
提示
· well-known *adj.* 熟知的

!文法
句型
· As the saying goes, ...　介紹諺語的句型

9. I believe that I will become an outstanding psychotherapist some day.

我相信我總有一天會成為一名傑出的精神治療師。

!字詞
提示
· outstanding *adj.* 傑出的

!文法
句型
·注意：some day　(未來的) 有一天

Step 5

1. burning [`bɜˋnɪŋ] *adj.* (情感) 強烈的

   The young boy has a burning desire for success.

   這位年輕的男孩對成功有強烈的渴望。

2. psychotherapist [ˌsaɪkoˋθɛrəpɪst] *n.* 精神治療師

   He sees a psychotherapist twice a month to treat his depression.

   他一個月去看兩次精神治療師，以治療他的憂鬱症。

3. recover [ˌrɪˋkʌvɚ] *v.* (+ from) 康復、復原

   It took Lisa a long while to recover from her heart operation.

   Lisa 花了很長一段時間才從心臟手術中恢復健康。

4. mental [`mɛntl̩] *adj.* 精神的，心理的

   Millions of people live with mental illnesses every day.

   數以百萬的民眾每天飽受精神疾病之苦。

5. regain [rɪˋgen] *v.* 恢復，重新獲得

   He made an effort to regain his self-control.　他努力恢復自制。

6. self-confidence [`sɛlfˋkɑnfədəns] *n.* 自信

   It is necessary for parents to help their children build up their self-confidence.

   父母幫助小孩建立自信是必要的。

7. increasing [ɪnˋkrisɪŋ] *adj.* 日益增多的

   The newlyweds are facing an increasing number of problems.

   這對新婚夫妻正面臨愈來愈多的問題。

8. observe [əbˋzɜˋv] *v.* 觀察

   It is important to observe your child's behavior and try to understand him.

   觀察你孩子的行為並試圖了解他是很重要的。

9. encounter [ɪnˋkaʊntɚ] *v.* 遭遇

   Along life's paths, each of us will encounter numerous obstacles and challenges.

   在人生的旅途上，我們每一個人都會遭遇許多障礙和挑戰。

10. barrier [`bærɪɚ] *n.* 障礙

    Overcoming the barriers to participation in digital economy requires appropriate policies.　要有適當的政策才能克服參與數位經濟的障礙。

11. day-to-day [`de tə `de] *adj.* 每天的

UNIT
21

UNIT
22

UNIT
23

UNIT
24

UNIT
25

UNIT
26

UNIT
27

UNIT
28

UNIT
29

UNIT
30

UNIT
31

UNIT
32

UNIT
33

UNIT
34

UNIT
35

UNIT
36

UNIT
37

UNIT
38

UNIT
39

UNIT
40

Handicapped people have to make more effort to solve their day-to-day problems. 殘障者必須付出更多努力來解決他們每天遭遇的問題。

12. motivated [ˋmotəˏvetɪd] *adj.* 有積極性的

Our staff are hard-working and highly motivated.

我們的員工很勤勞，而且很積極。

13. well-known [ˋwɛlˋnon] *adj.* 熟知的

That was an well-known old song. Most of us heard it before.

那是一首大家都熟悉的老歌。我們之中大部份的人以前都聽過。

14. outstanding [ˋautˋstændɪŋ] *adj.* 傑出的

It is believed that the outstanding scientist will win the Nobel Prize this year.

據信那位傑出的科學家會贏得今年的諾貝爾獎。

文法句型 Grammar Points → Sentences

1. help + O + (to) + V.... 協助…做…

The US$10,000 loan from the bank helped John (to) start his own business.

這筆一萬美金的銀行貸款幫助 John 開創了自己的事業。

2. in recent years 近年來 (通常與現在完成式搭配使用)

In recent years, there has been an increase in the amount of violence on TV.

近年來，電視上出現越來越多的暴力。

3. keep + O + adj. 使…保持在某一狀態

The noise from my neighbor's party kept me awake all night.

鄰居開派對的喧鬧聲讓我一整晚都沒睡。

4. be getting + adj.-er and adj.-er/more and more + adj. 變得越來越…

The earth's climate is getting more and more unstable and unpredictable.

地球的氣候變得越來越不穩定，也越來越不容易預測。

5. cope with 應付 (困難等)

Lisa felt unable to cope with the heavy work load after her child was born.

Lisa 的小孩出生後，她覺得自己沒辦法應付隨之而來的沉重負擔。

6. Since + 過去時間 , S + have/has + V-en.... 自…以來，…就一直…

Jason and Kathy have been friends since childhood.

Jason and Kathy 是從小就認識的朋友。

7. S + V + how/what/when/where/why + S + V.... 名詞子句

I don't understand what you said. 我不懂你在說什麼。

Do you know where you went wrong? 你知道你什麼地方弄錯了嗎？

8. feel confident about 對⋯有信心

We feel confident about our e-business capability.

我們對自己的電子商務能力有信心。

9. ability to + V 做⋯的能力

Paul has the ability to help people solve their problems.

Paul 有幫助人們解決問題的能力。

10. make + O + 原形 V

使役動詞後接受詞再接原形動詞，表示「使受詞去做原形動詞的動作」。

The movie made me cry. It's so touching!

那部電影讓我哭了。真的很感人！

11. As the saying goes, ... 介紹諺語的句型

As the saying goes, "Many heads are better than one."

正如該諺語所說的：「三個臭皮匠，勝過一個諸葛亮。」

UNIT
21
UNIT
22
UNIT
23
UNIT
24
UNIT
25
UNIT
26
UNIT
27
UNIT
28
UNIT
29
UNIT
30
UNIT
31
UNIT
32
UNIT
33
UNIT
34
UNIT
35
UNIT
36
UNIT
37
UNIT
38
UNIT
39
UNIT
40

UNIT 22

Narrative Writing　敘事文

My Best English Class Ever　最棒的一堂英文課

北區公立高中 93 年第一次指考模擬考

請以 "My Best English Class Ever" 為題，寫一篇英文短文，文長約 120 至 150 字，描述從小到大你上過最充實而令你印象深刻的一堂英文課。

Write a short essay in 120 to 150 words under the title "My Best English Class Ever." Describe one English class you may have enjoyed the most during your previous schooling.

Step 1　聯想提示 Association　依人、事、時、地、物、原因和方法聯想與題目相關的事項

- 我上過最棒的一堂英文課是哪一堂？　Which English class is the best one ever?
- 我的老師在課堂上做了什麼事？　What did my teacher do during the class?
- 為什麼它是最棒的英文課？　Why is it the best English class?
- 它有何特別之處？　What was special about it?
- 我在課堂上做什麼？　What did I do during the class?

Step 2　組織大綱提示 Organization　依照想到的事項，定出寫作優先順序及細節

第一段

1. 主題句：我在同學面前發表演講的那堂英文課，是最棒的英文課。

2. 支持句：成功發表演講並非容易的事。

   a. 它需要規劃、演練並注意細節。

   b. 在規劃階段，我組織演講稿。

   c. 在演練階段，我練習演說技巧。

第二段

1. 演講前後，我觀察其他演講者。

2. 老師對如何提昇演講效果提了一些建議。

3. 老實說，比起整堂課都靜靜地坐著，我比較喜歡口語表達訓練。

Step 3 範文 Model Composition

My Best English Class Ever

My best English class ever is the one during which I delivered a speech in front of my classmates. Delivering a speech successfully is not an easy task. It requires planning, rehearsal, and attention to detail. During the planning stage, I collected information and organized my speech. During the rehearsal, I rehearsed my speech by means of various speech delivery strategies, including facial and voice expressions, gestures, and body movements.

While waiting my turn to speak or after finishing my speech, I was looking at the other speakers and trying to listen to what they were saying. The teacher ended the class with a few suggestions about what we might do before, during, and after a speech to improve it. I enjoyed this class a lot because I prefer oral presentation training to sitting throughout the whole class.

Step 4 寫句實戰分析 Analyzing Sentences

第一段

1. My best English class ever is the one during which I delivered a speech in front of my classmates.

   我上過最棒的一堂英文課就是我在同學面前發表演講的那堂英文課。

   ①字詞提示　• deliver v. 發表 (演說)

   ①文法句型　• in front of 在…之前
   　　　　　　• 注意：不定代名詞 one 代替 class

2. Delivering a speech successfully is not an easy task.

   成功發表演講並非容易的事。

UNIT
21
UNIT
22
UNIT
23
UNIT
24
UNIT
25
UNIT
26
UNIT
27
UNIT
28
UNIT
29
UNIT
30
UNIT
31
UNIT
32
UNIT
33
UNIT
34
UNIT
35
UNIT
36
UNIT
37
UNIT
38
UNIT
39
UNIT
40

ⓘ**文法 句型** ・注意：本句為動名詞當主詞的用法。

3. It requires planning, rehearsal, and attention to detail.

它需要規劃、演練並注意細節。

ⓘ**字詞 提示**
- require *v.* 需要
- rehearsal *n.* 排演
- attention *n.* 注意
- detail *n.* 細節

4. During the planning stage, I collected information and organized my speech.

在規劃階段，我收集資訊並組織演講稿。

ⓘ**字詞 提示** ・ organize *v.* 組織

5. During the rehearsal, I rehearsed my speech by means of various speech delivery strategies, including facial and voice expressions, gestures, and body movements.　在演練階段，我利用各種演說策略：包括臉部表情、聲調、手勢和肢體動作，來排練我的演講。

ⓘ**字詞 提示**
- rehearse *v.* 演練，排練
- delivery *n.* 演說的方式或姿態
- strategy *n.* 策略
- facial *adj.* 臉部的
- expression *n.* 表情，聲調的感情
- gesture *n.* 手勢，姿勢

ⓘ**文法 句型** ・ by means of　用…，以…

第二段

1. While waiting my turn to speak or after finishing my speech, I was looking at the other speakers and trying to listen to what they were saying.　在我等待輪到我演講及完成演講後的期間，我觀察其他演講者，並試著聽他們的演講內容。

ⓘ**文法 句型** ・ wait sb's turn　等待輪到某人

129

2. The teacher ended the class with a few suggestions about what we might do before, during, and after a speech to improve it.

老師針對演講前、中、後我們可以如何使我們的演說更進步提了一些建議，作為這堂課的結束。

> ⓘ 文法句型 ・ end sth. with sth.　以…結束…

3. I enjoyed this class a lot because I prefer oral presentation training to sitting throughout the whole class.

我很喜歡這堂課，因為比起整堂課都靜靜地坐著，我比較喜歡口語表達訓練。

> ⓘ 字詞提示 ・ throughout *prep.* 在…的整個期間

> ⓘ 文法句型 ・ prefer A to B　喜歡 A 勝於 B

Step 5　用字遣詞 Words → Sentences

1. deliver [dɪˋlɪvɚ] *v.* 發表 (演說)

   The student delivered a passionate speech against war.

   這名學生發表了一場激昂的反戰演說。

2. require [rɪˋkwaɪr] *v.* 需要

   Most plants require sunlight.　大部分的植物都需要陽光。

3. rehearsal [rɪˋhɝsl] *n.* 排演

   We didn't have time for rehearsal before the performance.

   表演之前我們沒有時間排演。

4. attention [əˋtɛnʃən] *n.* 注意

   An article in the magazine caught my attention.

   這本雜誌裡的一篇文章吸引了我的注意。

5. detail [ˋditel] *n.* 細節

   Linda told me every detail in her first date, including what the boy wore, where they went, what they talked about, and so on.

   Linda 跟我說了她第一次約會的所有細節，包括那個男生穿了什麼，他們去了哪裡，聊了什麼等等。

6. organize [ˋɔrgənˏaɪz] *v.* 組織

   We should try to organize our time better.

UNIT 21

UNIT 22

UNIT 23

UNIT 24

UNIT 25

UNIT 26

UNIT 27

UNIT 28

UNIT 29

UNIT 30

UNIT 31

UNIT 32

UNIT 33

UNIT 34

UNIT 35

UNIT 36

UNIT 37

UNIT 38

UNIT 39

UNIT 40

我們應該試著更有條理地安排我們的時間。

7. rehearse [rɪ`hɝs] v. 演練，排練

On his way to the job interview, Nathan rehearsed what he would say.

在去工作面試的途中，Nathan 演練了一下要說的話。

8. delivery [dɪ`lɪvərɪ] n. 演說的方式或姿態

The poem sounded so beautiful with the professor's delivery.

透過這位教授的呈現，這首詩聽起來真美。

9. strategy [`strætədʒɪ] n. 策略

The company is working on new strategies to improve their share of the market.

這家公司正在研擬新的策略，以提昇其市場佔有率。

10. facial [`feʃəl] adj. 臉部的

Do you remember the robber's facial features?

你記得那名搶匪的臉部特徵嗎？

11. expression [ɪk`sprɛʃən] n. 表情，聲調的感情

There was a worried expression on Paul's face.

Paul 的臉上出現了擔心的表情。

12. gesture [`dʒɛstʃɚ] n. 手勢，姿勢

Dan made a rude gesture towards the taxi driver.

Dan 對計程車司機比了一個粗魯的手勢。

13. throughout [θru`aʊt] prep. 在…的整個期間

The national park is open to the tourists throughout the year.

這個國家公園一年到頭都對觀光客開放。

文法句型 Grammar Points → Sentences

1. in front of　在…之前

The bus stopped right in front of our house.

這輛公車剛好就停在我們的房子前面。

2. by means of　用…，以…

We crossed the river by means of a boat.　我們以船渡河。

3. wait sb's turn　等待輪到某人

Please be patient and wait your turn.　請耐心等候輪到你。

4. end sth. with sth.　以…結束…

We ended the farewell party with a song.

我們以一首歌結束這場歡送派對。

5. prefer A to B　喜歡 A 勝於 B

Jerry prefers cats to dogs.　Jerry 喜歡貓勝過於狗。

UNIT 21

UNIT 22

UNIT **23**

UNIT 24

UNIT 25

UNIT 26

UNIT 27

UNIT 28

UNIT 29

UNIT 30

UNIT 31

UNIT 32

UNIT 33

UNIT 34

UNIT 35

UNIT 36

UNIT 37

UNIT 38

UNIT 39

UNIT 40

UNIT 23

Expository Writing 　説明文

My Favorite Sport　我最喜愛的運動

　　寫一篇大約 120 個字的英文作文，談談你最喜愛的運動。把文章分成兩段：第一段說明該項運動的規則或玩法；第二段列舉該項運動的好處。

　　Write a short essay on your favorite sport in about 120 words. Organize the essay into two paragraphs. In paragraph one, explain the rules of the sport or how to play it; in paragraph two, list the benefits the sport may bring.

Step 1　聯想提示 Association 　　依人、事、時、地、物、原因和方法聯想與題目相關的事項

- 我最喜歡的運動是什麼？　What is my favorite sport?
- 這項運動怎麼玩？　How is this sport played?
- 我為什麼喜歡這項運動？　Why do I like the sport?
- 這項運動有什麼特點？　What is the sport about?
- 這項運動有哪些優點？　What advantages does the sport have?

Step 2　組織大綱提示 Organization 　　依照想到的事項，定出寫作優先順序及細節

第一段

1. 主題句：我最喜愛的運動是籃球。

2. 支持句：規則簡介

　　a. 它是一種團隊運動。通常需要兩隊各五名球員。

　　b. 目標是將球投進籃框得分。

　　c. 球員必須具備的基本技巧：運球和傳球。

3. 結論：合作是贏球的關鍵因素。

第二段

1. 主題句：打籃球帶給我很多好處。

2. 支持句：打籃球的優點。

　　a. 打籃球運動有助我保持健康。

　　b. 籃球訓練我如何和別人合作。

　　c. 打籃球讓我減輕壓力、增進活力。

3.結論：打籃球既好玩又刺激。

Step 3 範文 Model Composition

My Favorite Sport

My favorite sport is basketball. It is a team sport usually involving two teams with five players each. The purpose of the game is to shoot the ball through the basket. Basically, the players must be good at dribbling the ball and passing it. Since it is a team sport, the key factor of winning is cooperation.

Basketball is good exercise providing me with a variety of benefits. First of all, playing basketball is an excellent way to keep fit and healthy. Second, basketball, as a team sport, also trains me to cooperate with others. In addition, playing basketball enables me to relieve stress and boost my energy. On the whole, basketball is fun and exciting to play.

Step 4 寫句實戰分析 Analyzing Sentences

第一段

1. My favorite sport is basketball. 我最喜愛的運動是籃球。

① 字詞提示 · favorite *adj.* 最喜愛的

2. It is a team sport usually involving two teams with five players each.
它是一種團隊運動，通常需要兩隊各五名球員參加。

① 字詞提示 · involve *v.* 包含，涉及

① 文法句型 · 本句為限定關係子句改為現在分詞片語的用法，原句為 It is a team sport which usually involves....

3. The purpose of the game is to shoot the ball through the basket.
比賽的目的是把球投進籃框裡。

UNIT
21

UNIT
22

UNIT
23

UNIT
24

UNIT
25

UNIT
26

UNIT
27

UNIT
28

UNIT
29

UNIT
30

UNIT
31

UNIT
32

UNIT
33

UNIT
34

UNIT
35

UNIT
36

UNIT
37

UNIT
38

UNIT
39

UNIT
40

ⓘ 字詞
提示　・ purpose *n.* 目的

4. Basically, the players must be good at dribbling the ball and passing it.

基本上，所有球員必須擅長運球和傳球。

ⓘ 字詞
提示　・ dribble *v.* 運球

5. Since it is a team sport, the key factor of winning is cooperation.

因為它是一項團隊性運動，贏球的關鍵因素就是合作。

ⓘ 字詞
提示　・ factor *n.* 因素
　　　　・ cooperation *n.* 合作

第二段

1. Basketball is good exercise providing me with a variety of benefits.

籃球是很好的運動，提供我很多好處。

ⓘ 文法
句型　・ provide sb. with sth.　提供某物給某人
　　　　・ a variety of　各種不同的
　　　　・注意：原句為 Basketball is good exercise which provides me....

2. First of all, playing basketball is an excellent way to keep fit and healthy.

第一，籃球運動是保持健康的絕佳方式。

ⓘ 字詞
提示　・ excellent *adj.* 極佳的

ⓘ 文法
句型　・ keep fit　保持健康

3. Second, basketball, as a team sport, also trains me to cooperate with others.

第二，作為團隊運動，籃球也訓練我如何和他人合作。

ⓘ 字詞
提示　・ cooperate *v.* 合作

4. In addition, playing basketball enables me to relieve stress and boost my energy.

此外，打籃球讓我可以釋放壓力並增強活力。

ⓘ 字詞
提示　・ boost *v.* 增加

> ⚠️ 文法句型
> · enable sb. to V 使某人能夠…

5. On the whole, basketball is fun and exciting to play.

整體而言，打籃球既好玩又刺激。

> ⚠️ 文法句型
> · adj. to V to V 作副詞片語，修飾形容詞

Step 5 用字遣詞 Words → Sentences

1. favorite [`fevrɪt] *adj.* 最喜愛的

    I have dozens of blue shirts in my closet because my favorite color is blue.

    我的衣櫃裡有很多藍色襯衫，因為我最喜歡的顏色是藍色。

2. involve [ɪn`vɑlv] *v.* 包含，涉及

    A salesperson's job usually involves communicating with people.

    銷售員的工作內容通常包含了與人溝通。

3. purpose [`pɝpəs] *n.* 目的

    The purpose of this book is to inform the audience of what causes global warming.　這本書的目的是讓讀者知道是什麼造成溫室效應的。

4. dribble [`drɪbl] *v.* 運球

    The basketball player dribbles the ball very fast.

    這個籃球選手運球運得很快。

5. factor [`fæktɚ] *n.* 因素

    Mr. Wang's leadership quality is the key factor in his success.

    王先生的領導才能是他成功的關鍵因素。

6. cooperation [ko,ɑpə`reʃən] *n.* 合作

    The exchange student program stimulated the cooperation between the two universities.　交換學生計畫促進了兩個大學之間的合作。

7. excellent [`ɛkslənt] *adj.* 極佳的

    Studying abroad is an excellent chance to meet people from another country.

    出國唸書是個絕佳的機會，能夠認識其他國家的人。

8. cooperate [ko`ɑpə,ret] *v.* 合作

    The two companies cooperate in developing new products.

    這兩個公司合作生產新商品。

9. boost [bust] *v.* 增加

UNIT
21

UNIT
22

UNIT
23

UNIT
24

UNIT
25

UNIT
26

UNIT
27

UNIT
28

UNIT
29

UNIT
30

UNIT
31

UNIT
32

UNIT
33

UNIT
34

UNIT
35

UNIT
36

UNIT
37

UNIT
38

UNIT
39

UNIT
40

Winning this contest really boosted my confidence.

贏得這項競賽真的增進了我的信心。

文法句型 Grammar Points → Sentences

1. 限定關係子句改為現在分詞片語的用法

限定關係子句中若有一般動詞，可將關係代名詞去掉，將動詞改為現在分詞，即構成現在分詞片語。

It is a team sport usually involving two teams with five players each.

→ It is a team sport which usually involves two teams with five players each.

它是一種團隊運動，通常需要兩隊各五名球員參加。

I know the people who live next door.

→ I know the people living next door.　我認識住在隔壁的人。

2. provide sb. with sth.　提供某物給某人

The parents failed to provide their children with food and clothing.

這對父母沒有辦法提供他們的孩子食物和衣服。

3. a variety of　各種不同的

I have a variety of interests. I like to swim, sing, and play chess.

我有各種不同的興趣。我喜歡游泳，唱歌，還有下西洋棋。

4. keep fit　保持健康

Sophia goes jogging every morning to keep fit.

Sophia 每天早上都去慢跑以維持健康。

5. enable sb. to V　使某人能夠…

The software enables us to access the Internet in seconds.

這套軟體讓我們可以在幾秒鐘內就連接上網路。

6. adj. to V　to V 作副詞片語，修飾形容詞

I am glad to hear that Sarah is going to get married.

我很高興聽到 Sarah 要結婚了。

UNIT 24

Narrative Writing 敘事文

Olivia and Her Kittens　Olivia 和她的小貓

96 年學科能力測驗

　　根據下列四張連環圖畫的內容，將圖中所發生的事件作一合理的敘述。文長 120 個英文字左右。

　　Reasonably narrate a whole series of events according to the following four-frame comic strip. Write your essay in 120 words or so.

Step 1　看圖聯想 Association　依人、事、時、地、物、原因和方法聯想與題目相關的事項

Step 2　組織大綱提示 Organization　依照想到的事項，定出寫作優先順序及細節

圖一：**Olivia** 巧遇一隻小貓

1. 在一個晴朗的秋天午後，Olivia 到她家附近的一座公園玩。

2. 她遇到一隻可愛的小流浪貓並停下來和牠玩耍。

圖二：**Olivia** 和小貓玩耍

3. 又有其他幾隻貓跑到 Olivia 前面。

4. Olivia 很喜歡牠們，於是把牠們帶回家。

圖三：**Olivia** 纏著她媽媽

5. Olivia 告訴媽媽找到小貓的經過，希望收養小貓。

6. 媽媽點頭答應了，條件是牠們必須受到細心照顧。

圖四：**Olivia** 達成願望

7. 這些小貓每天都可以陪伴 Olivia 了，雖然牠們有時候是那麼地調皮，把客廳弄得亂七八糟。

UNIT 21
UNIT 22
UNIT 23
UNIT **24**
UNIT 25
UNIT 26
UNIT 27
UNIT 28
UNIT 29
UNIT 30
UNIT 31
UNIT 32
UNIT 33
UNIT 34
UNIT 35
UNIT 36
UNIT 37
UNIT 38
UNIT 39
UNIT 40

Step 3 範文 Model Composition

Olivia and Her Kittens

On a clear autumn afternoon, Olivia went to the park in her neighborhood. While strolling around in the park, she came across a stray kitten. She stopped to play with it because it was so cute and cuddly. Little by little, some other kittens came around one after another. Olivia was so pleased with their tameness and friendliness that she took them home. She went to tell her mom how she had found these lovely kittens in the park and ask to take them in. Her mom nodded her approval on condition that they should be coddled. Much to Olivia's delight, these kittens could keep her company every day, even though they were so naughty sometimes as to make a mess in the living room.

Step 4 寫句實戰分析 Analyzing Sentences

1. On a clear autumn afternoon, Olivia went to the park in her neighborhood.

   在一個晴朗的秋天午後，Olivia 到她家附近的一座公園。

   ⚠ 字詞
   提示　· neighborhood *n.* 鄰近地區，街區

   ⚠ 文法
   句型　· 注意：公園前面加 the 表特定的一座公園。

2. While strolling around in the park, she came across a stray kitten.

   在公園裡漫步時，她遇到一隻小流浪貓。

   ⚠ 字詞
   提示　· stroll *v.* 散步，漫步
   　　　· stray *adj.* 走失的，流浪的

   ⚠ 文法
   句型　· come across　偶遇
   　　　· 注意：While 子句省略了主詞 she，並且把動詞改成 V-ing 的形式，為分詞構句。

3. She stopped to play with it because it was so cute and cuddly.

她停下來和牠玩耍，因為牠很可愛，讓人想要抱牠。

> !字詞提示
> - cuddly *adj.* 令人想緊摟的，逗人喜愛的

4. Little by little, some other kittens came around one after another.

漸漸地，又有其他幾隻陸續來到跟前。

> !文法句型
> - little by little　漸漸地

5. Olivia was so pleased with their tameness and friendliness that she took them home.　Olivia 很喜歡這些小貓的溫馴和友善，所以把牠們帶回家。

> !字詞提示
> - tameness *n.* 溫馴

6. She went to tell her mom how she had found these lovely kittens in the park and ask to take them in.

她跟媽媽說她是怎麼在公園裡發現這些可愛的小貓，並請求收留牠們。

> !文法句型
> - S + V + how/when/where/what/who + S + V....
>   疑問詞引導名詞子句當受詞

7. Her mom nodded her approval on condition that they should be coddled.

她媽媽點頭答應了，條件是牠們必須受到細心照顧。

> !字詞提示
> - nod *v.* 點頭
> - approval *n.* 贊成
> - coddle *v.* 悉心照料

> !文法句型
> - on condition that + S + V　只要…，條件是…

8. Much to Olivia's delight, these kittens could keep her company every day, even though they were so naughty sometimes as to make a mess in the living room.

讓 Olivia 非常開心的是，這些小貓每天都可以陪伴她了，雖然牠們有時候是那麼地調皮，把客廳搞得亂七八糟。

> !字詞提示
> - naughty *adj.* 頑皮的，淘氣的

UNIT 21
UNIT 22
UNIT 23
UNIT 24
UNIT 25
UNIT 26
UNIT 27
UNIT 28
UNIT 29
UNIT 30
UNIT 31
UNIT 32
UNIT 33
UNIT 34
UNIT 35
UNIT 36
UNIT 37
UNIT 38
UNIT 39
UNIT 40

① 文法 句型
- keep sb. company　陪伴某人
- make a mess　弄髒，弄亂

Step 5

用字遣詞 Words → Sentences

1. neighborhood [`nebɚˌhʊd] *n.* 鄰近地區，街區

   We live in a nice and quiet neighborhood.　我們住在一個宜人安靜的區域。

2. stroll [strol] *v.* 散步，漫步

   I like to stroll along the riverbank in the summer afternoons.

   我喜歡在夏日午後沿著河岸散步。

3. stray [stre] *adj.* 走失的，流浪的

   Lily heard a stray cat crying at the door.

   Lily 聽到一隻流浪貓在門口哭叫。

4. cuddly [`kʌdlɪ] *adj.* 令人想緊摟的，逗人喜愛的

   Danny has been a very cuddly child. Everyone likes to hug him.

   Danny 一直是惹人愛的小孩。每個人都想抱抱他。

5. tameness [`temnɪs] *n.* 溫馴

   I like rabbits a lot because of their tameness.

   我喜歡兔子因為牠們很溫馴。

6. nod [nɑd] *v.* 點頭

   The lady nodded to me in a friendly fashion.　這位女士友善地跟我點頭。

7. approval [ə`pruvl̩] *n.* 贊成

   Mr. Thompson gave his son a nod of approval.

   Thompson 先生對他的兒子點頭表示同意。

8. coddle [`kɑdl̩] *v.* 悉心照料

   The mother coddled her son when he was sick.

   這個媽媽在她的兒子生病時用心照顧他。

9. naughty [`nɔtɪ] *adj.* 頑皮的，淘氣的

   The boy is very naughty. He always makes trouble at school.

   這個男孩非常調皮。他在學校總是惹麻煩。

文法句型 Grammar Points → Sentences

1. come across　偶遇

On my way to school, I came across my English teacher.

上學途中，我遇見了我的英文老師。

2. little by little   漸漸地

Gina found that she fell in love with Eric little by little.

Gina 發現她漸漸地愛上了 Eric。

3. S + V + how/when/where/what/who + S + V....   疑問詞引導名詞子句當受詞

I wonder how Michael finished the project alone.

我納悶 Michael 是如何獨自完成專案的。

I don't know where Ray lives.   我不知道 Ray 住在哪裡。

4. on condition that + S + V   只要…，條件是…

Jack said that he only lends me two thousand dollars on condition that I pay it back tomorrow.   Jack 說只要我明天可以還他兩千塊，他就借給我。

5. keep sb. company   陪伴某人

I'll keep you company till you fall asleep.   我會陪你到你睡著。

6. make a mess   弄髒，弄亂

The boy always makes a mess in his room.

這個男孩總是把他的房間弄得髒兮兮的。

UNIT
21
UNIT
22
UNIT
23
UNIT
24
UNIT
25
UNIT
26
UNIT
27
UNIT
28
UNIT
29
UNIT
30
UNIT
31
UNIT
32
UNIT
33
UNIT
34
UNIT
35
UNIT
36
UNIT
37
UNIT
38
UNIT
39
UNIT
40

UNIT 25

Informative Writing　訊息文

On Knowledge　論知識

以「論知識」為題，從正、反兩面來討論知識。文長至少 120 個英文字。

Write an essay entitled "On Knowledge." Discuss the pros and cons of knowledge. Write your essay in no less than 120 words.

Step 1 聯想提示 Association　依人、事、時、地、物、原因和方法聯想與題目相關的事項

- 知識像什麼？ What is knowledge like?
- 知識為何重要？ Why is knowledge important?
- 知識如何影響人類？ How does knowledge influence humans?
- 知識帶給人類什麼好處？ What benefits does knowledge bring to humans?
- 知識帶給人類什麼壞處？ What harm does knowledge bring to humans?
- 我們應如何看待知識？ How should we deal with knowledge?

Step 2 組織大綱提示 Organization　依照想到的事項，定出寫作優先順序及細節

第一段

1. 主題句：知識，就如同海上的指南針一樣，將人類導向更好的人生。

2. 支持句：沒有知識，人類就不可能發明日常所需的用品。

3. 結論：我們吸收的知識愈多，從中獲益愈多。

第二段

1. 主題句：知識可能遭濫用而衍生出無數問題。

2. 支持句：知識會誤導人們觸法犯紀。

3. 結論：這些都是造成道德淪喪的原因。

第三段

1. 主題句：隨著科技日新月異，知識的獲得和累積更加容易。

2. 轉折：但更重要的是如何妥善運用知識。

3. 結論：總之，知識讓知道如何善用它的人們獲益。

Step 3 範文 Model Composition

On Knowledge

Knowledge, like a compass at sea, enables humans to navigate their way to a better life. Without knowledge, humans couldn't have invented things needed for daily use, such as paper, electricity, furniture, and so forth. Indeed, the more knowledge we absorb, the more we benefit from it.

On the other hand, knowledge may also be misused to produce countless problems that plague people. It is knowledge that misleads people into committing crimes and other evil deeds. All these are responsible for the moral deterioration of the world.

As technology improves day by day, it is much easier to acquire and accumulate knowledge. However, what matters more is how to use knowledge appropriately. In conclusion, knowledge benefits people who know how to make wise use of it.

Step 4 寫句實戰分析 Analyzing Sentences

第一段

1. Knowledge, like a compass at sea, enables humans to navigate their way to a better life.

   知識，就如同海上的指南針一樣，讓人類導向更好的人生。

   ⚠️字詞提示
   - compass *n.* 指南針
   - navigate *v.* 導航

   ⚠️文法句型
   - 注意：enable + O + to + V

2. Without knowledge, humans couldn't have invented things needed for daily use, such as paper, electricity, furniture, and so forth.

UNIT 21
UNIT 22
UNIT 23
UNIT 24
UNIT 25
UNIT 26
UNIT 27
UNIT 28
UNIT 29
UNIT 30
UNIT 31
UNIT 32
UNIT 33
UNIT 34
UNIT 35
UNIT 36
UNIT 37
UNIT 38
UNIT 39
UNIT 40

沒有知識，人類就不可能發明日常所需的用品，例如紙、電、家具等。

⚠ 字詞提示
- invent *v.* 發明

⚠ 文法句型
- Without + N/V-ing..., S + could not have + V-en
  如果沒有…的話，就不可能…
- ..., and so forth/on …等等

3. Indeed, the more knowledge we absorb, the more we benefit from it.
的確，我們吸收的知識愈多，從中獲益就愈多。

⚠ 字詞提示
- absorb *v.* 吸收

⚠ 文法句型
- The + adj.-er..., the + adj.-er.... 越…，就越…

第二段

1. On the other hand, knowledge may also be misused to produce countless problems that plague people.
另一方面，知識也可能遭誤用而衍生出無數問題。

⚠ 字詞提示
- misuse *v.* 誤用，濫用
- countless *adj.* 無數的，數不盡的
- plague *v.* 使困擾，使煩惱

⚠ 文法句型
- on the other hand 另一方面

2. It is knowledge that misleads people into committing crimes and other evil deeds. 正是知識誤導人們觸法及做出其它惡行。

⚠ 字詞提示
- mislead *v.* 引入歧途，誤導
- commit *v.* 犯罪，做錯事
- crime *n.* 犯法 (行為)
- evil *adj.* 邪惡的
- deed *n.* 行為

⚠ 文法句型
- It is + 強調部分 + that + S + V.... 強調句型

3. All these are responsible for the moral deterioration of the world.

這些全都是造成世上道德淪喪的原因。

> (!) 字詞提示
> - moral *adj.* 道德 (上) 的
> - deterioration *n.* 惡化

第三段

1. As technology improves day by day, it is much easier to acquire and accumulate knowledge. 隨著科技日新月異，知識的獲得和累積更加容易。

> (!) 字詞提示
> - technology *n.* 科技
> - acquire *v.* 獲得
> - accumulate *v.* 累積

2. However, what matters more is how to use knowledge appropriately.

但更重要的是，如何妥善地運用知識。

> (!) 字詞提示
> - appropriately *adv.* 適當地

3. In conclusion, knowledge benefits people who know how to make wise use of it.

總之，知識讓知道如何善用它的人獲益。

> (!) 文法句型
> - make good/wise use of 善用

Step 5

用字遣詞 Words → Sentences

1. compass [ˋkʌmpəs] *n.* 指南針

   You need a map and compass to help you find your way in the forest.

   你需要一張地圖和指南針來幫助你在森林裡找路。

2. navigate [ˋnævə͵get] *v.* 導航

   Having no compass, we had to navigate our ship by the stars.

   因為沒有指南針，我們必須靠星星來導航我們的船隻。

3. invent [ɪnˋvɛnt] *v.* 發明

   Thomas Edison invented the light bulb.　愛迪生發明了電燈泡。

4. absorb [əbˋsɔrb] *v.* 吸收

   Trees absorb carbon dioxide and produce oxygen.

樹木吸收二氧化碳，產生氧氣。

5. misuse [mɪs`juz] *v.* 誤用，濫用

The government official is accused of misusing public funds.

這位政府官員遭指控濫用公共資金。

6. countless [`kauntləs] *adj.* 無數的，數不盡的

Ivy has countless reasons to break up with her boyfriend.

Ivy 有無數的理由來與她男友分手。

7. plague [pleg] *v.* 使困擾，使煩惱

Financial problems have been plaguing Henry for years since he lost his job.

自從失去工作，財務問題已困擾 Henry 多年。

8. mislead [mɪs`lid] *v.* 引入歧途，誤導

The boy was misled by his companions.

這名男孩因為他的同伴們而誤入歧途。

9. commit [kə`mɪt] *v.* 犯罪，做錯事

This man was sentenced to death for committing murder.

這名男子因為謀殺而被判死刑。

10. crime [kraɪm] *n.* 犯法 (行為)

Drunk driving is a serious crime. 酒醉駕車是嚴重的犯法行為。

11. evil [`ivl] *adj.* 邪惡的

Rules need to be set up to prevent people from doing evil things.

我們需要制定規定來防止人們做壞事。

12. deed [did] *n.* 行為

Children are encouraged to do good deeds. 我們鼓勵孩子們做好事。

13. moral [`mɔrəl] *adj.* 道德 (上) 的

Moral values of the candidates are what the voters are concerned about the most. 候選人的道德價值觀是選民最關切的議題。

14. deterioration [dɪ,tɪrɪə`reʃən] *n.* 惡化

The relations between the two countries have been in a continuing deterioration.

這兩國之間的關係持續惡化。

15. technology [tɛk`nɑlədʒɪ] *n.* 科技

Modern technology has made people's lives more convenient than before.

現代科技讓人們的生活更方便。

16. acquire [ə`kwaɪr] *v.* 獲得

Tom has acquired a good knowledge of English since he was a student.

UNIT 21
UNIT 22
UNIT 23
UNIT 24
UNIT 25
UNIT 26
UNIT 27
UNIT 28
UNIT 29
UNIT 30
UNIT 31
UNIT 32
UNIT 33
UNIT 34
UNIT 35
UNIT 36
UNIT 37
UNIT 38
UNIT 39
UNIT 40

自從 Tom 還是學生時，他就獲取很多英文的知識。

17. accumulate [ə`kjumjə,let] v. 累積

We have accumulated enough money to buy a new car.

我們已經累積了足夠的錢來買新車。

18. appropriately [ə`proprɪɪtlɪ] adv. 適當地

When attending a formal party, make sure you are appropriately dressed.

參加正式的宴會時，確定你穿著合適的服裝。

文法句型 Grammar Points → Sentences

1. Without + N/V-ing..., S + could not have + V-en　若沒有…的話，就不可能…

此句型為與過去事實相反的假設語氣。

Without your help, I couldn't have done it.

如果沒有你的幫助，我是不可能辦到的。　(事實上辦到了)

2. ..., and so forth/on　…等等

I like animals such as cats, dogs, rabbits, and so forth.

我喜歡動物，像是貓、狗、兔子等等。

3. The + adj.-er..., the + adj.-er....　越…，就越…

The more you eat, the fatter you become.　你吃得越多，就變得越胖。

4. on the other hand　另一方面

I'd like to go to that expensive restaurant, but on the other hand I don't want to spend a lot of money.

我想要去那家昂貴的餐廳，但另一方面我不想花很多錢。

5. It is + 強調部分 + that + S + V....　強調句型

本句型中的 It 沒有意義，只是用來改變句子結構，使原句的某一部分可以受到強調。

受到強調的部份可以是主詞、受詞、補語、修飾語。

I ran across Julie in the library yesterday.

我昨天在圖書館遇到 Julie。

→ It was I that ran across Julie in the library yesterday.　(強調主詞)

→ It was Julie that I ran across in the library yesterday.　(強調受詞)

→ It was yesterday that I ran across Julie.　(強調時間副詞)

→ It was in the library that I ran across Julie.　(強調地方副詞)

6. make good/wise use of　善用

We must make good use of our natural resources.

我們必須善用我們的天然資源。

UNIT
21

UNIT
22

UNIT
23

UNIT
24

UNIT
25

UNIT
26

UNIT
27

UNIT
28

UNIT
29

UNIT
30

UNIT
31

UNIT
32

UNIT
33

UNIT
34

UNIT
35

UNIT
36

UNIT
37

UNIT
38

UNIT
39

UNIT
40

UNIT 26

One Good Thing That Makes Me Happy 一件讓我覺得幸福美好的事

北區公立高中 95 年第一次指考模擬考

以 "One Good Thing That Makes Me Happy" 為題，寫一篇至少 120 個字的英文作文。

Write an essay entitled "One Good Thing That Makes Me Happy" in no less than 120 words.

Step 1 聯想提示 Association　依人、事、時、地、物、原因和方法聯想與題目相關的事項

- 什麼事情讓我覺得快樂？ What makes me happy?
- 為什麼它讓我覺得快樂？ Why does it make me happy?
- 它有什麼特殊的意義？ What special meanings does it have?

Step 2 組織大綱提示 Organization　依照想到的事項，定出寫作優先順序及細節

1. 主題句：讓我覺得快樂的事是得到我一直努力想得到的東西。

2. 支持句：舉例

　a. 當我考試成績進步時，會讓我感到自豪。

　b. 原因一：學業進步證明我有反敗為勝的能力。

　c. 原因二：我付出的努力會獲得父母及老師的肯定。

　　　他們會賦予我一種自我價值感，並且讓我知道我值得他們關愛。

3. 結論：的確，考試成績進步是一件讓我覺得快樂的事。

Step 3 範文 Model Composition

One Good Thing That Makes Me Happy

One good thing that makes me happy is getting something that I have been trying to get. For example, it makes me feel proud of myself when I get better

149

grades on tests. For one thing, the progress I make in my studies proves my ability to turn failure into success, which makes me a person who knows how to cope with adversity. For another, the effort I have made to improve my grades will certainly be recognized by my parents and my teachers. Their encouragement will give me a sense of achievement and let me know I deserve their attention and affection. Indeed, getting better grades on tests is a good thing that makes me happy.

Step 4 寫句實戰分析 Analyzing Sentences

1. One good thing that makes me happy is getting something that I have been trying to get. 讓我覺得快樂的事就是得到我一直努力想得到的東西。

   ⓘ 文法句型
   - 本句中有兩個 that 子句為關係代名詞的限定用法：
     a. One good thing that makes me happy....
     b. ...something that I have been....

2. For example, it makes me feel proud of myself when I get better grades on tests. 例如，當我考試成績進步時，那會讓我感到自豪。

   ⓘ 文法句型
   - feel 為連綴動詞，後接形容詞，修飾 me。
   - 注意：make + O + 原形 V

3. For one thing, the progress I make in my studies proves my ability to turn failure into success, which makes me a person who knows how to cope with adversity. 一方面，我在學業上的進步證明我有反敗為勝的能力，這讓我成為一個知道如何應付逆境的人。

   ⓘ 字詞提示
   - progress *n.* 進步
   - prove *v.* 證明
   - cope *v.* 對付
   - adversity *n.* 困境

   ⓘ 文法句型
   - For one thing.... For another....　一方面…另一方面…
   - turn A into B　將 A 變成 B
   - 注意：句中 which 引導的關係子句為非限定用法，which 代替前面提到的整件事 (學業進步證明反敗為勝的能力)。

UNIT 21
UNIT 22
UNIT 23
UNIT 24
UNIT 25
UNIT 26
UNIT 27
UNIT 28
UNIT 29
UNIT 30
UNIT 31
UNIT 32
UNIT 33
UNIT 34
UNIT 35
UNIT 36
UNIT 37
UNIT 38
UNIT 39
UNIT 40

4. For another, the effort I have made to improve my grades will certainly be recognized by my parents and my teachers.

另一方面，我為了使成績進步所付出的努力一定會獲得父母及老師的肯定。

⚠️字詞
提示　· recognize *v.* 表彰，認可

5. Their encouragement will give me a sense of achievement and let me know I deserve their attention and affection.

他們的鼓勵會給我成就感，並且讓我知道我值得他們關愛。

⚠️字詞
提示　· deserve *v.* 值得，應得
　　　· affection *n.* 鍾愛，關愛

6. Indeed, getting better grades on tests is a good thing that makes me happy.

的確，考試成績進步是一件讓我覺得快樂的事。

⚠️文法
句型　·注意：本句用動名詞片語做主詞，搭配單數動詞。

✒ Step 5 　用字遣詞 Words → Sentences

1. progress [ˋprɑgrɛs] *n.* 進步

The pitcher made great progress in every aspect after receiving intensive training.　接受密集訓練後，這位投手在每個層面都有長足的進步。

2. prove [pruv] *v.* 證明

We hope this new evidence will prove my client's innocence.

我們希望這項新證據將能證明我的當事人是無辜的。

3. cope [kop] *v.* 對付

We were amazed at the new employee's ability to cope with the difficult situation.　我們對於這位新員工處理困境的能力大感驚奇。

4. adversity [ədˋvɝsətɪ] *n.* 困境

He was always cheerful in adversity.　他在逆境中總是情緒高昂。

5. recognize [ˋrɛkəgˏnaɪz] *v.* 表彰，認可

The novelist's work is recognized as one of the best in his time.

這位小說家的作品被認為是他的年代中最傑出的作品。

6. deserve [dɪˋzɝv] *v.* 值得，應得

We all deserve a big meal after a day's hard work.

在一天辛苦工作後，我們應該得到一份大餐。

7. affection [əˋfɛkʃən] *n.* 鍾愛，關愛

The old lady has great affection for her hometown.

這位老婦人十分鍾愛她的故鄉。

文法句型 Grammar Points → Sentences

1. 關係代名詞的限定用法

　　a. 以關係代名詞引導關係子句，用以限定、修飾先行詞。

　　b. 關係代名詞前面不加逗號。

My sister who lives in Taipei works as a secretary.

我那個住在台北的姊姊是個秘書。

(限定用法，可能有很多個姊姊，但有一個住在台北，擔任秘書。)

My sister, who lives in Taipei, works as a secretary.

我姊姊在台北工作，她是個秘書。

(非限定用法，只有一個姊姊，關係子句補充說明姊姊住在台北。)

2. 連綴動詞 look/sound/smell/taste/feel + adj.

連綴動詞後接形容詞，作主詞補語，修飾主詞。

The food Joan cooks tastes good. 　Joan 煮的食物很好吃。

3. For one thing.... For another.... 　一方面…另一方面…

　　A: Why don't you come to Tokyo with me?

　　　你為什麼不跟我一起來東京？

　　B: For one thing, I don't like flying. For another, I can't afford it.

　　　一來，我不喜歡搭飛機。二來，我負擔不起。

4. turn A into B 　將 A 變成 B

The wizard has a magic power. He can turn stones into gold.

這個巫師有魔力。他可以把石頭變成黃金。

UNIT
21

UNIT
22

UNIT
23

UNIT
24

UNIT
25

UNIT
26

UNIT
27

UNIT
28

UNIT
29

UNIT
30

UNIT
31

UNIT
32

UNIT
33

UNIT
34

UNIT
35

UNIT
36

UNIT
37

UNIT
38

UNIT
39

UNIT
40

UNIT 27

Packing for a Year Abroad 出國遊學

　　在忙碌的課業中，你曾想過打包行李，出國一年，去親身體驗自己有興趣的事物嗎？請以 "Packing for a Year Abroad" 為題，描述在這一年中，你會選擇什麼地點，進行什麼樣的活動？你又會以什麼樣的態度來度過這在異鄉的一年？

　　During your busy school life, have you ever thought of packing for a year abroad to personally experience something interests you? Please use "Packing for a Year Abroad" as a title to discuss what place you would choose to go to, what activity you would engage in, and what attitude you would hold toward the year you might spend abroad.

Step 1 聯想提示 Association　依人、事、時、地、物、原因和方法聯想與題目相關的事項

- 我想去哪裡？　Where do I want to go?
- 為什麼我想去那裡？　Why do I want to go there?
- 它可能會如何影響我？　How could it influence me?
- 我暫住在哪裡？　Where do I want to stay?
- 我想在那裡做哪些特定的事情？　What specific things do I want to do there?

Step 2 組織大綱提示 Organization　依照想到的事項，定出寫作優先順序及細節

1. 主題句：出國遊學一年一直是我的夢想。
2. 支持句：
   原因：a. 我正打算以交換學生的身分到美國去。
   　　　b. 我想花一年的時間在那裡生活，念高中。
   　　　c. 曾聽說過有關美國的事物，但很模糊。
   決定：我決定親自造訪美國。
   影響：a. 在那裡念高中會讓我學到很多關於美國的語言、文化以及風俗。
   　　　b. 我可以拓展我的知識領域，開開眼界。
3. 結論：我希望我的夢想可以儘早實現。

Step 3 範文 Model Composition

Packing for a Year Abroad

Packing for a year abroad has been a dream of mine. I am planning to go to the United States as an exchange student. I would like to spend one year there studying in a high school, living with one or two host families, and traveling everywhere. I have heard and read about the United States, but I only have a very vague idea of it. That's why I have decided to visit the States personally; it will be worth it in the long run. I firmly believe that attending high school there will enable me to learn a lot of things about the American language, culture, and customs. All these benefits will not only enlarge my scope of knowledge, but also open my eyes to the world. I hope my dream will come true as soon as possible.

Step 4 寫句實戰分析 Analyzing Sentences

1. Packing for a year abroad has been a dream of mine.
   出國遊學一年一直是我的夢想之一。

   ⓘ字詞提示
   - pack *v.* 打包
   - abroad *adv.* 在國外，往海外

2. I am planning to go to the United States as an exchange student.
   我正打算以交換學生的身分到美國去。

   ⓘ字詞提示
   - exchange student *n.* 交換學生

3. I would like to spend one year there studying in a high school, living with one or two host families, and traveling everywhere.
   我想花一年的時間在那裡念高中、與寄宿家庭住在一起，並且到處去旅行。

UNIT 21
UNIT 22
UNIT 23
UNIT 24
UNIT 25
UNIT 26
UNIT 27
UNIT 28
UNIT 29
UNIT 30
UNIT 31
UNIT 32
UNIT 33
UNIT 34
UNIT 35
UNIT 36
UNIT 37
UNIT 38
UNIT 39
UNIT 40

⚠ 字詞提示　・ host family *n.* 寄宿家庭

⚠ 文法句型　・ spend + 時間 + V-ing　花時間做⋯

4. I have heard and read about the United States, but I only have a very vague idea of it.

　　我曾聽說並讀過有關美國的資訊，但只有一個很模糊的概念。

⚠ 字詞提示　・ vague *adj.* 模糊的

5. That's why I have decided to visit the States personally; it will be worth it in the long run.　因此，我決定親自造訪美國；就長遠來看是值得一試的。

⚠ 字詞提示　・ personally *adv.* 親自地

⚠ 文法句型
・ be worth it　值得的
・ in the long run　最後，終究

6. I firmly believe that attending high school there will enable me to learn a lot of things about the American language, culture, and customs.

　　我深信，在那裡念高中會讓我學到很多關於美國的語言、文化以及風俗。

⚠ 文法句型
・注意：attending high school there 為動名詞片語當關係子句的主詞。
　　　　enable + O + to + V　使⋯能夠

7. All these benefits will not only enlarge my scope of knowledge, but also open my eyes to the world.

　　這些好處不僅會拓展我的知識領域，也讓我能看看這個世界。

⚠ 字詞提示
・ enlarge *v.* 增大，擴大
・ scope *n.* 範圍，領域

8. I hope my dream will come true as soon as possible.

　　我希望我的夢想可以儘早實現。

⚠ 文法句型　・ as soon as possible　越快越好

Step 5 用字遣詞 Words → Sentences

1. pack [pæk] *v.* 打包

   We're leaving early tomorrow morning, so we'd better pack tonight.

   我們明天一早就出發，所以我們最好今晚就打包行李。

2. abroad [ə`brɔd] *adv.* 在國外，往海外

   My mom has not traveled abroad yet; the city she wants to visit the most is Paris. 我媽媽還沒有去過國外旅遊。她最想去的城市是巴黎。

3. exchange student [ɪks`tʃendʒ `studn̩t] *n.* 交換學生

   Exchange students from around the world go to the U.S. to study.

   世界各地的交換學生到美國去讀書。

4. host family [host `fæmlɪ] *n.* 寄宿家庭

   Some people stay with host families when they are visiting another country.

   有些人在造訪其他國家的時候，會和寄宿家庭住在一起。

5. vague [veg] *adj.* 模糊的

   After the teacher's explanation, I still only have a very vague idea about what the author wants to express.

   在老師解釋之後，我仍然對作者想要傳達的理念不太了解。

6. personally [`pɝsn̩lɪ] *adv.* 親自地

   I am sure we have everything we need for the party tomorrow, because I checked it personally.

   我確定明天的派對需要的東西我們都有了，因為我親自檢查過了。

7. attend [ə`tɛnd] *v.* 出席，定期去 (學校等)

   The teacher is upset because only 16 students attended the class today.

   老師很不高興，因為今天的課只有十六個學生出席。

8. enlarge [ɪn`lɑrdʒ] *v.* 增大，擴大

   We can enlarge our vocabulary by reading newspapers every day.

   我們可以藉由每天閱讀報紙來擴增字彙量。

9. scope [skop] *n.* 範圍，領域

   I guess that question is beyond the scope of this chapter.

   我想那個問題超過了這一章的範圍。

UNIT 21
UNIT 22
UNIT 23
UNIT 24
UNIT 25
UNIT 26
UNIT 27
UNIT 28
UNIT 29
UNIT 30
UNIT 31
UNIT 32
UNIT 33
UNIT 34
UNIT 35
UNIT 36
UNIT 37
UNIT 38
UNIT 39
UNIT 40

文法句型 Grammar Points → Sentences

1. spend + 時間 + V-ing　花時間做…

   I spent all the afternoon cleaning my room.

   我花了整個下午的時間打掃我房間。

2. be worth it　值得的

   We spent a lot of money on our house, but it was worth it.

   我們花很多錢在這棟房子上面，但那是值得的。

3. in the long run　最後，終究

   I'm confident that I'll succeed in the long run if I keep working hard.

   我有自信如果我繼續努力的話，我終究會成功的。

4. as soon as possible　越快越好

   Please come back as soon as possible. I miss you badly.

   請儘快回來。我很想你。

UNIT 28

Persuasive Writing 說理文

Reducing the Amount of Trash 垃圾減量

請寫一篇大約 120 個字的英文作文,主題為 "Reducing the Amount of Trash"。文分兩段:第一段說明垃圾問題的嚴重性;第二段提出垃圾減量的方法。

Use about 120 words to write a short essay of two paragraphs under the title "Reducing the Amount of Trash." Explain why trash is a serious problem in paragraph one and list several ways of reducing trash in paragraph two.

Step 1 聯想提示 Association 依人、事、時、地、物、原因和方法聯想與題目相關的事項

- 垃圾問題如何形成? How does the trash problem develop?
- 垃圾過多會產生什麼問題? What will happen when there is too much trash?
- 為什麼要垃圾減量? Why do we reduce the trash amount?
- 要如何達到垃圾減量? How do we reduce the trash amount?

Step 2 組織大綱提示 Organization 依照想到的事項,定出寫作優先順序及細節

第一段

1. 主題句:因人口增加及工業快速發展,我們正面臨嚴重的垃圾問題。

2. 支持句:垃圾問題帶來危害

　a. 室內戶外過量的垃圾總引來有害生物散播病毒和疾病。

　b. 垃圾也會滋生黴菌而導致疾病。

4. 結論:越來越多的垃圾正威脅著環境的衛生與大眾的健康。

第二段

1. 主題句:我們可以藉著把廢棄物轉換成有用的資源來減少垃圾。

2. 支持句:提出垃圾減量的方法

　a. 可將玻璃、金屬及紙類等物質重製成新產品。

　b. 可將廚餘製成堆肥並加入土壤,以幫助植物生長。

　c. 選擇可重複使用的產品,也要避免購買過度包裝的物品。

　d. 捐出舊的家具和家用品,供重複利用。

3. 結論:如果我們按照這些步驟去做,一定可以將垃圾減量。

UNIT 21
UNIT 22
UNIT 23
UNIT 24
UNIT 25
UNIT 26
UNIT 27
UNIT 28
UNIT 29
UNIT 30
UNIT 31
UNIT 32
UNIT 33
UNIT 34
UNIT 35
UNIT 36
UNIT 37
UNIT 38
UNIT 39
UNIT 40

Step 3 範文 Model Composition

Reducing the Amount of Trash

We are faced with a serious problem of the accumulation of trash due to the increasing population and rapid industrial development. Excess trash always draws rats, flies, and cockroaches, which carry viruses and spread disease. Mold and bacteria also grow on trash and cause sickness. Indeed, the increasing amount of trash is threatening public health.

We can reduce trash by turning waste materials into useful resources. Materials like glass, metal, and paper can be reprocessed into new products. Besides that, we should choose reusable products instead of disposable ones, and avoid buying over-packaged goods. Last but not least, we can donate our old furniture and household items for reuse. If we carry out these methods, we will certainly reduce the amount of trash.

Step 4 寫句實戰分析 Analyzing Sentences

第一段

1. We are faced with a serious problem of the accumulation of trash due to the increasing population and rapid industrial development.
由於人口增加和工業快速發展，我們正面臨嚴重的垃圾堆積問題。

⨀字詞提示
• accumulation *n.* 堆積，累積
• industrial *adj.* 工業的

⨀文法句型
• be faced with sth. 面臨… (問題、困難等)
• due to 由於

2. Excess trash always draws rats, flies, and cockroaches, which carry viruses and spread disease.
過量的垃圾總是引來老鼠、蒼蠅和蟑螂，牠們帶有病毒，並且散播疾病。

⚠️ 字詞提示　・ excess *adj.* 過多的，過量的

3. Mold and bacteria also grow on trash and cause sickness.

垃圾也會滋生黴菌和細菌，並導致疾病。

⚠️ 字詞提示
- mold *n.* 黴菌
- bacteria *n.* 細菌 (bacterium 的複數)

4. Indeed, the increasing amount of trash is threatening public health.

的確，越來越多的垃圾正威脅著大眾健康。

⚠️ 字詞提示　・ threaten *v.* 威脅

⚠️ 文法句型　・ the amount of ⋯的數量

第二段

1. We can reduce trash by turning waste materials into useful resources.

我們可以藉著把廢棄物變成有價值的資源來減少垃圾。

⚠️ 字詞提示　・ resource *n.* 資源

⚠️ 文法句型　・注意：turn A into B 把 A 變成 B

2. Materials like glass, metal, and paper can be reprocessed into new products.

像玻璃、金屬和紙張等物質可以重新製成新的產品。

⚠️ 字詞提示　・ reprocess *v.* 重製

⚠️ 文法句型　・注意：本句中的 like 可用 such as 替換。

3. Besides that, we should choose reusable products instead of disposable ones, and avoid buying over-packaged goods.　此外，我們應該選擇可以重複使用的產品來取代拋棄式的產品，並避免購買過度包裝的物品。

⚠️ 字詞提示　・ disposable *adj.* 拋棄式的

UNIT 21
UNIT 22
UNIT 23
UNIT 24
UNIT 25
UNIT 26
UNIT 27
UNIT 28
UNIT 29
UNIT 30
UNIT 31
UNIT 32
UNIT 33
UNIT 34
UNIT 35
UNIT 36
UNIT 37
UNIT 38
UNIT 39
UNIT 40

⚠ 文法句型
- instead of 代替，而不是
- 注意：avoid 後接動名詞。

4. Last but not least, we can donate our old furniture and household items for reuse.

最後而且很重要的是，我們可以捐出舊的家具和家用品，以供重複使用。

⚠ 字詞提示
- donate v. 捐出

⚠ 文法句型
- last but not least 最後但也很重要的 (用於強調)

5. If we carry out these methods, we will certainly reduce the amount of trash.

如果我們實行這些方法，我們一定可以減少垃圾量。

⚠ 文法句型
- carry out 執行
- 注意：If 子句用現在式動詞代替未來式，主要子句用未來式助動詞。

Step 5 用字遣詞 Words → Sentences

1. accumulation [ə,kjumjə`leʃən] n. 堆積，累積

   A glacier is an accumulation of ice, air, water, and stones.

   冰河是由冰、空氣、水和岩石所堆積而成的。

2. industrial [ɪn`dʌstrɪəl] adj. 工業的

   Industrial waste should be processed properly or it may cause serious pollution.

   工業廢棄物應該妥善處理，否則會造成嚴重汙染。

3. excess [ɪk`sɛs] adj. 過多的，過量的

   Excess intake of oil harms your health. 攝取過多油會傷害你的健康。

4. mold [mold] n. 黴菌

   The room smelled damp and there was mold on one wall.

   這房間聞起來潮濕，而且牆上有黴菌。

5. bacteria [bæk`tɪrɪə] n. 細菌 (bacterium 的複數)

   Some kinds of bacteria cause diseases.

   有些種類的細菌造成疾病。

6. threaten [`θrɛtn̩] v. 威脅

   The robber threatened people in the bank with a gun.

   這名搶匪用槍威脅銀行裡的人。

7. resource [rɪ`sors] *n.* 資源

We must protect and conserve our natural resources.

我們必須保護並保存我們的天然資源。

8. reprocess [rɪ`prɑsɛs] *v.* 重製

We collected the used materials to be reprocessed and reuse.

我們收集使用過的材料，用以重製並再利用。

9. disposable [dɪ`spozəbl] *adj.* 拋棄式的

For protecting the environment, we'd better not buy disposable products.

為了保護環境，我們最好不要買拋棄式的產品。

10. donate [do`net] *v.* 捐贈

This rich man donated millions of dollars to charity.

這個有錢人捐了幾百萬元給慈善機構。

文法句型 Grammar Points → Sentences

1. be faced with sth.　面臨… (問題、困難等)

We're faced with a problem of high unemployment rate in our country.

我國正面臨高失業率的問題。

2. due to　由於…

The game was put off due to the rain.　這場比賽因為下雨而延期。

3. instead of　代替，而不是

Let's have tea instead of coffee.　我們喝茶，不要喝咖啡。

4. last but not least　最後但也很重要的 (用於強調)

I would like to thank the publisher, editors, and, last but not least, my wife.

我要感謝我的出版社、編輯，以及最後但也很重要的一個人，也就是我太太。

5. carry out　執行

We have to work as a team to carry out the new project.

我們必須團隊合作來執行此計劃。

UNIT
21

UNIT
22

UNIT
23

UNIT
24

UNIT
25

UNIT
26

UNIT
27

UNIT
28

UNIT
29

UNIT
30

UNIT
31

UNIT
32

UNIT
33

UNIT
34

UNIT
35

UNIT
36

UNIT
37

UNIT
38

UNIT
39

UNIT
40

UNIT 29

Expository Writing 說明文

The First Class Reunion after Graduation 畢業後的第一次同學會

94 年指定科目考試

指定科目考試完畢後，高中同學決定召開畢業後的第一次同學會，你被推派負責主辦。請將你打算籌辦的活動寫成一篇短文。文分兩段，第一段詳細介紹同學會的時間、地點及活動內容，第二段則說明採取這種活動方式的理由。文長至少 120 個英文字。

After the college entrance examination, your class decided to hold the first class reunion after graduation and elected you chair of the reunion committee. Please write a two-paragraph essay about what you are planning to do for this reunion. List the details of this class reunion, including the time and the place in paragraph one; list the reasons why you decided to arrange things this way in paragraph two. Write your essay in no less than 120 words.

Step 1 聯想提示 Association　依人、事、時、地、物、原因和方法聯想與題目相關的事項

- 誰負責籌備工作？ Who is in charge of the preparatory work?
- 什麼時候舉辦？ When will it take place?
- 為什麼這樣安排？ Why is it arranged this way?
- 在哪裡舉辦？ Where will it take place?
- 我對它的期待？ How do I expect it to be?

Step 2 組織大綱提示 Organization　依照想到的事項，定出寫作優先順序及細節

第一段

1. 主題句：擔任畢業後第一次同學會的主席對我而言是一大榮幸。

2. 我和其他幾位委員會成員已決定舉辦晚餐派對。

3. 現在我們正在籌備這個即將到來的同學會。

第二段

1. 主題句：同學會之所以如此安排的理由如下。

2. 支持句：

　a. 利用目前的地址召集全班同學。

b. 當天晚上大家可以一起歡度一段輕鬆時光。

c. 在台北圓山大飯店，我們一定能夠享受永生難忘的盛宴。

3. 結論：且讓我們期待這第一次的同學會。

Step 3 範文 Model Composition

The First Class Reunion after Graduation

It is a great pleasure for me to serve as chair for our first class reunion after graduation. I, together with the other committee members, have decided to give a dinner party at the Taipei Grand Hotel on the first Sunday following the College Entrance Exam. Now we are working on this upcoming class reunion.

Here are the reasons why it is arranged this way. First, we could more easily gather the whole class together using their current addresses, which may change later this year. Second, we believe that evening should be a relaxing time when we may eat, drink and talk to our hearts' content. Third, the Taipei Grand Hotel is a five-star hotel. With its top-quality service, we are guaranteed an awesome feast. Let's look forward to this first class reunion.

Step 4 寫句實戰分析 Analyzing Sentences

第一段

1. It is a great pleasure for me to serve as chair for our first class reunion after graduation. 擔任畢業後第一次同學會的主席對我而言是一大榮幸。

!字詞提示
- pleasure *n.* 榮幸，樂趣
- reunion *n.* 團聚，重聚
- graduation *n.* 畢業

!文法句型
- serve as 擔任

2. I, together with the other committee members, have decided to give a dinner

UNIT 21
UNIT 22
UNIT 23
UNIT 24
UNIT 25
UNIT 26
UNIT 27
UNIT 28
UNIT 29
UNIT 30
UNIT 31
UNIT 32
UNIT 33
UNIT 34
UNIT 35
UNIT 36
UNIT 37
UNIT 38
UNIT 39
UNIT 40

party at the Taipei Grand Hotel on the first Sunday following the College Entrance Exam. 我和其他幾位委員會成員已決定於大學入學考試後的第一個星期日在台北圓山大飯店舉辦晚餐派對。

> ⓘ 字詞 提示　• committee *n.* 委員會

> ⓘ 文法 句型　• together with　連同

3. Now we are working on this upcoming class reunion.

現在我們正在籌備這個即將到來的同學會。

> ⓘ 字詞 提示　• upcoming *adj.* 即將來臨的

> ⓘ 文法 句型　• work on　從事，致力於

第二段

1. Here are the reasons why it is arranged this way.

同學會之所以如此安排的理由如下。

> ⓘ 文法 句型　• Here + be + S　為表示以下要介紹某些事物給某人的句型

2. First, we could more easily gather the whole class together using their current addresses, which may change later this year. 第一、我們可以利用目前的地址更容易地召集全班同學，這些地址可能在今年下半年會異動。

> ⓘ 字詞 提示　• gather *v.* 召集，聚集
> • current *adj.* 目前的

3. Second, we believe that evening should be a relaxing time when we may eat, drink and talk to our hearts' content.

第二、我們相信當天晚上應該是一段輕鬆的時光，我們可以盡情地吃、喝和聊天。

> ⓘ 文法 句型　• do sth. to sb's heart's content　盡情地做某事

4. Third, the Taipei Grand Hotel is a five-star hotel. With its top-quality service, we are guaranteed an awesome feast. 第三、台北圓山大飯店是一間五星級的飯店。由於

它頂級的服務，我們一定會有一次永生難忘的盛宴。

⚠️ 字詞
提示   • awesome *adj.* 很棒的

5. Let's look forward to this first class reunion.

且讓我們期待這第一次的同學會。

⚠️ 文法
句型   • look forward to N/V-ing 期待

✏️ Step 5 用字遣詞 Words → Sentences

1. pleasure [`plɛʒɚ] *n.* 榮幸，樂趣

   It's a great pleasure to work with Professor Chen.

   很榮幸能與陳博士共事。

2. reunion [ri`junjən] *n.* 團聚，重聚

   Traditionally, Chinese New Year is a time for family reunion.

   傳統上，中國新年是家人團聚的時刻。

3. graduation [ˌgrædʒʊ`eʃən] *n.* 畢業

   Teaching English is my first job after graduation from university.

   教英文是我大學畢業後的第一份工作。

4. committee [kə`mɪtɪ] *n.* 委員會

   The government set up a committee to promote environmental protection.

   政府成立了一個委員會來推動環境保護議題。

5. upcoming [`ʌp͵kʌmɪŋ] *adj.* 即將來臨的

   The Taipei City Government has completed its anti-flooding measures against the upcoming typhoon.

   台北市政府針對即將來臨的颱風做好了防洪措施。

6. gather [`gæðɚ] *v.* 召集，聚集

   The students gathered together in the hall, waiting for the speech to start.

   學生們聚集在演講廳中，等待演講開始。

7. current [`kɝənt] *adj.* 目前的

   Have you seen the current issue of *Time* magazine?

   你看過這一期的時代雜誌了嗎？

8. awesome [`ɔsəm] *adj.* 很棒的

   This is an awesome CD player. You can not only play CDs but also record your favorite radio show with it. 這是一台很棒的 CD 播放器。你不僅可以用它播放 CD，還可以把你喜歡的廣播節目錄下來。

文法句型 Grammar Points → Sentences

1. serve as 擔任

   Cindy was elected to serve as chairwoman of the party.

   Cindy 獲選擔任這個政黨的主席。

2. together with 連同

   I, together with my friends, decided to do some charity work for the Red Cross.

   我和我的朋友決定要為紅十字會做些慈善工作。

3. work on 從事，致力於

   The writer is working on a new novel. 這位作家正在寫一本新的小說。

4. Here + be + S 表示以下要介紹某些事物給某人的句型

   Here are the books you want. 這些是你要的書。

5. do sth. to sb's heart's content 盡情地做某事

   I spend my free time reading to my heart's content.

   我利用我的空閒時間盡情地閱讀。

6. look forward to N/V-ing 期待

   Susan is really looking forward to her holiday.

   Susan 真的很期待她的假期。

UNIT 21
UNIT 22
UNIT 23
UNIT 24
UNIT 25
UNIT 26
UNIT 27
UNIT 28
UNIT 29
UNIT 30
UNIT 31
UNIT 32
UNIT 33
UNIT 34
UNIT 35
UNIT 36
UNIT 37
UNIT 38
UNIT 39
UNIT 40

UNIT 30

The Importance of Trees　樹木的重要

　　寫一篇英文短文論述樹木與我們生活的密切關聯。文分兩段。第一段說明樹木重要的原因；第二段說明如何拯救並維護樹木。文長 120 個英文字左右。

　　Write a two-paragraph essay dealing with the close link between trees and our lives. Give the reasons why trees are important in paragraph one; list the ways to save and protect trees in paragraph two. Write your essay in 120 words or so.

Step 1　聯想提示 Association　依人、事、時、地、物、原因和方法聯想與題目相關的事項

- 樹木有多重要？　How important are trees?
- 樹木如何影響地球上的生物？　How trees influence life on earth?
- 樹木有什麼用途？　What can trees do?
- 我們可以做什麼來拯救並保護樹木？　What can we do to save and conserve trees?
- 政府針對這件事情可以做什麼？　What can the government do about this matter?

Step 2　組織大綱提示 Organization　依照想到的事項，定出寫作優先順序及細節

第一段

1. 主題句：樹木的重要性再怎麼強調都不為過。
2. 支持句：樹木可滿足地球萬物許多不可或缺的需求。

　　a. 例如，樹木釋放所有生物賴以維生的氧氣。

　　b. 日常生活中許多其他方面也仰賴樹木。

第二段

1. 主題句：樹木是值得拯救和保護的寶貴資源。
2. 支持句：如何拯救及保存樹木

　　a. 必須嚴懲盜伐樹木者。

　　b. 集思廣義來研究保護樹木的方法。

　　c. 呼籲鄰居在住家附近種植更多樹木。

UNIT
21

UNIT
22

UNIT
23

UNIT
24

UNIT
25

UNIT
26

UNIT
27

UNIT
28

UNIT
29

UNIT
30

UNIT
31

UNIT
32

UNIT
33

UNIT
34

UNIT
35

UNIT
36

UNIT
37

UNIT
38

UNIT
39

UNIT
40

Step 3 範文 Model Composition

The Importance of Trees

The importance of trees cannot be overemphasized. As a matter of fact, trees are invaluable resources which can be used to satisfy many purposes that are essential to all life on earth. For example, trees give off oxygen which all living things need to stay alive. Besides, many other aspects of our daily lives rely on trees, such as food, shelter, paper, furniture, and shade.

With all their benefits, it is clear that trees are precious resources worth saving and conserving. First of all, we suggest the government legislate to severely penalize those who fell trees illegally. Secondly, we should also pool the wisdom of the masses to look into ways to protect trees. Last but not least, we can call on our neighbors to plant more trees in our neighborhoods.

Step 4 寫句實戰分析 Analyzing Sentences

第一段

1. The importance of trees cannot be overemphasized.
   樹木的重要性再怎麼強調都不為過。

   文法句型 • cannot be overemphasized　再強調也不為過

2. As a matter of fact, trees are invaluable resources which can be used to satisfy many purposes that are essential to all life on earth.
   事實上，樹木是無價的資源，可用來滿足許多用途，這些用途對地球萬物而言是不可或缺的。

   字詞提示
   • invaluable *adj.* 無比珍貴的，無價的
   • resource *n.* 資源
   • essential *adj.* 必要的，不可或缺的

   文法句型 • as a matter of fact (= in fact)　事實上

169

3. For example, trees give off oxygen which all living things need to stay alive.

例如，樹木釋放所有生物賴以維生的氧氣。

> (!) 文法句型
> - give off　散發，釋放
> - stay + adj.　保持…

4. Besides, many other aspects of our daily lives rely on trees, such as food, shelter, paper, furniture, and shade.

此外，日常生活中許多其他方面也仰賴樹木，像是食物、庇護、紙張、傢俱、遮蔭。

> (!) 字詞提示
> - aspect *n.* 方面

> (!) 文法句型
> - rely on　依賴

第二段

1. With all their benefits, it is clear that trees are precious resources worth saving and conserving.

因為它們的好處，我們可以清楚明白樹木是值得拯救和保存的寶貴資源。

> (!) 字詞提示
> - precious *adj.* 珍貴的
> - conserve *v.* 維護，保育

> (!) 文法句型
> - be worth + V-ing　值得…

2. First of all, we suggest the government legislate to severely penalize those who fell trees illegally.

首先，我們建議政府立法嚴懲那些非法砍伐樹木的人。

> (!) 字詞提示
> - legislate *v.* 立法
> - penalize *v.* 處罰

> (!) 文法句型
> - S + suggest/insist/order/demand/require + (that) + S + (should) + V....　表建議、命令、要求的句型

3. Secondly, we should also pool the wisdom of the masses to look into ways to protect trees.　其次，我們也應該集思廣義來研究保護樹木的方法。

> (!) 字詞提示
> - pool *v.* 集中資源 (資金、物資、想法等)

UNIT 21
UNIT 22
UNIT 23
UNIT 24
UNIT 25
UNIT 26
UNIT 27
UNIT 28
UNIT 29
UNIT 30
UNIT 31
UNIT 32
UNIT 33
UNIT 34
UNIT 35
UNIT 36
UNIT 37
UNIT 38
UNIT 39
UNIT 40

· mass *n.* 大眾，民眾 (寫做 the masses)

⚠ 文法句型　· look into　深入研究，調查

4. Last but not least, we can call on our neighbors to plant more trees in our neighborhoods.

最後但同樣也很重要的是，我們可以呼籲鄰居在我們住家附近種植更多的樹木。

⚠ 文法句型　· call on sb. to + V　呼籲某人做⋯

Step 5　用字遣詞 Words → Sentences

1. invaluable [ɪnˋvæljəbḷ] *adj.* 無比珍貴的，無價的

   Working overseas will provide you with invaluable experience.

   在海外工作將提供你無比珍貴的工作經驗。

2. resource [rɪˋsors] *n.* 資源

   The most precious natural resource of our country is the forest.

   我們國家最珍貴的自然資源是森林。

3. essential [əˋsenʃəl] *adj.* 必要的，不可或缺的

   Hard work is essential to success.　想要成功就必須努力。

4. aspect [ˋæspɛkt] *n.* 方面

   Petroleum affects every aspect of our lives.

   石油影響了我們生活的每一個層面。

5. precious [ˋprɛʃəs] *adj.* 珍貴的

   Time is precious to us all.　時間對我們所有人來說都是寶貴的。

6. conserve [kənˋsɝv] *v.* 維護，保育

   The government passed new laws to conserve wildlife in the area.

   政府通過了新的法律來保育該地區的野生動物。

7. legislate [ˋlɛdʒɪsˌlet] *v.* 立法

   The government has legislated against gender discrimination in the workplace.

   政府已經立法防止工作場所內的性別歧視。

8. penalize [ˋpinḷˌaɪz] *v.* 處罰

   Students will be penalized for being late for classes.

   學生上課遲到將會被處罰。

9. pool [pul] *v.* 集中資源 (資金、物資、想法等)

Emmy's friends pooled their ideas to throw her a birthday party.

Emmy 的朋友集思廣益要幫她辦生日宴會。

10. mass [mæs] *n.* 大眾，民眾 (寫做 the masses)

Public libraries provide convenient access to books for the masses.

公立圖書館提供民眾借閱使用書籍的便利管道。

文法句型 Grammar Points → Sentences

1. cannot be overemphasized　再強調也不為過

The importance of prevention cannot be overemphasized.

預防的重要性再怎麼強調也不為過。

2. as a matter of fact (= in fact)　事實上

I knew Nina because we went to the same high school. As a matter of fact, she was my best friend in high school.

我認識 Nina，因為我們上同一所高中。事實上，她是我高中時最好的朋友。

3. give off　散發，釋放

The lovely flowers give off a sweet smell.

那些可愛的花散發出甜甜的味道。

4. stay + adj.　保持…

Amy has a good temper. She never stays angry for long.

Amy 脾氣很好。她從來不會生氣很久。

5. rely on　依賴

People nowadays rely on the Internet to keep in touch with friends.

現代人仰賴網路來和朋友保持聯繫。

6. be worth + V-ing　值得…

If you are looking for the wisdom in life, this book is worth reading.

如果你在尋找人生中的智慧，這本書值得一讀。

7. S + suggest/insist/order/demand/require + (that) + S + (should) + V....
表建議、命令、要求的句型

I suggest you call Jack before you drop by his house. He usually stays in the office late.

我建議你在順道拜訪 Jack 家之前先打電話給他。他通常會在辦公室待到很晚。

8. look into　深入研究，調查

The officials are looking into the possibility of merging the two banks.

官員們正在深入研究這兩家銀行合併的可能性。

9. call on sb. to + V 呼籲某人做…

The government is calling on all men and women over the age of 18 to join the army. 政府正呼籲所有年滿十八歲的男女入伍從軍。

UNIT 21
UNIT 22
UNIT 23
UNIT 24
UNIT 25
UNIT 26
UNIT 27
UNIT 28
UNIT 29
UNIT 30
UNIT 31
UNIT 32
UNIT 33
UNIT 34
UNIT 35
UNIT 36
UNIT 37
UNIT 38
UNIT 39
UNIT 40

UNIT 31

The Internet and My Life 網際網路和我的生活

北區公立高中 95 年第二次指考模擬考

以 "The Internet and My Life" 為題,寫一篇至少 120 字的英文作文。

Write an essay with the title "The Internet and My Life" in no less than 120 words.

Step 1 聯想提示 Association　依人、事、時、地、物、原因和方法聯想與題目相關的事項

- 網路為什麼重要？　Why is the Internet important?
- 我從它享受到什麼好處？　What advantages of the Internet do I enjoy?
- 網路有什麼缺點？　What disadvantages does the Internet have?
- 網路如何影響我的生活？　How does the Internet influence my life?
- 應如何看待網路？　How should I look at the Internet?

Step 2 組織大綱提示 Organization　依照想到的事項,定出寫作優先順序及細節

第一段

1. 主題句:網路在通訊和資訊兩方面扮演著關鍵性的角色。

2. 支持句:列出網路的好處

　　a. 可以透過搜尋引擎來搜尋資訊。

　　b. 可以利用電子郵件來和朋友保持聯繫。

　　c. 可以上網玩遊戲。

3. 結論:我熱愛網路,無法想像沒有網路的生活。

第二段

1. 主題句:網路並非毫無缺點。

2. 支持句:列出網路的缺點

　　a. 一直待在電腦前面,眼睛一直盯著螢幕看。

　　b. 全身痠痛因為在椅子上面坐太久了。

3. 結論:網路有優點也有缺點,端看你如何使用它。

UNIT 21
UNIT 22
UNIT 23
UNIT 24
UNIT 25
UNIT 26
UNIT 27
UNIT 28
UNIT 29
UNIT 30
UNIT 31
UNIT 32
UNIT 33
UNIT 34
UNIT 35
UNIT 36
UNIT 37
UNIT 38
UNIT 39
UNIT 40

Step 3 範文 Model Composition

The Internet and My Life

The Internet plays a crucial role in both communication and information in my life. For example, I can get the information I need via search engines, such as Google and Yahoo, in no time; I can stay in touch with my friends by email over the Internet; I can also play games which I find exciting and stimulating on the Internet. I love the Internet and I can't imagine life without it.

However, the Internet is not without disadvantages. While surfing the Internet, I keep staying in front of my PC with my eyes glued to the screen. As a result, my body aches all over from sitting too long in my chair. The Internet has its pros and cons. Whether it is good for you depends on how you use it.

Step 4 寫句實戰分析 Analyzing Sentences

第一段

1. The Internet plays a crucial role in both communication and information in my life. 網際網路在我生活中的溝通方面或是取得資訊方面都扮演著決定性的角色。

   文法句型
   · play a(n) crucial/important/key role in... 在某方面扮演關鍵／重要的角色
   · 注意：Internet 的首字母要大寫，前面要加定冠詞 the。

2. For example, I can get the information I need via search engines, such as Google and Yahoo, in no time; ....
   例如，我可以透過像 Google、Yahoo 等搜尋引擎來很快的找到我要的資訊；…

   字詞提示
   · via *prep.* 透過，經由
   · search engine *n.* 搜尋引擎

   文法句型
   · in no time　立即，很快

3. I can stay in touch with my friends by email over the Internet; ....

我也可以利用電子郵件，透過網路來和我的朋友保持聯繫；…

⚠ **文法句型**
- keep/stay in touch with + sb.　與某人保持聯繫
- 注意：over the Internet　經由、透過網路

4. I can also play games which I find exciting and stimulating on the Internet. I love the Internet and I can't imagine life without it.

我也可以在網路上玩一些我覺得興奮又刺激的遊戲。我愛網路而且我無法想像沒有網路的生活。

⚠ **字詞提示**
- stimulating *adj.* 有趣的，刺激人心的

第二段

1. However, the Internet is not without disadvantages.

然而，網路並非毫無缺點。

⚠ **字詞提示**
- disadvantage *n.* 缺點，不利之處

2. While surfing the Internet, I keep staying in front of my PC with my eyes glued to the screen.

當我上網時，我一直待在我的個人電腦前面，眼睛一直盯著螢幕看。

⚠ **字詞提示**
- surf *v.* 在網路上隨意瀏覽資訊
- glue *v.* 緊附著

3. As a result, my body aches all over from sitting too long in my chair.

結果，因為在椅子上面坐太久的關係，我全身痠痛。

⚠ **字詞提示**
- ache *v.* 疼痛

⚠ **文法句型**
- 注意：本句中的 from 表原因。

4. The Internet has its pros and cons. Whether it is good for you depends on how you use it.

網路有優點也有缺點，端看你要如何使用它。

UNIT 21
UNIT 22
UNIT 23
UNIT 24
UNIT 25
UNIT 26
UNIT 27
UNIT 28
UNIT 29
UNIT 30
UNIT 31
UNIT 32
UNIT 33
UNIT 34
UNIT 35
UNIT 36
UNIT 37
UNIT 38
UNIT 39
UNIT 40

⚠ **文法句型**
- pros and cons　好處與壞處
- 此句為 whether 引導名詞子句當主詞的句型。句中 Whether it is good for you 為主詞。

Step 5　用字遣詞 Words → Sentences

1. via [`vaɪə] *prep.* 透過，經由
I sent a message to Angela via her boyfriend.
我透過 Angela 的男朋友捎了一個訊息給她。

2. search engine [sɝtʃ `ɛndʒən] *n.* 搜尋引擎
Google provides a very powerful search engine. You can find all kinds of information with the click of your mouse.
Google 提供非常強力的搜尋引擎。只要點兩下滑鼠，你就可以找到各種資訊。

3. stimulating [`stɪmjə,letɪŋ] *adj.* 有趣的，刺激人心的
Ms. Potter is a good teacher; she makes the classes interesting and stimulating so that we stay focused all the time.
Potter 小姐是個好老師；她讓課程很刺激有趣，所以我們一直很專心。

4. disadvantage [,dɪsəd`væntɪdʒ] *n.* 缺點，不利之處
The only disadvantage of the neighborhood to me is that it's too far from my office.　這個社區對我來說唯一的缺點是離我的辦公室太遠了。

5. surf [sɝf] *v.* 在網路上隨意瀏覽資訊
I sometimes surf the Internet at night for news and interesting things.
有時候我會在晚上瀏覽網路，看看新聞和新奇的玩意兒。

6. glue [glu] *v.* 緊附著
Monica's eyes were glued to the television when the Yankee game was on.
當洋基隊的比賽在播放時，Monica 的眼睛一直緊盯電視。

7. ache [ek] *v.* 疼痛
My stomach aches when I see my math teacher.
我一看到數學老師就胃痛。

文法句型 Grammar Points → Sentences

1. play a(n) crucial/important/key role in...　在某方面扮演關鍵／重要的角色
Studies showed that sleep plays a crucial role in brain development in the early stage of our life.

研究顯示我們生命初期的睡眠可能在腦部發展上扮演著關鍵性的角色。

2. in no time　立即，很快

You'll learn how to use the software in no time.

你很快就會學會怎麼使用這套軟體。

3. keep/stay in touch with + sb.　與某人保持聯繫

I hope that we can stay in touch with each other.

我希望我們彼此可以保持連絡。

4. pros and cons　好處與壞處

Jill and I had discussed about the pros and cons of going to college. I think she will do it.　Jill 和我已經討論過上大學的好壞之處。我想她會去。

5. Whether 引導名詞子句當主詞的句型

Whether the typhoon comes or not will influence our decision to visit Hualien.

颱風來不來會影響我們去花蓮玩的決定。

UNIT
21

UNIT
22

UNIT
23

UNIT
24

UNIT
25

UNIT
26

UNIT
27

UNIT
28

UNIT
29

UNIT
30

UNIT
31

UNIT
32

UNIT
33

UNIT
34

UNIT
35

UNIT
36

UNIT
37

UNIT
38

UNIT
39

UNIT
40

UNIT 32

Narrative Writing　敘事文

The Most Unforgettable Exam I Have Ever Taken

最難忘的一次考試

　　小考、段考、複習考、畢業考、甚至校外其他各種大大小小的考試，已成為高中學生生活中不可或缺的一部分。請寫一篇 120 到 150 個字的英文作文，文分兩段，第一段以 "Exams of all kinds have become a necessary part of my high school life." 為主題句；第二段則以 "The most unforgettable exam I have ever taken is…" 為開頭並加以發展。

　　All kinds of exams, such as quizzes, monthly exams, review tests, graduation exams, and others outside the school, have become an essential part of life at high school. Please write a two-paragraph essay in about 120 to 150 words. Paragraph one begins with the topic sentence "Exams of all kinds have become a necessary part of my high school life." Paragraph two begins with "The most unforgettable exam I have ever taken is…" with some elaboration on it.

Step 1　聯想提示 Association　依人、事、時、地、物、原因和方法聯想與題目相關的事項

- 考試對我有什麼意義？　What do exams mean to me?
- 哪一次考試是最難忘的？　Which exam is the most unforgettable?
- 這次考試是在什麼時候？　When did the exam take place?
- 這次考試有什麼特殊之處？　What was special about it?
- 為什麼那次考試我沒考好？　Why didn't I do well on it?
- 我從這次經驗中學到什麼？　What have I learned from the experience?

Step 2　組織大綱提示 Organization　依照想到的事項，定出寫作優先順序及細節

第一段

1. 主題句：考試已成為高中生活中不可或缺的一部份。

2. 支持句：

　　a. 我已經被訓練成為考試機器，成績時好時壞。

　　b. 拿好成績沒有捷徑，要全力以赴，才能通過考試。

3. 結論：我真的相信勤奮的人才會成功。

第二段

1. 主題句：最難忘的一次考試是高中第一學期的生物期中考試。

2. 支持句：考試的經過

　　a. 考試前在網路上跟朋友聊天。

　　b. 沒有準備考試，所以抄同學的答案。

　　c. 作弊被抓到，所以成績以零分計算。

　　d. 我對自己犯下的錯事感到很羞愧。

3. 結論：我真的學到了教訓，永遠也無法忘記。

Step 3　範文 Model Composition

The Most Unforgettable Exam I Have Ever Taken

Exams of all kinds have become a necessary part of my high school life. I have been trained as an exam-taking machine. Sometimes I do pretty well on exams, but sometimes I do very poorly. There is no shortcut to better grades indeed. I should spare no effort to pass exams. I truly believe that diligence breeds success.

The most unforgettable exam I have ever taken is my first biology midterm during my first semester of high school. I chatted with a friend online the night before the exam. I was so poorly prepared for the exams that I could not help copying my classmate's answers. I got caught and received no score on my exam. I was so ashamed of myself for such a misdeed. I really learned a lesson, which I will never forget.

Step 4　寫句實戰分析 Analyzing Sentences

第一段

1. Exams of all kinds have become a necessary part of my high school life.
   各式各樣的考試已成為我高中生活中不可或缺的一部份。

UNIT
21

UNIT
22

UNIT
23

UNIT
24

UNIT
25

UNIT
26

UNIT
27

UNIT
28

UNIT
29

UNIT
30

UNIT
31

UNIT
32

UNIT
33

UNIT
34

UNIT
35

UNIT
36

UNIT
37

UNIT
38

UNIT
39

UNIT
40

⚠️ 文法
句型　· N + of all kinds　各式各樣的⋯

2. I have been trained as an exam-taking machine.

我已經被訓練成為一個考試機器。

⚠️ 文法
句型　· N-V-ing/V-en　複合形容詞。例：English-speaking country

3. Sometimes I do pretty well on exams, but sometimes I do very poorly. There is no shortcut to better grades indeed.

有時候我考的不錯，有時候我考的很差。的確，要拿更好的成績沒有捷徑。

⚠️ 字詞
提示　· shortcut *n.* 捷徑

⚠️ 文法
句型　· 注意：shortcut 後接 to 是介系詞，後面接名詞或動名詞。

4. I should spare no effort to pass exams.　我應該為了通過考試全力以赴。

⚠️ 文法
句型　· spare no effort to + V　不遺餘力，全力以赴

5. I truly believe that diligence breeds success.　我真的相信，勤奮才會成功。

⚠️ 字詞
提示　· diligence *n.* 勤勞
　· breed *v.* 引起，招致

第二段

1. The most unforgettable exam I have ever taken is my first biology midterm during my first semester of high school.

我考過最難忘的一次考試是高中第一學期的第一次生物期中考試。

⚠️ 字詞
提示　· biology *n.* 生物學
　· semester *n.* 學期

2. I chatted with a friend online the night before the exam. I was so poorly prepared for the exams that I could not help copying my classmate's answer.

前一天晚上，我一直跟朋友在網路上聊天。我考試準備得太糟了，所以忍不住抄了同學的答案。

3. I got caught and received no score on my exam.

我考試作弊被抓到，而且得到零分。

4. I was so ashamed of myself for such a misdeed.

我因為對自己犯下如此的錯事感到羞愧。

5. I really learned a lesson, which I will never forget.

我真的學到了教訓，永遠也不會忘記。

Step 5

用字遣詞 Words → Sentences

1. shortcut [`ʃɔrtˌkʌt] *n.* 捷徑

   There is no shortcut to success. 成功沒有捷徑。

2. diligence [`dɪlədʒəns] *n.* 勤勞

   With her diligence, Emma got promoted to manager of our department in her early thirties. 由於她的勤奮，Emma 三十出頭就被晉升為我們部門的經理。

3. breed [brid] *v.* 引起，招致

   Nothing breeds success like success. 一事成功，萬事順利。

4. biology [baɪ`ɑlədʒɪ] *n.* 生物學

   My favorite subject in school is biology, because I can learn a lot about the living things. 我在學校最喜歡的科目是生物學，因為我可以學到很多關於生物的知識。

5. semester [sə`mɛstɚ] *n.* 學期

   The first semester lasts from this September to next January.

UNIT 21
UNIT 22
UNIT 23
UNIT 24
UNIT 25
UNIT 26
UNIT 27
UNIT 28
UNIT 29
UNIT 30
UNIT 31
UNIT 32
UNIT 33
UNIT 34
UNIT 35
UNIT 36
UNIT 37
UNIT 38
UNIT 39
UNIT 40

第一學期從九月持續到隔年一月。

6. score [skor] *n.* 分數

Homework turned in late will not be marked and will get a score of zero.

遲交的家庭作業不會被批改，而且會得零分。

7. misdeed [mɪs`did] *n.* 壞事，惡行

The murderer felt guilty about his past misdeeds. He wanted to make it up by doing a lot of voluntary work.

這個殺人犯對於他過去的惡行有罪惡感。他想藉著做義工來彌補。

文法句型 Grammar Points → Sentences

1. N + of all kinds　各式各樣的

Tom is quite fascinated with insects of all kinds.

Tom 對於各式各樣的昆蟲相當著迷。

2. N-V-ing/V-en　複合形容詞

名詞後面加上分詞，中間用英文連字號相連，即形成複合形容詞。若有主動涵義的用現在分詞，有被動涵義的則用過去分詞。

English-speaking people　講英文的人

home-made salad　自家製的沙拉

3. spare no effort to + V　不遺餘力，全力以赴

We will spare no effort to protect wildlife.

我們將不遺餘力地去保護野生動物。

4. can not help + V-ing....　禁不住做了某事

I can not help laughing when I saw Ben in that hat.

當我見到 Ben 戴著那頂帽子時，我禁不住笑出來。

5. be ashamed of　對…感到羞愧

I don't think you have anything to be ashamed of.

我不覺得你有什麼好羞愧的。

UNIT 33

Informative/Narrative Writing　訊息文 / 敘事文

The Red Envelope—A Tradition of the Lunar New Year

紅包記趣——中國農曆新年傳統

除夕收到紅包是最快樂不過的事情。請寫一篇 120 到 150 個字的英文短文，分為兩段：第一段說明除夕發紅包的意義，第二段描述你個人收到紅包的過程和感受。

On the eve of the Lunar New Year, the most delightful thing is the giving of red envelopes. Please write a short essay about 120 to 150 words. Organize your essay into two paragraphs. In paragraph one, explain the meaning of the red envelope given on Lunar New Year's Eve; in paragraph two, describe how you get the red envelope and your feelings about it.

Step 1　聯想提示 Association 依人、事、時、地、物、原因和方法聯想與題目相關的事項

• 過年拿紅包在傳統中國社會中有什麼意義？

What does getting a red envelope in the Lunar New Year mean in traditional Chinese society?

• 我對紅包的感覺如何？　How do I feel about the red envelope?

• 我怎麼樣才能拿到紅包？　How can I get the red envelope?

• 我通常什麼時候拿到紅包？　When do I usually receive the red envelope?

• 我拿到紅包後會做什麼？　What do I do after receiving the red envelope?

Step 2　組織大綱提示 Organization　依照想到的事項，定出寫作優先順序及細節

第一段

1. 主題句：除夕家人團圓守歲是中國人的習俗。

2. 支持句：除夕發紅包，我們最開心了。

3. 小結論：紅包有給晚輩帶來好運的意義。

第二段

1. 主題句：每逢農曆新年，我都會很興奮地期待拿到紅包。

2. 支持句：

　a. 除夕夜我們全家人都會在爺爺奶奶家圍爐。

UNIT
21

UNIT
22

UNIT
23

UNIT
24

UNIT
25

UNIT
26

UNIT
27

UNIT
28

UNIT
29

UNIT
30

UNIT
31

UNIT
32

UNIT
33

UNIT
34

UNIT
35

UNIT
36

UNIT
37

UNIT
38

UNIT
39

UNIT
40

b.吃完年夜飯，要先在大人面前說些吉祥話，才能拿到紅包。

c.然後，我會迫不及待地數數看紅包袋裡的錢。

Step 3　範文 Model Composition

The Red Envelope－A Tradition of the Lunar New Year

Chinese people have a custom to stay up till dawn on Lunar New Year's Eve, when family members gather to say goodbye to the old year. Another New Year's Eve custom that delights us most is the giving of red envelopes with money enclosed. It is believed that a red envelope brings good luck to the younger generation.

When the Lunar New Year approaches, I cannot help but be excited in anticipation of this annual gift. All my family members gather together at our grandparents' house for a family reunion on the eve of the Spring Festival. At the end of the luxurious evening meal, I am required to say auspicious words in front of my elders before they hand out the red envelopes. Then, I cannot resist the temptation to count the money inside the red envelopes.

Step 4　寫句實戰分析 Analyzing Sentences

第一段

1. Chinese people have a custom to stay up till dawn on Lunar New Year's Eve, when family members gather to say goodbye to the old year.

中國人在除夕有守歲的習俗，這個時候家人會團聚，向舊的一年道別。

字詞
提示
· custom *n.* 習俗
· gather *v.* 集合，聚集

文法
句型
· stay up　熬夜（＝sit up）
· 關係副詞 when 的非限定用法：
　　a.關係副詞前面一定要有逗點。
　　b.關係副詞 when 引導的子句用來修飾表時間的先行詞。

2. Another New Year's Eve custom that delights us most is the giving of red envelopes with money enclosed.

另一個讓我們最開心的新年除夕習俗就是發裡面有裝錢的紅包。

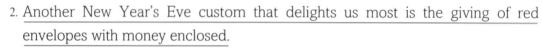 字詞提示
- delight *v.* 使高興，使愉悅
- envelope *n.* 信封，封套
- enclose *v.* (信封、包裹中) 附帶，附上

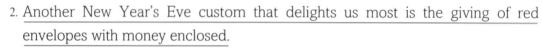 文法句型
- with + N (phrase) + V-en/V-ing　分詞修飾名詞（片語）的狀態

3. It is believed that a red envelope brings good luck to the younger generation.

一般認為，紅包可以為較年輕的一輩帶來好運。

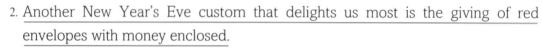 文法句型
- It is believed that + S + V....　一般認為…

第二段

4. When the Lunar New Year approaches, I cannot help but be excited in anticipation of this annual gift.

當農曆新年的腳步接近，我不禁會興奮地期待這一年一度的禮物。

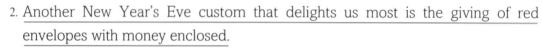 文法句型
- cannot (help) but + V　一定…，不禁…
- in anticipation of　期待，預期

5. All my family members gather together at our grandparents' house for a family reunion on the eve of the Spring Festival.

春節除夕，我們全家人會聚在爺爺奶奶家裡團聚。

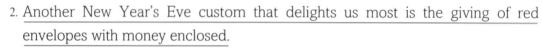 文法句型
- 注意：at + 地方 ; for + 目的 ; on + 時間
- the Spring Festival　春節
- family reunion　家人團聚

6. At the end of the luxurious evening meal, I am required to say auspicious words in front of my elders before they hand out the red envelopes.

豐盛的年夜飯結束後，我必須先在長輩面前說些吉祥話，他們才會發紅包。

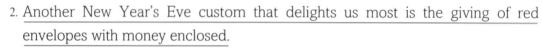 字詞提示
- luxurious *adj.* 奢華的
- auspicious *adj.* 吉利的

UNIT
21

UNIT
22

UNIT
23

UNIT
24

UNIT
25

UNIT
26

UNIT
27

UNIT
28

UNIT
29

UNIT
30

UNIT
31

UNIT
32

UNIT
33

UNIT
34

UNIT
35

UNIT
36

UNIT
37

UNIT
38

UNIT
39

UNIT
40

⚆ 文法
　　句型　· be required to + V　必須⋯

7. Then, I cannot resist the temptation to count the money inside the red envelopes.　然後，我就會忍不住誘惑想數數看紅包裡的錢。

⚆ 字詞
　　提示　· temptation *n.* 誘惑

Step 5

用字遣詞 Words → Sentences

1. custom [ˋkʌstəm] *n.* 習俗

   Most Americans have made it a custom to eat turkey on Thanksgiving.

   大多數美國人已經把感恩節吃火雞當成一種習俗。

2. gather [ˋgæðɚ] *v.* 集合，聚集

   My whole family gathered together at Greg's home.

   我們一家人都聚在 Greg 的家裡。

3. delight [dɪˋlaɪt] *v.* 使高興，使愉悅

   Brian's success in college delighted his family.

   Brian 在大學的成就讓他的家人很高興。

4. envelope [ˋɛnvəˏlop] *n.* 信封，封套

   Insert the letter into the envelope, seal it and put it into a mailbox.

   把信放入信封裡，將它密封起來，然後放到郵筒裡。

5. enclose [ɪnˋkloz] *v.* (信封、包裹中) 附帶，附上

   Please send the completed form back, enclosing a recent photograph.

   請將填妥後的表格寄回，並附上一張最近的照片。

6. luxurious [lʌgˋʒʊrɪəs] *adj.* 奢華的

   We stayed in a luxurious hotel during our visit to Kaohsiung.

   我們去高雄玩的時候，住在一個豪華的旅館裡。

7. auspicious [ɔˋspɪʃəs] *adj.* 吉利的

   It was an auspicious date for a wedding.　那是個結婚的好日子。

8. temptation [tɛmpˋteʃən] *n.* 誘惑

   Pandora couldn't resist the temptation to open the box.

   Pandora 忍不住想打開那個盒子的誘惑。

文法句型 Grammar Points → Sentences

1. stay up　熬夜 (= sit up)

   They stayed up late in the night talking.　他們熬夜聊天到三更半夜。

2. 關係副詞 when 的非限定用法：

   a. 關係副詞前面一定要有逗點。

   b. 關係副詞 when 引導的子句用來修飾表時間的先行詞。

   Please wait till Monday, when I will tell you everything.

   請等到禮拜一，到時候我會把所有的事情都告訴你。

3. with + N (phrase) + V-en/V-ing　分詞修飾名詞（片語）的狀態

   The boy is pointing to a factory with its chimney smoking.

   這個男孩正指著一座煙囪正在冒煙的工廠。

4. It is believed that + S + V....　一般認為…

   It is believed that the murderer has left the country.

   一般認為這個殺人兇手已經出境了。

5. cannot (help) but + V　一定…，不禁…

   If we persevere, we cannot (help) but succeed.　如果我們不屈不撓，一定會成功。

6. in anticipation of　期待，預期

   She bought extra food in anticipation of more people coming than she'd invited.

   她預期來的人會比她邀請的還多，所以就多買了些食物。

7. be required to + V　必須…

   Students are required to attend classes.　學生們必須上課。

UNIT
21

UNIT
22

UNIT
23

UNIT
24

UNIT
25

UNIT
26

UNIT
27

UNIT
28

UNIT
29

UNIT
30

UNIT
31

UNIT
32

UNIT
33

UNIT
34

UNIT
35

UNIT
36

UNIT
37

UNIT
38

UNIT
39

UNIT
40

UNIT 34

Procedural Writing 程序文

The Thing I Hope and Promise to Complete Before the End of High School

我希望在高中畢業前一定要完成的事

北區公立高中 93 年第二次指考模擬考

高中生涯即將進入尾聲 ，請想一想有沒有什麼事情是你希望並承諾在高中畢業前一定要完成的。文分兩段，第一段說明這件事是什麼，以及你為什麼希望並承諾在高中畢業前一定要完成這件事；第二段說明你將如何完成。

Your high school days will soon come to an end. Please think about one thing that you hope and promise to complete before the end of high school. Write an essay of two paragraphs. Describe the thing and explain why you hope and promise to complete it before the end of high school in paragraph one; explain how you would complete the thing in paragraph two.

Step 1 聯想提示 Association 依人、事、時、地、物、原因和方法聯想與題目相關的事項

- 我在高中畢業前最想完成什麼事？ What to do?
- 為什麼是這件事？ Why to do it?
- 這件事有什麼意義和重要性？ What is it about?
- 要怎樣才能完成這件事？ How to do it?
- 有哪些具體的方法？ Specific ways to do it?

Step 2 組織大綱提示 Organization 依照想到的事項，定出寫作優先順序及細節

第一段

1. 主題句：高中畢業前最想完成的事是通過全民英檢中級。

2. 這個目標兩年前就訂下了。

3. 突顯這項考試的重要性。

4. 闡述通過這項考試的意義及價值：建立英文能力的自信、對未來有幫助。

第二段

1. 主題句：提出達成這個目標的方法。

2. 列舉並闡述具體的做法：

a. 增加字彙，改善閱讀能力。

b. 多練習英文寫作。

c. 多聽英文廣播或看英語電視節目，增強聽力。

3. 結論：對達成目標的信心與自我評估。

Step 3 範文 Model Composition

The Thing I Hope and Promise to Complete Before the End of High School

The thing I hope and promise to complete before the end of high school is to pass the General English Proficiency Test (GEPT) at the Intermediate Level on May 1. I have been preparing for the test over the last two years. This test matters more to me than any test given in school. By passing it I can gain confidence in communicating in English, which will pave the way for a bright future.

To pass this challenging exam, I must continue with the following steps. First, I should read as much as possible to extend my vocabulary and improve my reading ability. Second, I have to practice writing in English constantly and ask my English teacher to help correct and improve my drafts. Third, it is also necessary for me to listen intensively to radio and television news reports to improve my listening and speaking skills. If I keep on doing what I have been doing, the probability of my passing the Intermediate GEPT will be greatly enhanced.

Step 4 寫句實戰分析 Analyzing Sentences

第一段

1. <u>The thing I hope and promise to complete before the end of high school is to pass the General English Proficiency Test (GEPT) at the Intermediate Level on May 1.</u>

我希望並承諾在高中畢業前一定要完成的事是通過五月一日的全民英檢中級測驗。

UNIT
21

UNIT
22

UNIT
23

UNIT
24

UNIT
25

UNIT
26

UNIT
27

UNIT
28

UNIT
29

UNIT
30

UNIT
31

UNIT
32

UNIT
33

UNIT
34

UNIT
35

UNIT
36

UNIT
37

UNIT
38

UNIT
39

UNIT
40

ⓘ 字詞
提示
· proficiency *n.* 熟練，精通
· intermediate *adj.* 中級的，中等程度的

ⓘ 文法
句型
· 注意：對等連接詞 and 前後各接一個現在式動詞。
　　　 主詞 the thing 後接一個省略掉關代的形容詞子句 I hope... 修飾主詞，整
　　　 個句子的動詞是 is，動詞後的不定詞於此作主詞補語。

2. I have been preparing for the test over the last two years.

過去兩年以來，我一直在準備應考。

ⓘ 文法
句型
· over/in/for the last/past + 一段時間常與完成 (進行) 式連用。

3. This test matters more to me than any test given in school.

對我而言，這項考試比校內任何考試都來的重要。

ⓘ 文法
句型
· 注意：matter 為動詞，matters more = is more important。
　　　 名詞 test 後接一個過去分詞片語 given... 做修飾。

4. By passing it I can gain confidence in communicating in English, which will pave
the way for a bright future.

藉由通過這次考試，我可以增加對英文溝通的信心，藉此為光明的未來鋪路。

ⓘ 字詞
提示
· communicate *v.* 溝通，交流

ⓘ 文法
句型
· gain confidence in N/V-ing　對…有信心
· pave the way for　為…預作安排
· 注意：介系詞 by 表示「藉由…」，後接動名詞。
　　　 主要子句後接逗點，再接關係代名詞 which 引導的子句修飾整個主句，為
　　　 關係代名詞的非限定（補述）用法。

第二段

1. To pass this challenging exam, I must continue with the following steps.

為了要通過這項具挑戰性的測驗，我必須繼續採取下列的措施。

ⓘ 文法
句型
· continue with　繼續…
· 注意：句首的不定詞 (To + V) 表目的。

2. First, I should read as much as possible to extend my vocabulary and improve

my reading ability.

第一，我應該儘可能多閱讀以擴充我的字彙並且改善我的閱讀能力。

⊙ 字詞
提示
· extend *v.* 擴展，延伸

⊙ 文法
句型
· as...as possible　儘可能地…

3. Second, I have to practice writing in English constantly and ask my English teacher to help correct and improve my drafts.

第二，我必須經常練習用英文寫作並請求英文老師幫忙訂正、改進我的草稿。

⊙ 字詞
提示
· constantly *adv.* 不斷地，時常地
· draft *n.* 草稿

4. Third, it is also necessary for me to listen intensively to radio and television news reports to improve my listening and speaking skills.

第三，我也有必要去密集地收聽收音機以及電視的新聞報導來增強我的聽力和口語能力。

⊙ 字詞
提示
· intensively *adv.* 密集地；深入地

⊙ 文法
句型
·注意：第一個 and 前後各接一個名詞；第二個 and 前後各接一個動名詞。

5. If I keep on doing what I have been doing, the probability of my passing the Intermediate GEPT will be greatly enhanced.

如果我持續做我一直在做的事，我通過全民英檢中級測驗的可能性就會大大提高。

⊙ 字詞
提示
· enhance *v.* 提升，增強

⊙ 文法
句型
· keep on + V-ing　繼續做
· the probability of one's V-ing　某人做…的可能性
·注意：在直述法中，if 子句用現在式動詞，主要子句用簡單未來式動詞，表示有可能發生的假設。

UNIT
21

UNIT
22

UNIT
23

UNIT
24

UNIT
25

UNIT
26

UNIT
27

UNIT
28

UNIT
29

UNIT
30

UNIT
31

UNIT
32

UNIT
33

UNIT
34

UNIT
35

UNIT
36

UNIT
37

UNIT
38

UNIT
39

UNIT
40

Step 5

用字遣詞 Words → Sentences

1. proficiency [prə`fɪʃənsɪ] *n.* 熟練，精通

   It is said in the job ad that applicants need to have proficiency in at least two languages.　求才廣告中表示申請者需精通至少兩種語言。

2. intermediate [ˌɪntə`midɪɪt] *adj.* 中級的，中等程度的

   This textbook is too difficult for intermediate students of English.

   這本教科書對英文中級程度的學生來說太難了。

3. communicate [kə`mjunə,ket] *v.* 溝通，交流

   People who can't speak can communicate in sign language.

   不能說話的人可以用手語溝通。

4. extend [ɪk`stɛnd] *v.* 擴展，延伸

   Careful maintenance can extend the life of your car.

   小心保養能延長你車子的壽命。

5. constantly [`kɑnstəntlɪ] *adv.* 不斷地，時常地

   Mary talked constantly about her new boyfriend.

   Mary 不斷提到她的新男友。

6. draft [dræft] *n.* 草稿

   Jeff asked me to check the draft of his proposal.

   Jeff 要我幫他檢查提案的草稿。

7. intensively [ɪn`tɛnsɪvlɪ] *adv.* 密集地；深入地

   This case has been intensively studied.　這件案子已經被深入地研究過了。

8. enhance [ɪn`hæns] *v.* 提升，增強

   They did nothing to enhance the reputation of the company.

   他們對於提升公司的形象並未採取任何行動。

文法句型 Grammar Points → Sentences

1. over/in/for the last/past + 一段時間　最近…以來 (搭配完成式動詞)

   Jack's company has been promoting their new product over the past few months.　過去幾個月來，Jack 的公司一直在促銷他們的新商品。

2. gain confidence in N/V-ing　對…有信心

   I've gained more confidence in making English speeches in public.

   我對於公開發表英文演講更有信心了。

3. pave the way for 為…預作安排

Scientists hope the data will pave the way for a more detailed exploration of Mars. 科學家希望這些資料能為進一步的火星探索預作準備。

4. continue with 繼續…

Does your brother intend to continue with his studies?

你哥哥打算繼續他的學業嗎？

5. as...as possible 儘可能地…

Try to give as much detail as possible in your description.

試著儘可能地仔細描述。

6. keep on + V-ing 繼續做…

John kept on asking me questions over the whole period.

John 整堂課都在問我問題。

7. the probability of one's V-ing 某人做…的可能性

The probability of his winning the championship is slim.

他贏得冠軍的可能性微乎其微。

UNIT
21

UNIT
22

UNIT
23

UNIT
24

UNIT
25

UNIT
26

UNIT
27

UNIT
28

UNIT
29

UNIT
30

UNIT
31

UNIT
32

UNIT
33

UNIT
34

UNIT
35

UNIT
36

UNIT
37

UNIT
38

UNIT
39

UNIT
40

UNIT 35

Tomorrow 明天

以 "Tomorrow" 為題，寫一篇 120 到 150 字的英文短文，文分兩段。第一段必須以 "There is always a tomorrow giving you a glimmer of hope." 為主題句。

Write a short essay of two paragraphs with the title "Tomorrow" in 120 to 150 words. Paragraph one should begin with the topic sentence "There is always a tomorrow giving you a glimmer of hope."

Step 1 聯想提示 Association 依人、事、時、地、物、原因和方法聯想與題目相關的事項

- 明天代表什麼意義？　What does tomorrow mean?
- 明天有什麼好處？　What is good about tomorrow?
- 明天可以帶給我們什麼？　What can tomorrow bring us?
- 我們應該如何面對明天？　How should we face tomorrow?
- 我們應該如何面對今天？　How should we face today?
- 為什麼我們應如此面對今天？　Why should we face today this way?

Step 2 組織大綱提示 Organization 依照想到的事項，定出寫作優先順序及細節

第一段

1. 主題句：明天總是帶給你一線希望。

2. 支持句：

　　a. 也許你今天陷入困境，需要一個新的機會來改善情況。

　　b. 舉例：可能今天小考考不好，而需要新的一天來恢復信心。

3. 結論：常言道，明天又是新的一天。

第二段

1. 主題句：然而，你不可以完全依賴明天。

2. 支持句：

　　a. 必須充分把握今天。

　　b. 利用今天來完成昨天未完成的事。

　　c. 利用今天來檢查做過的事，看看有哪裡可能做錯了。

d. 切記：「明日復明日，明日何其多。」

3. 結論：畢竟，誰知道明天會有什麼變化呢？

Step 3 範文 Model Composition

Tomorrow

There is always a tomorrow giving you a glimmer of hope. If you are in a difficult situation today, you may need another chance to make things better tomorrow. For example, if you feel sorry for poor performance on a quiz today, you may need another chance tomorrow to regain your confidence. As the saying goes, "Tomorrow is another day."

However, you cannot count entirely on tomorrow to help you. You must also make the most of today. You can use today to complete the task that was half done yesterday. You can also use today to check what you have done and where you may have gone wrong. Keep in mind another saying: "Tomorrow never comes." After all, who knows what changes tomorrow may bring?

Step 4 寫句實戰分析 Analyzing Sentences

第一段

1. There is always a tomorrow giving you a glimmer of hope.

明天總是帶給你一線希望。

⚠字詞提示 · glimmer *n.* 跡象，少許

⚠文法句型 · 注意：原句為 There is always a tomorrow which gives you....

2. If you are in a difficult situation today, you may need another chance to make things better tomorrow.

如果你今天陷入困境，你明天或許需要一個新的機會來改善情況。

UNIT 21
UNIT 22
UNIT 23
UNIT 24
UNIT 25
UNIT 26
UNIT 27
UNIT 28
UNIT 29
UNIT 30
UNIT 31
UNIT 32
UNIT 33
UNIT 34
UNIT 35
UNIT 36
UNIT 37
UNIT 38
UNIT 39
UNIT 40

ⓘ **文法句型** ・注意：本句中的 things 是「情況，情形」的意思，用複數形。

3. For example, if you feel sorry for poor performance on a quiz today, you may need another chance tomorrow to regain your confidence.

例如，你可能今天小考考不好，而需要新的一天來幫助你恢復信心。

ⓘ **字詞提示** ・ regain *v.* 取回，恢復
・ confidence *n.* 信心

4. As the saying goes, "Tomorrow is another day."

常言道：「明天又是新的一天。」

ⓘ **文法句型** ・ As the saying goes, "...." 如諺語所說的，… (介紹諺語、格言的句型)

第二段

1. However, you cannot count entirely on tomorrow to help you.

然而，你不可以完全依賴明天。

ⓘ **字詞提示** ・ entirely *adv.* 完全地

ⓘ **文法句型** ・ count on 依賴，指望

2. You must also make the most of today. 你也必須充分把握今天。

ⓘ **文法句型** ・ make the most of 充分利用

3. You can use today to complete the task that was half done yesterday.

你可以利用今天來完成昨天未完成的事。

ⓘ **文法句型** ・注意：本句中的 half 是副詞，修飾形容詞 done，意為「完成一半的」。

4. You can also use today to check what you have done and where you may have gone wrong. 你也可以利用今天來檢查做過的事，看看有哪裡可能做錯了。

ⓘ **文法句型** ・ go wrong 出錯

5. Keep in mind another saying: "Tomorrow never comes."

切記:「明日復明日,明日何其多。」

⚠ 字詞提示　• saying *n.* 諺語,格言

⚠ 文法句型　• keep in mind　牢記在心

6. After all, who knows what changes tomorrow may bring?

畢竟,誰知道明天會有什麼變化呢?

⚠ 文法句型　• after all　畢竟

Step 5

用字遣詞 Words → Sentences

1. glimmer [ˋglɪmɚ] *n.* 跡象,少許

   After talking to the teacher, I felt a glimmer of hope for the future.

   跟老師談過之後,我對未來感到一絲希望。

2. regain [rɪˋgen] *v.* 取回,恢復

   Regular exercise can help you regain your health and energy.

   規律的運動可以幫助你恢復健康和活力。

3. confidence [ˋkɑnfədəns] *n.* 信心

   Sharon has strong confidence in her swimming ability.

   Sharon 對她的游泳能力很有信心。

4. entirely [ɪnˋtaɪrlɪ] *adv.* 完全地

   The baseball player admitted that losing the game was entirely his fault. He was the one to blame.　這個棒球球員承認輸掉這場比賽完全是他的錯。全都該怪他。

5. saying [ˋseɪŋ] *n.* 諺語,格言

   Never forget the old saying, "Never put off till tomorrow what you can do today."　永遠不要忘記這句老格言:「永遠不要把今天可以做的事情拖到明天才做。」

文法句型 Grammar Points → Sentences

1. As the saying goes, "...."　如諺語所說的,…(介紹諺語、格言的句型)

   As the saying goes, "practice makes perfect."　就像諺語所說的,熟能生巧。

2. count on　依賴,指望

   No matter what happens, I know I can count on my best friend, Jim.

不論發生什麼事，我都知道我可以依靠我最好的朋友，Jim。

3. make the most of　充分利用

We must make the most of our life.　我們必須充分利用我們的人生。

4. go wrong　出錯

If you do what Mr. Wang tells you, you can't go wrong.

如果你照王先生告訴你的去做，就不會出差錯。

5. keep in mind　牢記在心

Keep your goal in mind, and try hard to achieve it.

把你的目標牢記在心，然後努力達成它。

6. after all　畢竟

Don't be so mad at what your sister said. After all, she's still young.

不要對你妹妹說的話太生氣。畢竟，她年紀還輕。

UNIT 21
UNIT 22
UNIT 23
UNIT 24
UNIT 25
UNIT 26
UNIT 27
UNIT 28
UNIT 29
UNIT 30
UNIT 31
UNIT 32
UNIT 33
UNIT 34
UNIT 35
UNIT 36
UNIT 37
UNIT 38
UNIT 39
UNIT 40

UNIT 36

Travel Is the Best Teacher　旅行是最好的老師

　　請以 "Travel Is the Best Teacher" 為主題，寫一篇至少 120 個字的英文作文。第一段說明旅行的優點。並在第二段舉自己在國內或國外的旅行經驗，以印證第一段的說明。

　　Please write an essay in no less than 120 words with the title "Travel Is the Best Teacher." In paragraph one, explain the advantages of travel. In paragraph two, use one of your experiences of traveling, home or abroad, to prove the explanation given in paragraph one.

Step 1　聯想提示 Association　依人、事、時、地、物、原因和方法聯想與題目相關的事項

- 為什麼旅行是最好的老師？　Why is travel the best teacher?
- 旅行有什麼優點？　What advantages does travel have?
- 我們可以從旅行學到什麼？　What can we learn from travel?
- 我最近曾經去哪裡旅行？　Where have I traveled recently?
- 這趟旅行期間我做了什麼？　What did I do during the trip?
- 我喜歡這趟旅行的哪些部份？　What do I like about the trip?

Step 2　組織大綱提示 Organization　依照想到的事項，定出寫作優先順序及細節

第一段

1. 主題句：旅行是最佳良師，總是帶給我們難以磨滅的學習經歷。

2. 支持句：舉例

　a. 旅行有數不盡的好處。

　b. 旅行可以擴展我們的知識領域。

　c. 旅行幫我們減輕工作上的壓力。

3. 結論：的確，越常去旅行，就越了解這個世界。

第二段

1. 主題句：去年暑假我花了一個半月的時間在美國到處旅行。

2. 支持句：旅行細節

UNIT 21
UNIT 22
UNIT 23
UNIT 24
UNIT 25
UNIT 26
UNIT 27
UNIT 28
UNIT 29
UNIT 30
UNIT 31
UNIT 32
UNIT 33
UNIT 34
UNIT 35
UNIT 36
UNIT 37
UNIT 38
UNIT 39
UNIT 40

a. 我去了好幾個觀光勝地，如大峽谷等等。

b. 在美國的旅行期間，我體驗了許多事物：美景、佳餚，也增進了英文能力。

3. 結論：我真的玩的很開心，也期待下一次的旅行。

Step 3　範文　Model Composition

Travel Is the Best Teacher

Travel is the best teacher and always results in the most enduring lessons. The advantages of travel are countless. First of all, it can widen our scope of knowledge. Traveling to another place, we expose ourselves to a new learning environment, where we gain new knowledge. Second, travel helps us relieve the pressure of work. We all need some time off to refresh ourselves, experiencing new things. Indeed, the more often we travel, the more we learn about the world.

Last summer vacation, I spent one month and a half traveling around the United States. I went to several popular holiday resorts, including the Grand Canyon, Las Vegas, and Yosemite National Park. During my travels in the United States, I experienced different landscapes, enjoyed some views of breathtaking beauty, tasted a large assortment of delicious foods, and improved my English. I really did have a wonderful time and look forward to another trip.

Step 4　寫句實戰分析　Analyzing Sentences

第一段

1. Travel is the best teacher and always results in the most enduring lessons.
   旅行是最好的老師，總是帶來難以磨滅的學習經驗。

   ⓘ 字詞提示　• enduring *adj.* 持久的，耐久的

   ⓘ 文法句型　• result in　導致

2. The advantages of travel are countless. First of all, it can widen our scope of knowledge.　旅行的好處是數不清的。第一，它可以拓展我們的知識領域。

> 🄌 字詞提示
> ・scope *n.* 範圍，眼界

> 🄌 文法句型
> ・First of all, ...　第一，…(用在列舉數點時的第一點)

3. Traveling to another place, we expose ourselves to a new learning environment, where we gain new knowledge.

到另一個地方旅行，讓我們置身在新的學習環境，在那裡我們會獲得新的知識。

> 🄌 文法句型
> ・expose sb. to sth.　使某人接觸…(新想法，新環境等)
> ・...a new learning environment, where we gain.... 為關係副詞 where 的非限定用法，where 引導子句補充說明先行詞 environment。

4. Second, travel helps us relieve the pressure of work.

第二，它有助於我們紓解工作的壓力。

> 🄌 字詞提示
> ・relieve *v.* 減緩

5. We all need some time off to refresh ourselves, experiencing new things.

我們都需要放個假，充電一下，體驗新事物。

> 🄌 字詞提示
> ・off *adv.* 休假，休息
> ・refresh *v.* 消除疲勞，重振精神

6. Indeed, the more often we travel, the more we learn about the world.

的確，我們越常去旅行，就越了解這個世界。

> 🄌 文法句型
> ・注意：此為 The more..., the more.... 的句型，為「越…，就越…」之意。

第二段

1. Last summer vacation, I spent one month and a half traveling around the United States.　去年暑假我花了一個半月的時間在美國到處旅行。

> 🄌 文法句型
> ・注意：「一個半月」有兩種寫法：one month and a half/one and a half months。注意後者為複數，所以 month 要加 s。

UNIT 21
UNIT 22
UNIT 23
UNIT 24
UNIT 25
UNIT 26
UNIT 27
UNIT 28
UNIT 29
UNIT 30
UNIT 31
UNIT 32
UNIT 33
UNIT 34
UNIT 35
UNIT 36
UNIT 37
UNIT 38
UNIT 39
UNIT 40

2. I went to several popular holiday resorts, including the Grand Canyon, Las Vegas, and Yosemite National Park.

我還去了好幾個觀光勝地，如大峽谷、拉斯維加斯、優勝美地國家公園等等。

① 字詞提示 · resort *n.* 度假勝地，名勝

① 文法句型 · S + V..., including.... 包括了…

3. During my travels in the United States, I experienced different landscapes, enjoyed some views of breathtaking beauty, tasted a large assortment of delicious foods, and improved my English.

在美國的旅行期間，我體驗了不同的景觀，欣賞了令人讚嘆的美景、品嚐了各色佳餚美食，也增進了我的英文能力。

① 字詞提示 · landscape *n.* 風景，景色
· breathtaking *adj.* 令人讚嘆的
· assortment *n.* 各式各樣

4. I really did have a wonderful time and look forward to another trip.

我真的玩的很開心，也期待下一次的旅行。

① 文法句型 · 本句在肯定句的動詞前加助動詞 did，表強調。

Step 5

用字遣詞 Words → Sentences

1. enduring [ɪn`djʊrɪŋ] *adj.* 持久的，耐久的
   Madonna is a famous singer and has enduring popularity.
   瑪丹娜是個有名的歌星，受歡迎的程度歷久不衰。

2. scope [skop] *n.* 範圍，眼界
   The professor restricted the scope of his research to see if he will get different result. 這位教授限制研究的範圍，看看會不會得到不同的結果。

3. relieve [rɪ`liv] *v.* 減緩
   Henry rubbed his arm to relieve the pain from carrying his suitcase.
   Henry 揉一揉他的手臂，以減緩因為提著他的行李箱所帶來的疼痛。

4. off [ɔf] *adv.* 休假，休息

I took a day off because I caught a cold. 我請了一天假，因為感冒了。

5. refresh [rɪˋfrɛʃ] v. 消除疲勞，重振精神

I feel refreshed after taking a hot bath. 在洗個熱水澡之後，我覺得精神好多了。

6. resort [rɪˋzɔrt] n. 度假勝地，名勝

Las Vegas is one of the world's most popular holiday resorts.

拉斯維加斯是世界上最受歡迎的渡假勝地之一。

7. landscape [ˋlænskep] n. 風景，景色

Through the window of our hotel room, we can see the beautiful landscape around this area. 由我們旅館房間的窗戶看出去，可以看到附近的美麗景色。

8. breathtaking [ˋbrɛθ͵tekɪŋ] adj. 令人讚嘆的

The Niagara Falls are the most breathtaking scenes I have ever seen.

尼加拉大瀑布是我所見過令人讚嘆的美景。

9. assortment [əˋsɔrtmənt] n. 各式各樣

The bakery has a great assortment of cookies and cakes for customers to choose from. 這個麵包店裡有各式各樣的餅乾和蛋糕供顧客挑選。

文法句型 Grammar Points → Sentences

1. result in 導致

Their luxurious lifestyle resulted in bankruptcy.

他們奢華的生活方式導致了破產。

2. First of all, …. 第一，… (用在列舉數點時的第一點)

There are several reasons that I want to go to university. First of all, I can learn new things. Second, I can meet a lot of people.

我想上大學有幾個理由。第一，我可以學習新事物。第二，我可以接觸到很多人。

3. expose sb. to sth. 使某人接觸… (新想法，新環境等)

It's good to expose children to a variety of activities to let them learn more.

讓孩子接觸多元化的活動是很好的，可以讓他們學習更多事物。

4. S + V..., where + S + V.... 關係副詞 where 的非限定用法

關係副詞 where 的非限定用法，主要是用來補述前面主要子句的不足，修飾表地點的先行詞。關係副詞的前面必須加逗點。

After the war, my grandpa moved to Taiwan, where he spent the rest of his life.

→ After the war, my grandpa moved to Taiwan, in which he spent the rest of his life.

→ After the war, my grandpa moved to Taiwan, and he spent the rest of his life here.　戰爭結束後，我爺爺搬到台灣來，並在這度過餘生。

5. S + V..., including....　包括了…

Six people were killed in the riot, including a policeman.

有六個人在暴動中喪命，包括一名警察。

6. S + do/does/did + V....　強調句型

在肯定句的動詞前加上助動詞 do/does/did 表強調，意為「的確，一定」。

Sarah said she did see her boyfriend walking hand in hand with another girl.

Sarah 說她真的看到她男朋友跟另一個女孩手牽手走著。

UNIT 21
UNIT 22
UNIT 23
UNIT 24
UNIT 25
UNIT 26
UNIT 27
UNIT 28
UNIT 29
UNIT 30
UNIT 31
UNIT 32
UNIT 33
UNIT 34
UNIT 35
UNIT 36
UNIT 37
UNIT 38
UNIT 39
UNIT 40

UNIT 37

Narrative Writing　敘事文

Waiting for a Call　等電話

　　根據下列三幅連環圖畫的內容，將圖中女子等電話的心情作一合理的敘述。文長120 個英文字左右。

　　Reasonably narrate how the girl felt while she was waiting for a call according to the following three-frame comic strip. Write your essay in 120 words or so.

Step 1　看圖聯想 Association　依人、事、時、地、物、原因和方法聯想與題目相關的事項

Step 2　組織大綱提示 Organization　依照想到的事項，定出寫作優先順序及細節

第一段 (圖 1)

　1.主題句：某一個星期五的傍晚，Helen 獨自待在家裡。

　2.支持句：細節

　　a.她坐在沙發上等她男友 Bob 的電話。

　　b.她除了一等再等，什麼事也沒做，臉上露出無聊的表情。

第二段 (圖 2)

　1.主題句：她等了二十分鐘，開始不耐煩了。

　2.支持句：Helen 的心情

　　a.猜想男友是否太忙而沒有打電話給她。

　　b.擔心男友因發生意外而無法打電話。

UNIT
21

UNIT
22

UNIT
23

UNIT
24

UNIT
25

UNIT
26

UNIT
27

UNIT
28

UNIT
29

UNIT
30

UNIT
31

UNIT
32

UNIT
33

UNIT
34

UNIT
35

UNIT
36

UNIT
37

UNIT
38

UNIT
39

UNIT
40

c. 氣男友沒有快點打電話給她。

第三段 (圖 3)

1. 主題句：就在她想放棄等待之前，電話鈴響了。

2. 支持句：細節

a. 她從沙發上跳起來並衝去接電話。

b. 她邊跑邊想：「一定是他。我終於可以和他講電話了。」

3. 結論：終於，她又滿面笑容了。

Step 3　範文 Model Composition

Waiting for a Call

One Friday evening, Helen stayed home alone. She sat on the sofa, waiting for a call from her boyfriend, Bob. She did nothing but wait, and there was a bored expression on her face.

She'd been waiting for twenty minutes and was getting impatient. Sometimes, she wondered if he was too busy to give her a call. Sometimes, she worried that an accident had happened and made him unable to make a call. Sometimes, she felt angry with him for not calling her sooner.

Right before she wanted to give up waiting for the call from Bob, the phone rang. She jumped out of the sofa and rushed to get the phone. She ran and thought, "It must be him. Yes, I can finally talk to him on the phone." Finally, she was all smiles again.

Step 4　寫句實戰分析 Analyzing Sentences

第一段

1. One Friday evening, Helen stayed home alone.

某一個星期五的傍晚，Helen 獨自待在家裡。

⚠ 文法
句型
・注意：本文全篇用過去式動詞，敘述已經發生的事情。作文時，全篇時態盡量統
一。

2. She sat on the sofa, waiting for a call from her boyfriend, Bob.

她坐在沙發上等她男友 Bob 的電話。

① 文法句型 ・注意：..., waiting for a call.... 為分詞構句，原句為 ..., and (she) waited for a call....

3. She did nothing but wait, and there was a bored expression on her face.

除了等之外，她什麼都沒做，臉上露出無聊的表情。

① 字詞提示 ・ expression *n.* 表情；臉色

① 文法句型 ・ do nothing but + V　除了…什麼事也沒做

第二段

1. She'd been waiting for twenty minutes and was getting impatient.

她等了二十分鐘，開始變得不耐煩了。

① 字詞提示 ・ impatient *adj.* 沒有耐心的

① 文法句型 ・...had been waiting.... 為過去完成進行式，表在過去某時已經持續一段時間的動作。

2. Sometimes, she wondered if he was too busy to give her a call.

一會兒，她猜想他是否太忙而沒有打電話給她。

① 字詞提示 ・ wonder *v.* 猜想

① 文法句型 ・ wonder if/whether + S + V　想知道是否…

3. Sometimes, she worried that an accident had happened and made him unable to make a call.　一會兒，她擔心他因發生意外而無法打電話給她。

① 文法句型 ・...make him unable.... 中的 make 為使役動詞，後接受詞，再接形容詞，修飾受詞 him。

4. Sometimes, she felt angry with him for not calling her sooner.

一會兒，她氣他沒有快點打電話給她。

UNIT 21
UNIT 22
UNIT 23
UNIT 24
UNIT 25
UNIT 26
UNIT 27
UNIT 28
UNIT 29
UNIT 30
UNIT 31
UNIT 32
UNIT 33
UNIT 34
UNIT 35
UNIT 36
UNIT 37
UNIT 38
UNIT 39
UNIT 40

⚠ **文法句型** ・注意：feel 為連綴動詞，後接形容詞做主詞補語，修飾主詞。

第三段

1. Right before she wanted to give up waiting for the call from Bob, the phone rang.

   就在她想放棄等待 Bob 的電話之前，電話鈴響了。

⚠ **文法句型** ・注意：give up 為放棄之意，後接 V-ing。

2. She jumped out of the sofa and rushed to get the phone.

   她從沙發上跳起來並衝過去接電話。

⚠ **字詞提示** ・rush *v.* 衝，急著做…

3. She ran and thought, "It must be him. Yes, I can finally talk to him on the phone."　她邊跑邊想：「一定是他。我終於可以和他講電話了。」

⚠ **文法句型** ・注意：講電話的介系詞用 on。

4. Finally, she was all smiles again.　終於，她又滿面笑容了。

⚠ **文法句型** ・be all smiles　滿臉笑容

✎ Step 5

用字遣詞 Words → Sentences

1. expression [ɪk`sprɛʃən] *n.* 表情；臉色

   The expression on my boyfriend's face told me something was wrong.

   我男友臉上的表情告訴我有事情不對勁。

2. impatient [ɪm`peʃənt] *adj.* 沒有耐心的

   Don't be so impatient—wait until it is your turn to speak.

   不要那麼沒耐心——等到輪到你再說話。

3. wonder [`wʌndɚ] *v.* 猜想

   We were wondering why Annie refused to go out with Jim. She liked Jim a lot.

   我們在想為什麼 Annie 不跟 Jim 出去。她很喜歡 Jim。

4. rush [rʌʃ] *v.* 衝，急著做…

Harry got up late in the morning, so he rushed to catch the school bus.

Harry 早上起床遲了，所以他衝去趕校車。

文法句型 Grammar Points → Sentences

1. do nothing but + V　除了…什麼事也沒做

   My friends and I did nothing but talk and laugh last night.

   我跟我的朋友昨晚除了說說笑笑之外，什麼也沒做。

2. had been + V-ing　過去完成進行式

   過去完成進行式表示過去一段期間裡的持續性動作，比句中的過去式早發生。

   We had been talking for over an hour before Tom arrived.

   Tom 抵達之前，我們已經談話談了超過一個小時。

3. wonder if/whether + S + V　想知道是否…

   Jamie didn't talk to me all day long. I wonder if she is mad at me.

   Jamie 一整天都沒有跟我說話。我想知道她是否在生我氣。

4. make + O + adj.　使役動詞

   使役動詞後可接受詞，再接形容詞做受詞補語。

   Ian's leg wound made him unable to walk.　腿上的傷讓 Ian 沒有辦法走路。

5. be all smiles　滿臉笑容

   The father gave a new pencil box to his daughter, and she was all smiles.

   那個父親給了他女兒一個新鉛筆盒，她滿臉都是笑容。

UNIT 21
UNIT 22
UNIT 23
UNIT 24
UNIT 25
UNIT 26
UNIT 27
UNIT 28
UNIT 29
UNIT 30
UNIT 31
UNIT 32
UNIT 33
UNIT 34
UNIT 35
UNIT 36
UNIT 37
UNIT 38
UNIT 39
UNIT 40

UNIT 38

Informative Writing　訊息文

What Can Replace the Role of a TV in the Living Room?

什麼可以取代電視在客廳的角色？

　　請以 "What Can Replace the Role of a TV in the Living Room?" 為題。首先於第一段中簡要說明電視在客廳扮演何種角色，並於第二段中建議一項或多項可以替代電視機來營造良好家庭氣氛的物品，並說明其原因。

　　Write an essay with the title "What can replace the role of TV in the living room?" In the first paragraph, briefly describe the role of TV in the living room. In the second paragraph, suggest one or more items which can replace the TV set and create a good family atmosphere. Give the reasons in the second paragraph.

Step 1 聯想提示 Association 　依人、事、時、地、物、原因和方法聯想與題目相關的事項

- 電視在客廳裡扮演什麼角色？　What role does a TV play in the living room?
- 電視提供什麼樣的節目？　What kinds of programs does a TV provide?
- 電視帶給我們什麼樣的好處？　What benefits does a TV bring to us?
- 我們可以如何善用這些東西？　How can we make good use of these things?
- 其他什麼東西可發揮同樣的功能？　What other things can serve the same function?

Step 2 組織大綱提示 Organization 　依照想到的事項，定出寫作優先順序及細節

第一段

1. 主題句：客廳裡的電視機是家庭娛樂最重要的部份。
2. 支持句：電視帶給我們什麼？
   a. 它提供我們每週最精采的電視節目。
   b. 它提供我們各式各樣的資訊。
3. 結論：的確，它提供我們機會來拓展知識領域。

第二段

1. 主題句：客廳裡還有其它的東西可以取代電視的角色。
2. 支持句：取代電視的活動

a. 我們可以聽音樂來紓解壓力。

b. 我們還可以閱讀書籍或雜誌，讓我們接觸新知識。

c. 西洋棋可以鍛鍊我們的頭腦。

3. 結論：這些當中的任何一樣都可取代電視扮演的角色。

Step 3 範文 Model Composition

What Can Replace the Role of a TV in the Living Room?

A television set in a living room is the centerpiece of home entertainment. It offers us weekly TV program highlights, such as variety shows, soap operas, and basketball games. It also provides us with all kinds of information to expand our horizons. Indeed, it provides us with the opportunities to enlarge our knowledge and adapt to new ways of observing the world.

However, there are some other things which can replace the role of a TV. We can listen to music to relieve stress. We can also read books or magazines, which expose us to new thoughts. Chess is also excellent because it exercises our brains. Any one of these could be a replacement for the role a TV performs in the living room.

Step 4 寫句實戰分析 Analyzing Sentences

2. A television set in a living room is the centerpiece of home entertainment.

客廳裡的電視機是家庭娛樂最重要的部份。

字詞提示
• centerpiece *n.* 最重要的部份

2. It offers us weekly TV program highlights, such as variety shows, soap operas, and basketball games.

它提供我們每週最精采的電視節目，例如：綜藝節目、連續劇和籃球賽。

字詞提示
• highlight *n.* 最精采的部份，最吸引人的部份
• variety show *n.* 綜藝節目

UNIT 21
UNIT 22
UNIT 23
UNIT 24
UNIT 25
UNIT 26
UNIT 27
UNIT 28
UNIT 29
UNIT 30
UNIT 31
UNIT 32
UNIT 33
UNIT 34
UNIT 35
UNIT 36
UNIT 37
UNIT 38
UNIT 39
UNIT 40

· soap opera *n.* 連續劇

3. It also provides us with all kinds of information to expand our horizons.

它還提供我們各式各樣的資訊，拓展我們的眼界。

⚠ 文法句型
· provide sb. with sth.　提供某人某物
· expand one's horizons　開闊某人的眼界

4. Indeed, it provides us with the opportunities to enlarge our knowledge and adapt to new ways of observing the world.

的確，它提供我們機會來拓展知識領域，並適應以新的方式來觀察世界。

⚠ 字詞提示
· opportunity *n.* 機會

⚠ 文法句型
· adapt to　適應

第二段

1. However, there are some other things which can replace the role of a TV.

然而，一些其它的東西可以取代電視的角色。

⚠ 字詞提示
· replace *v.* 取代

2. We can listen to music to relieve stress.　我們可以聽音樂來紓解壓力。

⚠ 字詞提示
· relieve *v.* 解除，緩解

3. We can also read books or magazines, which expose us to new thoughts.

我們也可以閱讀書籍或雜誌，讓我們接觸新的想法。

⚠ 文法句型
· 注意：expose sb. to sth.　使某人接觸⋯(新想法，新環境等)

4. Chess is also excellent because it exercises our brains.

西洋棋也很棒，它可以鍛鍊我們的頭腦。

⚠ 字詞提示
· excellent *adj.* 優秀的，極好的

5. Any one of these could be a replacement for the role a TV performs in the living

room. 這些當中的任何一樣都可以取代客廳裡的電視及它所扮演的角色。

> ⓘ **字詞提示** · replacement *n.* 替代品

✎ Step 5

用字遣詞 Words → Sentences

1. centerpiece [`sɛntɚˌpis] *n.* 最重要的部份

   The artist's work is the centerpiece of this exhibition.

   這位藝術家的作品是本次展覽中最重要的部份。

2. highlight [`haɪˌlaɪt] *n.* 最精采的部份，最吸引人的部份

   My dance class is the highlight of my week.

   我的舞蹈課是我一個星期中最精彩的部份。

3. variety show [vəˈraɪətɪ ʃo] *n.* 綜藝節目

   I like variety shows because I always find the comedy skits in the shows interesting. 我喜歡綜藝節目，因為我總是覺得裡面的小短劇很有趣。

4. soap opera [sop ˈɑpərə] *n.* 連續劇

   Friends is my favorite soap opera, for it talks a lot about friendship.

   《六人行》是我最喜歡的連續劇，因為它討論很多有關友誼的事。

5. opportunity [ˌɑpɚˈtjunətɪ] *n.* 機會

   I am going to have dinner with Rita tonight, and it's a perfect chance to let her know how I feel about her.

   我今晚會跟 Rita 吃晚餐。這是一個絕佳的機會，讓我告訴她我對她的感覺。

6. replace [rɪˈples] *v.* 取代

   Teachers will never be replaced by computers. 老師絕不會被電腦所取代。

7. relieve [rɪˈliv] *v.* 解除，緩解

   I relieve stress by doing yoga. 我做瑜珈來紓解壓力。

8. excellent [`ɛkslənt] *adj.* 優秀的，極好的

   Ivy's performance on the stage was excellent. I couldn't take my eyes off her.

   Ivy 在台上的演出太棒了。我無法不盯著她看。

9. replacement [rɪˈplesmənt] *n.* 替代品

   The computer has been used for years and needs a replacement.

   這台電腦已經用了很多年，需要買一台替代的。

文法句型 Grammar Points → Sentences

1. provide sb. with sth.　提供某人某物

   Homes provide us with shelter and love.　家提供我們庇護及愛。

2. expand one's horizons　開闊某人的眼界

   Travel can expand our horizons.　旅行可以開闊我們的眼界。

3. adapt to　適應

   Children are quick to adapt to new circumstances.

   小孩子很快就可以適應新環境。

UNIT 21
UNIT 22
UNIT 23
UNIT 24
UNIT 25
UNIT 26
UNIT 27
UNIT 28
UNIT 29
UNIT 30
UNIT 31
UNIT 32
UNIT 33
UNIT 34
UNIT 35
UNIT 36
UNIT 37
UNIT 38
UNIT 39
UNIT 40

UNIT 39

Expository/Narrative Writing　說明文／敘事文

What Makes a Good Friend? 好朋友

請以 "What Makes a Good Friend?" 為主題，寫一篇至少 120 個字的英文作文。第一段針對文章主題，說明什麼樣的朋友才算是「好朋友」，並在第二段舉自己的交友經驗為例，以印證第一段的說明。

Please write an essay under the title "What Makes a Good Friend?" in no less than 120 words. Explain what kind of friend is good in paragraph one; exemplify your own experience of making friends in paragraph two to prove what you mention in paragraph one.

Step 1 聯想提示 Association　依人、事、時、地、物、原因和方法聯想與題目相關的事項

- 怎樣才算是好朋友？　What makes a good friend?
- 我的好朋友是誰？　Who is my good friend?
- 為什麼這個人是我的好朋友？　Why is this person my good friend?
- 這個人對我做了什麼事？　What did this person do to me?
- 這件事是在哪裡發生的？　Where did it happen?

Step 2 組織大綱提示 Organization　依照想到的事項，定出寫作優先順序及細節

第一段

1. 主題句：好友難覓。

2. 支持句：

  a. 泛泛之交很多，可是摯友難尋。

  b. 問：怎樣才算是好朋友？

  c. 答：好朋友絕不會背叛我們。

  d. 答：好朋友會安慰、鼓勵、幫助我們。

第二段

1. 主題句：在一個夏日的午後，我和 John 一起去游泳。

2. 支持句：

  a. 我們在海灘游泳，突然間我的腳抽筋。

UNIT 21
UNIT 22
UNIT 23
UNIT 24
UNIT 25
UNIT 26
UNIT 27
UNIT 28
UNIT 29
UNIT 30
UNIT 31
UNIT 32
UNIT 33
UNIT 34
UNIT 35
UNIT 36
UNIT 37
UNIT 38
UNIT 39
UNIT 40

b. 我幾乎因劇痛而失去意識。

c. 為了求生，我奮力掙扎。

d. John 一發現我溺水，便立刻盡全力救我。

e. 他把我帶到岸上，並對我施行心肺復甦術。

3. 結論：他救了我一命，也讓我確信「患難見真情」。

Step 3　範文 Model Composition

What Makes a Good Friend

Good friends can be hard to find. Acquaintances and associates are found in abundance, but a true friend is scarce and worth treasuring. However, what makes a good friend? A good friend is one who never betrays us. Instead, a good friend comforts and encourages us and is always willing to help out when we are in a difficult situation.

One summer afternoon, I went swimming with John. We were swimming at a popular beach in northeastern Taiwan when I suddenly got a cramp in leg. It was so painful that I almost lost consciousness. I was floundering in the sea and feeling my life was in danger. Upon hearing my cry for help, John came to rescue me from drowning with all his strength. He finally brought me to shore and performed CPR on me. He saved my life and convinced me that "A friend in need is a friend indeed."

Step 4　寫句實戰分析 Analyzing Sentences

第一段

1. Good friends can be hard to find.　好朋友可能難尋。

!文法句型　· be + adj. + to V　不定詞作副詞片語修飾前面的形容詞

2. Acquaintances and associates are found in abundance, but a true friend is scarce and worth treasuring.

泛泛之交和同僚夥伴多的是，可是真正的朋友卻少之又少而且彌足珍貴。

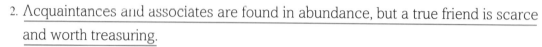 **字詞提示**
- acquaintance *n.* 認識的人
- associate *n.* 同事，夥伴
- abundance *n.* 豐富，充足
- scarce *adj.* 稀罕的，難得的

文法句型
- be worth + V-ing　值得…

3. However, what makes a good friend? A good friend is one who never betrays us.

然而，怎樣才算是好朋友呢？好朋友就是絕不會背叛我們的人。

字詞提示
- betray *v.* 背叛，出賣

文法句型
- 注意：關係代名詞的先行詞是單數時，後面要接單數動詞。

5. Instead, a good friend comforts and encourages us and is always willing to help out when we are in a difficult situation.

相反地，當我們處在困境時，好朋友會安慰、鼓勵我們，而且總是願意幫助我們。

文法句型
- be willing to + V　願意…

第二段

1. One summer afternoon, I went swimming with John.

一個夏日的午後，我和 John 一起去游泳。

文法句型
- 注意：go + V-ing 表示從事某種活動。

2. We were swimming at a popular beach in northeastern Taiwan when I suddenly got a cramp in leg.

我們在台灣東北角一處很有名的海灘游泳，突然間我的腳抽筋。

字詞提示
- cramp *n.* 抽筋

UNIT 21
UNIT 22
UNIT 23
UNIT 24
UNIT 25
UNIT 26
UNIT 27
UNIT 28
UNIT 29
UNIT 30
UNIT 31
UNIT 32
UNIT 33
UNIT 34
UNIT 35
UNIT 36
UNIT 37
UNIT 38
UNIT 39
UNIT 40

①文法句型 ・ S + was/were + V$_1$-ing...when + S + V$_2$　過去一段時間裡發生兩個動作，短時間的用過去簡單式，長時間的用過去進行式。

3. It was so painful that I almost lost consciousness. I was floundering in the sea and feeling my life was in danger.

我痛到差點失去意識。我在海中奮力掙扎，而且覺得有生命危險。

①字詞提示 ・ consciousness *n.* 知覺，意識
・ flounder *v.* 掙扎

①文法句型 ・ so...that + S + V　如此…以致於…

4. Upon hearing my cry for help, John came to rescue me from drowning with all his strength.

一聽見我的呼救聲，John 就馬上盡全力來救我，以免我溺斃。

①文法句型 ・ Upon/On + N/V-ing..., S + V....　一…就…
・ rescue sb. from sth.　救援…使不至於…
・ with all one's strength　盡某人的全力

5. He finally brought me to shore and performed CPR on me.

他最後終於把我帶到岸上，並對我施行心肺復甦術。

①文法句型 ・ perform CPR on sb.　對…施行心肺復甦術

6. He saved my life and convinced me that "A friend in need is a friend indeed."

他救了我一命，也讓我確信「患難見真情」。

①字詞提示 ・ convince *v.* 使信服

①文法句型 ・ A friend in need is a friend indeed. 【諺】患難見真情。

Step 5

用字遣詞 Words → Sentences

1. acquaintance [ə`kwentəns] *n.* 認識的人

Hillary has a wide circle of friends and acquaintances.

Hillary 的交遊廣闊。

2. associate [ə`soʃɪɪt] *n.* 同事，夥伴

Sam and Paul are associates in business.　Sam 和 Paul 是事業上的夥伴。

3. abundance [ə`bʌndəns] *n.* 豐富，充足

Fruit and vegetables grow in abundance on the island.

這個島上長了很多的水果蔬菜。

4. scarce [skɛrs] *adj.* 稀罕的，難得的

Good fruit is scarce just now, and it costs a lot.

好的水果現在很稀有，而且很貴。

5. betray [bɪ`tre] *v.* 背叛，出賣

The soldier was accused of betraying his country during the war.

這名士兵被控在戰爭期間背叛他的國家。

6. cramp [kræmp] *n.* 抽筋

Liz's got a cramp in her foot.　Liz 的腳抽筋。

7. consciousness [`kɑnʃəsnɪs] *n.* 知覺，意識

My grandpa did not regain consciousness and died the next day.

我爺爺沒有恢復意識，而且隔天就過世了。

8. flounder [`flaʊndɚ] *v.* 掙扎

The fish floundered on the river bank, struggling to breathe.

這條魚在河岸上掙扎，拼了命地想要呼吸。

9. convince [kən`vɪns] *v.* 使信服

It's no use trying to convince Janet that she doesn't need to lose any weight.

想說服 Janet 她完全不需要減肥是沒用的。

文法句型 Grammar Points → Sentences

1. be + adj. + to V　不定詞作副詞片語修飾前面的形容詞

English is easy to learn but hard to master.

英文學起來很容易，但要精通卻很難。

2. be worth + V-ing　值得…

This idea is well worth considering.　這個想法很值得考慮。

3. be willing to + V　願意…

I'm willing to overlook your mistakes.　我願意寬恕你的錯誤。

4. S + was/were + V_1-ing...when + S + V_2

過去一段時間裡發生兩個動作，短時間的用過去簡單式，長時間的用過去進行式。

George was taking a bath when the telephone rang.

當電話響的時候，George 正在洗澡。

5. so...that + S + V　如此…以致於…

I'm so tired that I could sleep in this chair.

我累到可以在這張椅子上睡著。

6. Upon/On + N/V-ing..., S + V....　一…就…

On arriving home, I discovered my parents had left.

一到家，我就發現我爸媽已經離開了。

7. rescue sb. from sth.　救援…使不至於…

The managers tried to rescue the company from bankruptcy.

經理們試圖拯救這家公司，使它免於倒閉。

8. with all one's strength　盡某人的全力

Brian pushed against the rock with all his strength.

Brian 用盡全力推這顆岩石。

9. perform CPR on sb.　對…施行心肺復甦術

The lifeguard performed CPR on the unconscious girl as soon as he dragged her onto the shore.

救生員一把那無意識的女孩拖到岸上，就立刻對她施行心肺復甦術。

10. A friend in need is a friend indeed.【諺】患難見真情

When I was down-and-out, only Gary lent me a helping hand. A friend in need is a friend indeed.

當我窮途潦倒的時候，只有 Gary 對我伸出援手。真是患難見真情啊。

UNIT 21
UNIT 22
UNIT 23
UNIT 24
UNIT 25
UNIT 26
UNIT 27
UNIT 28
UNIT 29
UNIT 30
UNIT 31
UNIT 32
UNIT 33
UNIT 34
UNIT 35
UNIT 36
UNIT 37
UNIT 38
UNIT 39
UNIT 40

UNIT 40

Who Should Do the Household Chores? 誰來做家事？

你會幫忙做家事嗎？你認為應該幫忙做家事嗎？請以 "Who Should Do the Household Chores?" 為題，說明你對做家事的看法，並詳細說明理由。

Would you help with the household chores? Do you think you should help do the household chores? Please use "Who Should Do the Household Chores?" as a title to explain your views on doing the household chores with detailed reasons.

Step 1 聯想提示 Association 依人、事、時、地、物、原因和方法聯想與題目相關的事項

- 做家事的理由？ What are the reasons to do the household chores?
- 小孩可以做什麼？為什麼？ What can kids do and why do they do it?
- 父母可以做什麼？為什麼？ What can parents do and why do they do it?
- 做家事有什麼意義？ What does doing household chores mean?

Step 2 組織大綱提示 Organization 依照想到的事項，定出寫作優先順序及細節

1. 主題句：要保持家庭和諧平順，所有家庭成員都要幫忙做家事。
2. 支持句：原因
   a. 小孩有必須做的家事來練習分擔責任。
   b. 雙親也應該共同分擔家事，做為小孩的榜樣。
3. 結論：做家事不僅是每個家庭成員的日常工作，也是為享有快樂健康的家庭生活所應承擔的責任。

Step 3 範文 Model Composition

Who Should Do the Household Chores?

In order to keep a home running smoothly, all members of the family

UNIT 21
UNIT 22
UNIT 23
UNIT 24
UNIT 25
UNIT 26
UNIT 27
UNIT 28
UNIT 29
UNIT 30
UNIT 31
UNIT 32
UNIT 33
UNIT 34
UNIT 35
UNIT 36
UNIT 37
UNIT 38
UNIT 39
UNIT 40

should help with the household chores, such as washing the dishes, taking out the garbage, tidying their rooms, vacuuming, and so on. The kids have chores they are required to do to practice sharing responsibility. Doing the household chores is also the responsibility of both the parents, whose participation in the domestic chores makes their relationship stronger and sets a good example for their kids to follow. To sum up, doing the household chores is not only a matter of daily routine for all family members, but also a responsibility they should take on to enjoy a happy and healthy home life.

Step 4　寫句實戰分析 Analyzing Sentences

1. In order to keep a home running smoothly, all members of the family should help with the household chores, such as washing the dishes, taking out the garbage, tidying their rooms, vacuuming, and so on.
   要保持家庭和諧平順，所有家庭成員都要幫忙做家事，比如像洗碗、倒垃圾、清理房間、吸塵等等。

   ⓘ 字詞提示
   - household *adj.* 家庭的，家用的
   - chore *n.* 雜務
   - tidy *v.* 整理，使整潔
   - vacuum *v.* 用吸塵器打掃

2. The kids have chores they are required to do to practice sharing responsibility.
   小孩有必須做的家事來練習分擔責任。

   ⓘ 文法句型
   - 注意：be required to + V　必須
   - to practice sharing responsibility 為不定詞片語，表示「目的」。

3. Doing the household chores is also the responsibility of both the parents, whose participation in the domestic chores makes their relationship stronger and sets a good example for their kids to follow.
   做家事也是父母親共同的責任，父母親參與家事可以加強夫妻關係，也可以給孩子們樹立好榜樣，以供效仿。

   ⓘ 字詞提示
   - participation *n.* 參與
   - domestic *adj.* 家庭的

223

① 文法
句型
- whose 為關係代名詞所有格，引導子句修飾先行詞，為所有格，用於表示屬於先行詞的人或物。
- set an example for sb. 為某人樹立榜樣

4. To sum up, doing the household chores is not only a matter of daily routine for all family members, but also a responsibility they should take on to enjoy a happy and healthy home life. 總之，做家事不僅是每個家庭成員的日常工作，也是為享有快樂健康的家庭生活所應承擔的一份責任。

① 字詞
提示
- daily routine 日常工作、慣例

① 文法
句型
- to sum up 總結
- a matter of 關於…的問題
- take on 承擔

Step 5

用字遣詞 Words → Sentences

1. household [ˈhaʊsˌhold] *adj.* 家庭的，家用的
   The supermarket offers a variety of household appliances.
   這個超級市場提供各式各樣的家庭用品。

2. chore [tʃor] *n.* 雜務
   I'll go shopping after I finish my chores. 處理完家裡的雜事之後，我要去逛街。

3. tidy [ˈtaɪdɪ] *v.* 整理，使整潔
   Linda usually helps her little sister tidy her room.
   Linda 通常幫她小妹整理她的房間。

4. vacuum [ˈvækjʊəm] *v.* 用吸塵器打掃
   We vacuum our carpet once a week. 我們每個星期用吸塵器清潔地毯一次。

5. participation [pɚˌtɪsəˈpeʃən] *n.* 參與
   We would like to thank you for your participation in our wedding ceremony.
   我們要感謝您參與我們的婚禮。

6. domestic [dəˈmɛstɪk] *adj.* 家庭的
   I always share domestic chores with my family members.
   我都會跟我的家人分擔家事。

UNIT 21
UNIT 22
UNIT 23
UNIT 24
UNIT 25
UNIT 26
UNIT 27
UNIT 28
UNIT 29
UNIT 30
UNIT 31
UNIT 32
UNIT 33
UNIT 34
UNIT 35
UNIT 36
UNIT 37
UNIT 38
UNIT 39
UNIT 40

文法句型 Grammar Points → Sentences

1. whose 關係代名詞所有格

   whose 引導子句修飾先行詞，為所有格，用於表示屬於先行詞的人或物。

   A man was shouting at a driver whose car was blocking the street.

   一名駕駛的車把街道堵住了，一名男子對著這名駕駛大吼。

2. set an example for sb. 為某人樹立榜樣

   What David did set a good example for the other students.

   David 的所作所為給其他學生樹立了一個好榜樣。

3. to sum up 總結

   To sum up, if you want to lose weight, all you have to do is eat less and exercise more. 總之，如果你想要減肥，你只要少吃多運動就好了。

4. a matter of 關於⋯的問題

   Jeff is really hard-working. It's only a matter of time for him to be successful.

   Jeff 真的很認真工作。對他來說，成功只是時間的問題而已。

5. take on 承擔

   Cindy took on too much responsibility and made herself ill.

   Cindy 承擔了太多責任，而讓自己病倒了。